De Montfort's Crown

Book 14 in the Border Knight Series

By

Griff Hosker

de Montfort's Crown

Published by Sword Books Ltd 2023

Copyright ©Griff Hosker First Edition 2023

Contents

De Montfort's Crown i
Prologue 3
Chapter 1 7
Chapter 2 16
Chapter 3 25
Chapter 4 34
Chapter 5 45
Chapter 6 53
Chapter 7 60
Chapter 8 74
Chapter 9 82
Chapter 10 91
Chapter 11 102
Chapter 12 112
Chapter 13 123
Chapter 14 131
Chapter 15 138
Chapter 16 145
Chapter 17 155
Chapter 18 165
Chapter 19 176
Chapter 20 190
Epilogue 203
Glossary 206
Historical Note 207
Other books by Griff Hosker 210

Historical figures

King Henry III of England son of King John

Richard of Cornwall- 1st Earl of Cornwall second son of King John and also the King of the Romans

Prince Edward- heir to the throne and known as **The Lord Edward**

Prince Edmund- putative King of Sicily and brother to The Lord Edward

Henry of Almain- the son of Richard of Cornwall

William de Valance- The Earl of Pembroke. King Henry's half-brother through his mother, Isabella of Angoulême

John de Warenne – Earl of Surrey

Guy de Lusignan-King Henry's half-brother through his mother, Isabella of Angoulême

Simon de Montfort- The Earl of Leicester

Simon de Montfort the younger - the son of the Earl of Leicester

Guy de Montfort - the son of the Earl of Leicester

Henry de Montfort - the son of the Earl of Leicester

Aymer de Lusignan- King Henry's half-brother through his mother, Isabella of Angoulême

King Louis IX of France-also known as St. Louis

Leonor of Castile- Later Eleanor and the great-great-granddaughter of Henry II of England

King Alexander III of Scotland (The Glorious born in 1241) King Henry's son-in-law

Charles, King of Naples

Llewelyn ap Gruffudd- Prince of Wales

Lord Rhys Fychan- The Welsh lord given Gwynedd by King Henry

Richard de Clare- 5th Earl of Gloucester

Gilbert de Clare – 6th Earl of Gloucester and the son of Richard de Clare

Roger Bigod- 4th Earl of Norfolk

Hugh Bigod- the brother of the Earl of Norfolk

Roger Mortimer -1st Baron Mortimer of Wigmore

Dugald mac Ruari – King of the Isles

King Magnus – King of Man

The Land of the Warlord

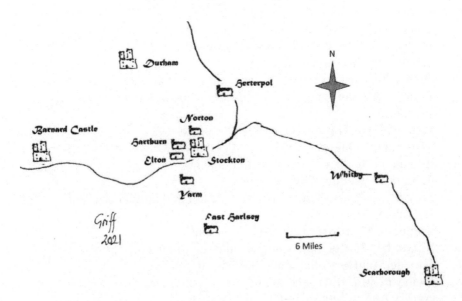

Prologue

Sir Henry Samuel

I am Baron Henry Samuel of Elton but when my uncle Earl William of Stockton dies, I shall be the earl and hold the lands north of the Tees for the king. I pray that I will be an old man when that day comes but we live in parlous times. King Henry of England came perilously close to losing his kingdom to the man who would be king, Simon de Montfort, the Earl of Leicester. I was partly responsible for thwarting him. The visit of the king and the earl to Paris had removed the Provisions of Oxford but the chains that had shackled him remained. The king hung on to his crown but the snake was not yet scotched. He plotted and he planned in his lands in France. My uncle had put us on a war footing from that moment on. We spent money arming and training warriors for a war that we knew was coming.

Matthew was my cousin and my squire. Alfred and Samuel, my sons, were pages and he was training them. I rarely left the valley, apart from times of war, but sometimes it was necessary. Whenever I did, I went well protected. Assassins had tried to kill not only me but those close to me. In addition to my squire and two pages I also had four men at arms, led by Jack and four archers. The visit to York was necessary otherwise I would not have left my home. My uncle had been summoned by the High Sherriff of Yorkshire, John de Oketon, who had not been in office long and he wished to consult with my uncle who protected the northern part of his domain. My uncle was not well enough to ride and I went in his place. I had met with the Sherriff and assured him that we would continue to serve both the king and England. The north was safe.

We had taken advantage of York's market and we had laden sumpters as we headed north and passed through Easingwold. The land here was a mixture of farmland and forest. We always rode cautiously through the forested areas. The archers would string their bows while we did so and my men at arms would pull their shields a little tighter. On the way south we had enjoyed a peaceful journey and there was no reason why, on the way back, we should not have the same degree of safety. When we neared the forested parts we would form a single file. Two archers would ride at the fore and two at the rear with two men at arms and the sumpters. My other two men at arms would protect my sons. We rode along the road through the forest in silence for our ears were weapons we could use to our advantage. It was one of the newly joined archers, Alan son of Robbie who held up his hand and stopped. While he and the other archers nocked an arrow the rest of us, my sons included, drew a sword. In the boys' cases, it was a long dagger. As we listened, I heard the sound of voices raised to our right, in the forest. Many people would have ridden on determining that it was not their concern. My family, descended from the warlord, had a keen sense of duty. Someone was in trouble and we were duty-bound to help.

Alan looked around and every face turned to me. I waved my sword to the right and Alan led us through the trees. I turned to Robert and Rafe and said quietly, "Stay here with my sons and the sumpters."

I saw the look of disappointment on the faces of Alfred and Samuel but they nodded. Alan had to pick his way through the trees and saplings for there was no clear trail. The noise we heard grew and it became clear that there were angry voices ahead of us. Alan reined in to locate the source of the noise and I waved the others into a hunter's line. I still allowed Alan to lead for he had shown that he knew how to track, especially sounds.

It was a threatening northern voice that we heard, "We will take your fingers one by one if we have to. Where is your treasure? These pieces of parchment are worthless."

"I beg you. Leave my son and me alone. You have killed our men and I have told you we do not carry treasure with us."

"You are Jews! We know you are all rich men."

Those few words told me all that I needed to know. These were bandits and they had found a Jew and his servants. This was a robbery. Through the trees, I saw movement. I waved to Alan and Edgar, my two remaining archers to dismount and I led Matthew, my squire, and my men at arms towards the men who were in some sort of clearing. I had not instructed Alan and Edgar but they would know what to do. As we entered the clearing I saw three bodies and a line of horses. Ten men surrounded a Jew, clearly identified by his dreadlocks and a boy who looked to be of an age with Alfred. The bodies of the dead had clearly been mutilated.

As our horses edged into the clearing, we were seen and eight of the men turned to face us. The leader shook his head, "Leave us, my lord, for we can deal with this Jew. It is not only the Earl of Leicester who punishes the killers of Christ."

"I am Baron Henry Samuel of Elton and I command you to lay down your weapons."

"They are Jews!"

"And I am a knight. Disobey me at your peril."

They outnumbered us by two to one and the leader, keeping his sword at the old Jew's throat shouted to his men, "Kill them and we double our profit."

Two of the men were archers and they raised their bows while the others grabbed pole weapons and ran at us, clearly intent on unhorsing us. The two arrows that slammed into the backs of the two archers came as a complete shock to the two men who died without knowing I had archers with me. At the same time, the six of us rode at the men who came at us. The least experienced of us was Matthew, but as it would not be long before he was knighted, he was skilled with both sword and horse. He easily avoided the swing from the billhook and his sword hacked into the man's head. As the man with the poleaxe came at me I made Raven rear and his hooves clattered into the man's hands making him drop his weapon. He barely turned before my sword split open the back of his skull. My men were ruthlessly efficient. The only one who survived was the leader and he used the old Jew as a shield and put his sword at the old man's throat.

"One step closer and he dies."

"You are outnumbered. Surrender."

He laughed, "So that you may hang me? This old Jew is my guarantee of …"

He got no further for an arrow sprouted from the side of his head, the feathers embedded up to his ear. His body slid to the ground.

"Jack, see if there are any more."

I dismounted and went to the old man. His son was shaking with fear. "Are you hurt?"

The old man smiled, "No, but had you not come then we would have been. I am Cok fil Isaac and this is my son, Abraham. I am grateful, my lord, and surprised that you came to our aid."

Matthew helped the boy to his feet and I said, "Why surprised?"

"We Jews are not popular, my lord. Men seek us out when they need money but they shun us."

I nodded, "My great-grandmother was a Jewess and my name is Henry Samuel."

His face broke into a smile, "You are from Stockton. Then all is clear. We have heard of your family and we are lucky that you came to our aid."

"What brings you on this road?"

"We had been to Durham. One of the Prince Bishop's knights borrowed money from another Jew, in Leicester. Since the earl expelled them from the city they find it hard to move around the country. I am a relative and undertook to make the negotiations for him. They are kinder men in York and in Durham."

Jack came back with a string of mangy-looking animals, "We found some sumpters tethered to trees. I think they are only fit for eating."

I nodded, "Put the dead servants on the animals. John of Parr, take Hob with you and accompany Master Isaac back to York." I threw him a purse. "Stay the night and we will see you back in Elton."

The Jew shook his head, "You need not, my lord, you have done more than enough."

Smiling I said, "I am just being the good Christian."

Once we were back on the road Alfred and Samuel pestered me with questions once Matthew had told them the story. "Why was there no treasure, Father? Everyone knows that Jews are money lenders."

"They use parchment and that represents money. Cok fil Isaac will have given the paper from Leicester to a Jew in Durham and he would have supplied the money. They have a good system."

"And what will happen to the bodies of the bandits?"

"If we had time we might have buried them but I wish to be home as soon as we can. If they have families they might find them and bury them. If not then the animals and birds of the forest will feast on their flesh. That is the price such men pay."

Alan, his brother and his father had been forced to live in the forest and, overhearing our words he said, "There are bandits, Master Alfred, who only rob for food. They do not enjoy the life but sometimes it is forced on them. The ones we slew were bad men with black hearts. They need not be mourned. I could smell their evil."

My sons had not been in any real danger but the experience was a lesson for them. They were learning what it was to be of the blood of the warlord.

Chapter 1

Henry Samuel

The conspiracy

When the king's nephew, Henry of Almain, arrived at the castle I knew that the knights of the valley would be asked to ride forth once more. As we awaited him, for he had to use the ferry to cross the river, I spoke with my uncle. He was well-wrapped against the wind coming from the east as Earl William was no longer a young man.

He shook his head, "I know of no war in which England is involved. Since the king gave away Normandy to hang on to Gascony we have been at peace with the French."

I nodded, "And now that the king's daughter is wed to King Alexander of Scotland there is no war north of the border."

Matthew shrugged, "Then it will be the Welsh once more."

"I hope not for Eirwen's sake."

My uncle hoped for a peaceful life, "Speculation is idle, nephew. Perhaps this is just a social visit."

As we headed down the stairs of the gatehouse to greet the son of the King of the Romans I laughed, "And since when has a Plantagenet ever travelled north unless there was some request to be made? We had better sharpen our swords for war will come."

"Until the Earl of Leicester returns then we shall have peace."

I liked Lord Henry Almain. He was a warrior and a likeable man. He had with him just four oathsworn and they looked like soldiers too. Their horses and their cloaks showed all the signs of having been ridden hard.

Sir Henry bowed, "Earl, I have been sent by my uncle and I apologise for the lack of warning. It is not the way to do such things."

My uncle put his arm around the young noble and said, "This is not the court. We are border knights and make welcome every traveller. The accommodation will be comfortable and we dine well here in the north no matter what they think in London." He waved over Edgar, the new steward. "Take these lords to the chambers in the west tower. They should be comfortable there."

"Yes, my lord." Edgar had a weary sound to his voice as he knew the visitors would necessitate a great deal of work for the servants under his command and he would have to watch them closely to ensure that everything was just so for a royal visitor. There was food but Edgar planned a week of meals and this would upset them. He would cope but he would be like a bear with a sore head as far as the servants were concerned. He would smile and bow but inside he would be unhappy. I knew that one day Stockton would be mine and these problems would become mine. I was in no rush to be the earl.

My brother Alfred lived at Elton with me and my former squire and cousin, Sir Richard of Stockton, also lived in the manor. I still called him Dick, if only to avoid confusion with my friend and fellow knight, Sir Richard of Hartburn.

"We will see you when you have cleaned up from the journey, Sir Henry." After they had gone he said, "Whatever the king asks we do not have to do, Henry Samuel. I know you and you are duty-driven. You have suffered enough in the service of the king."

"We can listen and the king needs our support. I would not have the crown on Simon de Montfort's head. He wishes it to be so but I have come to know that the man is evil. It is evil of the worst kind because he hides it behind a mask of good deeds. He boasts of being a crusader and yet he blinded whole villages and slaughtered women and children. Whatever the king asks then I am inclined, already, to agree, if only to keep him on the throne and the crown on his head."

We sat in the solar and James, one of the hall servants, brought over a jug of wine and some goblets. If it had just been my uncle and me then we would have used beakers but a royal visitor demanded well-made goblets. Dick had been hunting and he strode into the hall still wearing his hunting gear. "I saw strange horses in the stables. We have visitors?"

His father said, "Lord Henry Almain."

Dick poured himself some wine and drank half of it in one swallow, "Then action will be forthcoming. Good."

My uncle sighed, "Dick, put your mind to a wife and producing grandchildren for me. You have warred enough for one so young."

"There will be time, father, for you are still hale."

"Hale? I cannot walk far and the last time I rode…well, I cannot even remember."

"It was the mad Parliament, uncle, at Oxford."

He smiled at the memory, "That was where you showed Simon Montfort that the knights of the north know how to fight." I had fought a combat to the death with one of de Montfort's knights.

Dick finished his wine and shook his head, "And yet I am berated for wanting action. I shall go and change. Mother will be less than pleased if I let the family down before the nephew of the king."

As his son left my uncle shook his head, "Will the boy never become the man?"

"Dick is who he is, uncle. Thomas took time to become the man he is today and that was not an easy journey for Sir Robert is not the best of teachers. Each man makes and follows his own path."

Dick changed and returned at the same time as Lord Henry Almain and his knights. The four knights sat apart and I poured Lord Henry Almain some wine. He shivered, despite the proximity of the fire, "Is the wind always as cold here in the north?"

I nodded, "When it blows from the east then it is always so. I believe the sea makes it thus."

My uncle was impatient and cut to the chase, "What brings the king's nephew all the way north to visit this outpost of the realm?"

Sir Henry smiled and I shrugged, "To the point; you are right Sir William. Such a long journey has to have purpose and here it is. You know that my cousin, the king's daughter, is married to King Alexander of Scotland?"

"I do. They were married before the two of them were twelve, I believe."

"They were and are happy. King Alexander now has an heir. King Henry is well-disposed towards his son-in-law. He rules well and is popular in Scotland. We no longer need to fear the threat from the north."

"And yet here you are, in the north and speaking of Scotland."

"You are right, Sir William." He drank some wine and continued, "King Alexander wishes to unite all his kingdom. The islands to the north and west of his realm represent a threat. He would have them ruled from Edinburgh. King Hakon of Norway not only ferments trouble in the isles but he is also trying to take them over. King Alexander is raising an army to fight him."

My uncle shook his head, "Then I see no reason why you have visited. We are not under threat and if there is a war, then from your words it will be to the north and west of this land."

Lord Henry Almain glanced at Dick and me and then said, "King Henry would have a conroi of knights of the valley join King Alexander and act as advisors."

My uncle laughed and shook his head, "Once more the blood of the warlord will be spilt so that King Henry gets his way. My father often spoke of the misery caused by King John and he hoped that his son would be cut from a different cloth." He leaned forward, "And the king will pay for this service?"

Lord Henry Almain was uncomfortable and he shook his head, "Since the Earl of Leicester upset it Parliament is loath to release the money that King Henry needs. There will be no money for this."

My uncle sat back and emptied his goblet.

Lord Henry Almain endured the uncomfortable silence for a moment or two and then said, "Sir Henry Samuel, you have not yet spoken."

"My uncle is the earl and the lord of this land. He has spoken."

Sir William said, "You wish the leader of this conroi to be my nephew?"

Spying a glimmer of hope Lord Henry Almain leaned forward, "It was not only King Henry who suggested that Sir Henry Samuel leads the conroi but also my cousin, The Lord Edward." He smiled at me, "You have skills on the battlefield, Sir Henry, and a reputation for honour and chivalry. King Alexander is young and like a piece of unformed clay. Your hands could make him a warrior."

"You flatter me, Sir Henry, but what you ask would take men away from the valley for at least six months. I have lost years of my life already in the service of King Henry. I would watch my children grow and not miss those times of change."

He nodded, "I confess that this is a challenge but we thought that the heirs of the warlord would continue their service to the crown."

My uncle rose, "The honour we have shown the crown has rarely been reciprocated. The hall will need to be prepared for the feast." He was dismissing our visitors and it seemed to me rude.

"Come, Lord Henry, Dick and I will give you a tour of the castle. It will give an appetite for food." I stood and smiled, "You will need your cloak."

We left the hall and I led the five of them across the inner bailey to the river wall. We climbed the steps and when we reached the fighting platform then the wind gusted from the east. I nodded to the sentries who headed for the guard room. It would afford us privacy and while we walked the walls, they would not need to do a duty. I pointed to the river that the men had crossed, "That is our greatest defence and bars any invader from the north from ravaging the lands to the south of us. We protect the jewel that is York."

"And that is why there is no bridge."

"We have the ferry and that is enough." I led them to the east tower. "There lies the sea. It can take days if the tides and winds are wrong, to reach the sea. Herterpol is a busier port than Stockton these days." When we reached the north wall, he saw the town of Stockton below us. "We have a strong wall to protect our town and men who are willing to fight." I turned to face Lord Henry Almain, "We maintain, at our own

10

expense, a larger retinue than most knights. My uncle would not have that expense wasted fighting for another country."

He nodded, "Bluntly put." He leaned his hands on the stone and said, "My cousin will reimburse you for any losses." He turned to me, "He has his own income from Gascony. Let Sir Henry and I speak alone." His men moved out of our hearing. He looked at Dick.

I smiled, "You should know, Lord Henry Almain, that as close as you are to The Lord Edward, I am closer to Sir Richard here. If you wish to speak in confidence to me then do so before him. I would tell him what you said in any case."

"I am sorry, Sir Richard, I am more used to the knights at court whose smiles hide daggers."

Dick grinned, "I am not offended, my lord."

"War is coming, Sir Henry. My cousin and I know that. The Earl of Leicester might still be abroad but he ferments trouble. His allies in this land harry and harass the Jews. It is to make King Henry more dependent than ever on Parliament for the money paid to him is drying up. The intervention of the King of France was but a stay of execution. We need King Alexander to be grateful to us so that when the earl does return, we shall not have to leave the knights of the north watching the northern border. I am not saying that if we do not help King Alexander he will join de Montfort but The Lord Edward would do all in his power to secure the best warriors when war does come."

"I thank you for your honesty. You do not require a large conroi do you?" He shook his head. "If I have read you aright then in reality you just need me."

"I suppose but it would look better if there were others with you."

"Quite. I am just thinking of how to present this to my uncle."

He brightened, "Then you will do it?"

I shook my head, "It will be Sir William's decision. I am his heir and he may not wish to risk losing me. The needs of the borderlands are ingrained in us. Enjoy the food this night and the company this night. We shall see."

We headed back to the guard room and I nodded to the men there, "Thank you for the privacy."

"You are welcome, my lord, and we enjoyed the sit down and the warm."

As we headed back to the hall Lord Henry Almain said, "You have a loose relationship with your men, do you not?"

I stopped and looked at him. I could never understand why lords further south distanced themselves from their men as though they were somehow different. "Of course. When we fight then we are all placed in danger. The battlefield does not divide into nobles and villeins. When we die we all face the same God."

We entered the hall, "I begin to see why the knights of this land enjoy such success. My cousin needs you to do this, Sir Henry Samuel."

I had confirmation of who was taking the reins of power and I nodded, "I know and The Lord Edward is England's hope."

Left alone with Dick, my cousin said, "You know that my father will agree with whatever you have decided?"

I smiled, "I do."

"And you have already decided that you will go."

"Of course, but it will do no harm to make the royal family worry that we might refuse."

"And you will take me?"

I stopped and faced him, "Dick, these are not knights that we will face. These are Vikings. These are the wild warriors who fight on even though there is no hope. King Alexander will have to risk all if he is to defeat them."

"Still, cuz, I would follow your banner once more."

My bookish brother William was present at the feast. He was more like a monk than anything and his fingers were always ink-stained, no matter how much he scrubbed them. He had a thirst for knowledge that amazed me and he threw question after question at Lord Henry Almain during the feast. Aunt Mary was a stickler for behaving properly and she rolled her eyes at him when he took out his wax tablet to record some nugget of information. That she did not reprimand him was because of the presence of my mother, Matilda. My mother was still the matriarch of the family and she indulged my younger brother. I think that while she loved all her children, William was special to her. For one thing, she knew he would never go to war and that she would never have to weep for him.

Lady Mary also had a sense of duty and my uncle had not told her the purpose of Lord Henry Almain's visit. When she heard she beamed, "I have heard that King Alexander and Queen Margaret are a well-matched couple. It will be good to have warriors from this land help them."

My uncle wiped his mouth on the cloth he had over his shoulder and shook his head, "There will be no payment for our service and so we shall not send men."

Lady Mary gave her husband a shocked look, "Are we mercenaries now that we do not draw swords without gold?"

12

My mother said, mildly, "Mary, as we sit at home and sew the scenes of battles on tapestries while our sons fight them, I think we should leave those decisions to Earl William."

An awkward silence fell upon the table. My little brother, William said, "Of course, there is a precedent, uncle."

"Precedent?"

He nodded, "More than one in fact. The Warlord famously fought Stephen and the Scots without any payment from the royal household and Sir Thomas, the hero of Arsuf, took his sword to fight in the Baltic crusade."

I saw my chance and I seized it, "So, William, if I were to go as an advisor to King Alexander then I would be doing what our forebears have always done, the right thing?"

He nodded. "I have discovered that Ridley, who began this line, did so when he followed Lord Aelfraed to Miklagård. He understood duty better than any."

Once more silence fell. My uncle wiped his hands and shook his head, "It is some years since I fought on a battlefield and I never yielded my sword when I did but I can see that I am outnumbered and despite my objections, Henry Samuel will be acting as King Alexander's advisor. I hope you understand, wife, that this will be putting our son Matthew in danger as he is Henry Samuel's squire."

"And me, mother, for Henry Samuel would not leave behind the bravest knight." Dick pre-empted my decision.

Earl William shook his head, "How you get your head into a helmet these days amazes me, my son."

Lord Henry Almain was, of course, delighted. The next day he spent the morning with me. There was a parchment from King Henry to introduce me to King Alexander. I doubted that many of his men would need an introduction. The ones who lived close to the Tweed had encountered me many times.

"I am happy that I can be of service to King Henry and The Lord Edward but if my advice is ignored or I am not needed then I shall return. I do not feel obligated to the Scots."

"That is understood but you should know that King Alexander asked for this help. He did not name you specifically but when he visited with the king, he asked for a knight who knew how to fight and to win to be his advisor."

Once I had gleaned all that I could the knight and his oathsworn road to Herterpol where they would seek a passage back to England. They would not endure the hard journey they had made when they had travelled north.

I sat with my uncle, brother, William, and my two cousins, Sir Richard and Matthew, my squire. William had his inevitable wax tablet. He was never happier than when he was making marks on either wax or parchment. He also gave us the benefit of his sharp mind. My uncle said little for he felt he had been badgered into the commitment.

William was an organised man, "So, brother, how many men will you lead?"

I looked at Dick, "You have yet to choose a squire. Who would you have? One of the men at arms?"

He shook his head, "I have been approached by a young warrior who wishes to be my squire. I thought to choose him."

"Good. Who is it?"

"Your son, Alfred."

I was annoyed for neither had yet spoken to me and both owed me that duty. "He is too young. It is out of the question."

"Cousin, I was your squire at the same age."

I looked at Matthew and began to understand how my uncle felt. It seemed like a conspiracy. William nodded, "It makes sense, brother. You will be there to see that he is trained well and if you are to be advisors then you should not need to draw a sword."

I rounded on William, "In war, William, especially fighting Vikings, there is no safe place to be, except, perhaps, sheltering behind the walls of a castle."

He did not react to the barb but just nodded, "You are right. I know nothing of war but I do know that Matthew has grown as your squire and, thanks to you, will soon be ready for his spurs. The same will be true of Alfred."

I said nothing but I knew they were all right. Eirwen would not be happy. "Then that will mean two knights and two squires. We need at least four archers and four men at arms. I would not take those who have families. The brothers Alan and Robert are my first choice for archers."

Dick knew my men as well as I did, "Ned and Leofwine are both single and good archers."

I nodded and William added their names to his tablet. Matthew asked, "Will you take Jack?"

I laughed, "I cannot see Jack being willing to be left behind. He would lead the familia."

"Then Harold, John Long Leg and Will Grey Streak would be the best men at arms. They are all young and Jack trained them all."

"Good. I am not sure what King Alexander will have in the way of equipment. We will need four sumpters with three tents."

"Lances?"

I shook my head, "No, Dick. I am unsure about Scottish horsemen. I would not ride in a charge with men I did not know. We take our swords. That should be enough."

We spent another hour identifying all that we might need. "We will leave on the morrow. Tonight is the time for goodbyes."

"Will you take a ship, brother?"

I shook my head, "We ride. I will take Raven." I looked at Dick, "And you had better ensure that my son has all that he needs."

Dick said, cheerfully, "Oh, he does. He began to prepare last night. We spoke of it while we ate."

As the four of us rode to Elton I wondered how my son, Samuel, would take it. He was being left at home and yet was only slightly younger than his brother.

The complete conspiracy was made clear to me when I reached my hall. Alfred was all packed and he and Samuel were grooming his horse. Eirwen clearly knew that Alfred was going and there was no sign of tears. I was confounded. Even Samuel seemed resigned to staying at home. That evening, as we ate, Samuel said, philosophically, "I am the younger son. I will go to war next time. This way I can continue my training under John of Parr's eagle eye."

Alfred nodded, "And as you are taking Jack then my teacher will be there to continue, if he has need, to offer advice for me."

When Eirwen lay in my arms that night I asked, "Why are you not more upset?"

She chuckled in the dark, "Would you have me teary-eyed and fretful? You are a warrior and your sons take after you. Had they chosen to be like their Uncle William then they might well have lived lives of peace but they are both warriors. You are a good man, Henry Samuel, and you will watch over them. It is you I worry about. You are the one who puts yourself in danger. This time you go to advise a king. Good. Advise and leave your sword sheathed. That way all my men will come home to me."

I kissed her, "And I am lucky to have a wife such as you."

Chapter 2

Henry Samuel

The King and the Steward

We navigated our way north by way of the castles that protected this land: Durham, Prudhoe, Morpeth and Norham. At each one, I questioned the castellan about the border and was relieved to know that it was quiet. There were still raids but they were not ones that heralded war. They were cross-border raids by men on both sides who had grudges or feuds. In some cases, it was just to steal cattle. The castellans did not condone such action and punished any that they caught but to the warring families who lived in this land, it was more like a game than anything.

When we reached Norham there was surprise that we were going to aid the Scots. "Given your family history, Sir Henry, I would have thought that you would be the last man to help an enemy."

I smiled at the bishop's knight, Sir Roger, "First and foremost I am an Englishman and I serve my king and my country. This visit of mine might well result in peace on this border. Your life would be easier as would mine."

He nodded, "We have enjoyed peace here for some time and it seems that it is closer to London where the king has his problems."

"And I have had dealings with the Earl of Leicester, he is a far greater danger to England than an army of Scotsmen."

We crossed the Tweed and headed for Edinburgh. The Romans had built two roads when they had come north. One passed through Jedburgh but we took the one that ran closer to the coast. We did not stay in castles for I did not wish to risk running into an old enemy. Instead, we stayed in holy houses. We paid for our beds, food and stables. It was strange to ride through this land with our mail on sumpters and our shields hung from our cantles. Cowled cloaks and hoods replaced coifs and armour. Our archers had unstrung bows and we rode in an uneasy silence. When we neared Edinburgh then word of our arrival was sent to the king. By the time we reached his castle, he had word of our arrival. Edinburgh Castle still had timber buildings but I could see that there were stone ones being constructed. Its position made any attack by an enemy difficult.

King Alexander greeted us at the gate. I dismounted and bowed, "King Henry has sent me, my lord, and put me at your command." I handed him the parchment. The young king, I took him to be in his early twenties, studied the parchment and then handed it to a mailed man.

I learned that the mailed man was Alexander of Dundonald, Steward of Scotland and King Alexander's general.

The king looked at me, "You did not bring many men, Baron Elton."

I smiled, "I was told that Scotland had enough brave men and you needed my advice."

"I can see that you are a diplomat too. That is good." He waved forward a man dressed in the royal tunic and said, "Have the baron's men housed. I will speak alone with our English ally."

By alone he meant the three of us for the steward came with us. That the king was popular was clear as we entered the mighty hall and headed for a chamber with a fine aspect of the firth. Men bowed but did so with a smile. The king showed that he knew how to win over people for he smiled back. We passed a room filled with women and I saw the queen nursing her child.

"My love, we have a countryman of yours to stay with us. Sir Henry Samuel of Elton."

Queen Margaret beamed, "I have heard much about your family, Sir Henry. My father often speaks of the debt he owes the family of the warlord. I hope to hear much from your lips when we dine."

"It will be an honour, my lady."

Once in the solar, the king waved his steward and me to sit. He nodded to the steward to begin speaking, "I do not know how much you know of our situation here, Sir Henry."

"I know that the lords and kings of the isles owe allegiance to King Hakon of Norway and that cannot be a good thing."

"You are right, King Alexander has offered to buy the islands from Norway but they have rejected our offer. We have no choice, if we wish to hold the islands, but to take them by force."

I nodded, "And I am guessing that the lords and kings of the isles will not take kindly to that and that they would resist."

"They would and as they control the seas we have something of a stalemate. We have devised a strategy that will, we hope, give us a greater chance of victory without losing too many men."

I warmed to this general, "A fine trick if you can manage it."

"We know that we will be outnumbered if King Hakon brings all of his ships to war. It is rumoured he has a thousand ships and as each ship can carry thirty to forty men then we could not defeat them in open battle."

He hesitated and the king nodded, "Speak openly, Sir Alexander, for we know that Sir Henry is an honourable man and can be trusted."

The steward nodded, "If we summoned every warrior in Scotland we would still be outnumbered and there are some who might use such a request for men as an opportunity to show their disobedience. We intend to fight our enemy with just the men from Ayr, my men. My son, Earl of Menteith, is gathering our men now for we have heard that a Norwegian fleet is approaching from Shetland. We have time. Had you taken any longer to reach us then we might have had to leave without you."

"I left as soon as the message came from King Henry."

King Alexander nodded, "Aye, well the Norwegians have chosen not to give us the time we thought we had. I would have been happier if you had brought more men. The handful you have will not determine the outcome of the battle."

"You know the story of Arsuf, King Alexander?"

"I know that King Richard won a mighty victory there."

"He did but he almost lost the battle. Thomas of Stockton, my grandsire, was a squire then and he stood alone with a standard and a sword protecting his father's body. He did so and it turned the battle. King Richard rallied his forces and defeated the Saracens. One man, the right man, can make all the difference."

They both nodded. The steward said, "There are spies in Edinburgh. The magnates from the islands watch us. We leave in two days' time and we shall sneak out before dawn. We wish to be close to Ayr before they know that we have left."

"My ambassadors are still negotiating with the Norwegians. The longer we can delay their sailing the more chance we have of victory."

"How so, my lord?"

"It is late summer now and soon we will have the winds and the rain from the west. King Hakon's strength lies in his ships. We have to hope that nature will join with us in this endeavour so that we can, between us, defeat Norway and claim the islands that are ours by right."

The steward said, "The Norwegians and the men of the isles are mighty warriors. We have fought them many times. Perhaps we know each other too well for our battles are always bloody and rarely conclusive. The king thought that a new approach might succeed. We have suffered at the hands of the English and the Normans more times than we have bloodied England's nose." He waved a hand around the castle, "After King William's defeat at the hands of one of your forebears, this castle was English. Now that the king is married to England perhaps we will benefit from your wisdom, experience and advice."

My mind had begun working already and I nodded, "You say that it will be your men that will fight this battle?" He nodded. "I am guessing that your strength lies not in horsemen but in men who fight on foot."

"We have horsemen, aye, but not as many as the English."

"And archers?"

He frowned, "We have men who can use the bow but they cannot influence a battle such as this."

I smiled, "I have brought but four archers with me however if you let them command your archers then we may be able to give the Norsemen a surprise. It is the same with your horsemen. Even a few can be used on a battlefield to cause defeat. Often it is the smallest stone that begins an avalanche."

The king smiled, "I told you that new eyes might see what we cannot."

The steward nodded, "You are right, my lord. When we ride west, Sir Henry, I will enjoy picking through your mind."

I had been given a fine chamber which I shared with Dick and our squires. They awaited me within. "Now remember that we are here as guests. We do not get drunk and we do not lord our past victories and encounters over them. We will be humble and polite. This is a new venture for me but if we can succeed then our days of having to fend off attacks from the north may well be a thing of the past. At least while King Alexander rules."

"He is a friend then, cuz?"

"He seems to be and remember Queen Margaret is English. This bodes well."

When we ate at the feast, I confined my stories to those that did not involve the Scots. I spoke of our battles in Gascony and Wales. I talked of the past and my family's fights in the Holy Land and the Baltic. The queen had heard some of the tales but not all and King Alexander was hearing them for the first time.

It was on the next morning that I had a chance to speak with Jack and my men. I took them to the battlements and we talked while looking east towards Norway. "If I thought we would come here to fight with words I was wrong and for that, I apologise. The Scots will need our help. You four archers will command the Scottish archers. I know not their quality but I suspect that they are used to loosing arrows as individuals. You all know better than any the power of a shower of arrows. Did we bring plenty?"

Ned frowned, "We brought two warbags each, my lord. That is just forty-eight arrows."

"Then I shall see the steward and get more. Jack, the men at arms will need to be used to fight alongside their knights. We will need lances or long spears. That was my fault. I did not bring them for I did not think that they would be needed."

"I get on well with the captain of the guard. I will find them. We will only need six."

Dick said, "See if you can get some javelins. Matthew and Alfred might be able to cause some hurt to our enemies." He smiled, "I cannot see these young cockerels being happy to sit astride their horses and smile."

"Dick, we may have to fight but I want not a drop of our blood to be spilt. This is not our war. That war is coming but it will be fought in England and not here in Scotland."

My men at arms and archers left us. I was looking at my son but my words were intended for both squires, "You will both need all your wits when we ride west. Do not underestimate the Norse. Sir Thomas fought such men in the Baltic and even he found them hard men to defeat. There is no dishonour in fleeing from a berserker."

"Berserker?"

"A man, Alfred, who will throw off his clothes to fight naked until either all his enemies lie dead or he does. Three such men held a whole army at bay at the Battle of Stamford Bridge. The first in our family, Ridley, fought there." I shook my head, "I would have you in mail, Alfred, but you are still growing. When we return home we will commission the weaponsmith to make you, Matthew, a hauberk."

"Then am I ready for knighthood?"

"Perhaps but that will be your father's decision. Even if you are knighted there will be no manor for you, at least not yet."

"I do not mind. Dick here has no manor and seems happy enough."

Shaking his head Dick said, "With spurs comes the expectation from our parents that we shall wed. Enjoy this life while you can, little brother."

When we left, I felt like a sneak thief. We donned our mail and were cloaked as we slipped out of the gate and headed west. The hooves of the horses clattered and should have alerted any spies that there were men leaving the city but they would have all been abed and by the time they had risen we would be further west. Well mounted as we were the only way for a spy to pass us was to leave the road and take to the byways. The king had fifty knights with him. They were mainly from the eastern side of Scotland and most of them knew me. I had even

20

ransomed a couple. Had I not been there as the king's guest then there might have been trouble but, as it was, I only had to deal with a few baleful looks. One thing they all knew was my skill with a sword and a lance. My trial by combat at Oxford was well known and some of the young knights had asked me about it when we dined.

We did not have far to go. We stopped at Wishaw where Sir Robert Belhaven had a manor. He was one of the steward's knights and he had ridden ahead to ensure that all was prepared for the king. It had been chosen so that we could cross the nearby Clyde early in the morning. The castle at Ayr was a fine one. King William had built it between the rivers Doon and Ayr. It would be a hard castle to take and I saw why Sir Alexander had been chosen to be the steward of Scotland. He was the bastion against the Norsemen and Islanders. His role was the same as mine. His son, Walter Stewart the Earl of Menteith, was like him in every way and we got along with him and his knights. I suppose it helped that we had not fought against these knights and while they had heard of us there was no bad blood.

We were greeted with the news that the Norse fleet had been sighted further north. They could raid the Clyde if they chose. We held a council of war in the Great Hall.

"If we allow the Scots to raid then Glasgow could be in danger and if that was secured by our enemies then the road to Edinburgh would be open." The Bishop of Glasgow had a vested interest in the river and his cathedral.

There seemed to be a shortage of ideas as to what could be done. I sighed. I now knew why The Lord Edward had thought I was the right man for this task. "There is an island to the west of here, I believe, Arran?" There were nods. "And if it was to be attacked then might that not draw King Hakon further south if only to stop us taking his land?"

The Earl of Menteith said, "But we could not hold it, Sir Henry."

"I was not suggesting that we hold it. A raid on the island and hostages taken might well provoke a reaction."

The steward said, "Is it not dangerous to poke the bear?"

"If the bear is asleep, but this bear is prowling close by and if our stick is long enough then we might make him move in a direction that we determine."

The earl said, "It is worth a try. We might not outnumber the Norsemen but we have more than enough to take one of the settlements on Arran."

The steward said, "Then do so on the morrow and I will hasten the muster."

The earl said, "And would you and your men at arms come with us when we raid? It is your plan."

Things were not going the way I had expected but he was right. I had made the suggestion. "It would be an honour."

I waved over my archers, "I have spoken to the steward and he agrees that you four will command his archers. Begin today even though the muster has yet to be completed. I need not tell you what to do."

Ned smiled, "Aye, my lord, find out those who can loose an arrow as far as we can and then see how many arrows they can release in a count of thirty."

"And Jack, you and the men at arms stay here. I want our horses well protected. We four go just as advisors. We will not need to draw a sword. It is a sign of good faith only."

Jack shook his head, "I am not sure, Sir Henry. I would rather watch your back."

"And I would rather have horses to come back to. All will be well."

The earl took ten ships and just three hundred men to slip across the eighteen miles of sea to Arran. We had not taken horses for we would not need them. The aim was to raid the stronghold of Dugald mac Ruari and slight it. If we could we would bring back hostages. My plan was to provoke the Vikings to raid closer to King Alexander's army. As the ships nudged their way across the sea, I could hear the excited voices of my son and squire. I was doing that which I had said I would not, I was putting my son in harm's way.

When Dick spoke in my ear I almost jumped. "Sir Thomas would be as worried as you are, Henry Samuel, if he had made this decision but, like you, he would have made it. How many times did you ride at his side when you were little older than Alfred?"

"That is different. You cannot compare me with Sir Thomas. He was unique."

Dick shook his head, "You should speak to your brother more often. Since returning to Stockton I have spent many hours speaking to him about our family. He loves to delve into the parchments in the castle and he would tell you that there have been many such as Sir Thomas. Sir William, the Warlord's son, went to the Holy Land and won not only great honour but a bride. Sir Samuel fought in the Holy Land and his son was Alfred's age. It is what we do and although I do not understand it I believe that there is something in each of us that makes us different. Trust in Alfred and do not fret about him."

I knew that Dick was right but it did not make it any easier.

The man who led the fleet was an islander himself. He had fallen out
with Dugald and was eager for vengeance. He led us to a small beach
just half a mile from the stronghold. We disembarked and the ships
stood out to sea. They would turn and sail towards the port and distract
the night watch while we approached from the land. The idea, once I
had heard of the man's knowledge, was mine. In my experience, you
kept a better watch to the side where the sea lay than the land you ruled.
I was with the earl, Calum, a local who knew the area, and the earl's
oathsworn. We led the men across the open ground. There were roads
but we crossed turf and dunes. Less than thirty of us were mailed and so
there was little jingling of mail. We were not silent but the noise was
carried away to the south and west by the slight breeze that had brought
us to the island.

We stopped two hundred paces from the wooden palisade. The sight
of the sails of our ten ships drew the four guards to the port side of the
walls and the earl waved forward ten young men who raced at the wall
and using shields sprang up the unguarded top. It was ridiculously easy
and when the gates were open, we flooded in. I would have preferred
silence but the men led by the earl had endured raids from the islands
and this was their chance for vengeance. They screamed war cries and
ran through the port.

The earl's oathsworn locked ranks and I said, "Matthew and Alfred,
stay behind Dick and me. Guard our backs."

The problem with wild men racing through a settlement is that
houses are not cleared. The four of us were quickly overtaken as our
raiders sought victims in houses that were less mean than the ones we
passed. The six men who emerged from the dwelling to our left must
have armed themselves and waited until they heard the screams and
shouts pass them.

"Behind!"

It was Alfred's voice that made us spin. The six men had axes, clubs
and swords. They each wore a helmet but none wore mail. We must
have looked like easy victims and, perhaps we were. Alfred wore just a
leather jack and helmet. He had a shield and a sword but it was a shorter
one than mine. There were screams as women and children fled from
the house and headed for the opened gates behind us.

Dick and I put our shields before us as Matthew and Alfred swashed
their swords before them and then stepped to the side. The axe that
struck Alfred's shield was a well-struck blow but my son's shield was a
good one and although I knew it would have made his arm shiver, it
held. Our swords were slashing weapons and I slashed across the
unprotected neck of the nearest warrior. Sharpened and unused as yet it

23

gave him a warrior's death. I punched my shield at the face of the next man as Matthew's sword hacked across his thigh. Unprotected as he was the blade bit through to the bone and he tumbled to the ground screaming in pain. With the odds now in our favour and as Dick and I were mailed, we were able to use our shields to protect us while our swords ripped and slashed through unprotected flesh. The last warrior was little more than a youth and he turned and ran for the gates when his comrades were slain.

Alfred made to follow but I said, "Leave him. Let us check the houses for any who still shelter within."

We found none but we looked inside every house as we followed the trail of carnage and destruction wreaked by the earl's men. The sun was just rising over the mainland when we reached the port. The ships had moored and the town was ours. We had passed enough bodies to know that the earl had lost men. The Islanders had lost far more but better led we might have suffered fewer deaths.

The earl was in an ebullient mood. I nodded, "Well done, my lord, but now is the time to load the ships, fire the town and walls and sail home."

One of his men said, "We could take the island, Sir Henry."

I shook my head, "And hold it with less than three hundred men? I think not. Take the victory. We surprised them and we won. We destroy their town, their walls and their ships. The aim is to bring King Hakon to us not for us to die on Arran."

The young earl had been carried away with the victory but as the sun came up he nodded his agreement, "You are right, Sir Henry. Load the hostages and treasure. Set fire to the gates and the houses to the west and place kindling in these homes. The wind will do the rest."

It took some hours to load the ships and as we left to tack our way home, the pall of smoke that rose would tell the king of the isles and King Hakon that we had struck the first blow. It took far longer to get home for the winds were contrary and we were laden but once back in Ayr, the king and the steward were delighted with both the raid and the hostages.

The steward came to speak to me, "Thank you, Sir Henry. I am not sure we would have envisaged such a bold strategy. You gave good advice despite your youth."

"We shall see for we now await the reaction of the Vikings. Will they take the bait?"

Chapter 3

Henry Samuel

The Battle of Largs

The fleet that arrived off the Ayrshire coast was the largest assembly of ships I had ever seen. King Hakon had not taken kindly to our raid and was coming to punish us. The steward had called upon the levy and we had an army to defend the land but it was dwarfed by the Vikings we saw aboard their ships.

King Alexander was kept safe inside the fortress that was Ayr where we held a council of war.

The steward said, "We cannot sit idly by and let them ravage this land."

The king said, "But we do not have enough men to bring them to battle here."

Once more it was incumbent upon me, as the advisor, to offer a suggestion, "What you have, King Alexander, is mobility. You have horsemen and they do not. They outnumber your army but by judicious use of horsemen you can outnumber their raiding parties." Every eye turned to me. "You have asked me here as an advisor and here it is. Fill these walls with foot soldiers and have every mounted man without. Let them bleed upon these walls. Let your archers whittle them down while we make them bleed without." I pointed to the west. "You told me, Lord High Steward, that the weather and nature can come to our aid. Let us trust in God and the sea to do so."

The earl nodded, "That is a good plan for we have too many horses to be housed and fed in these walls. Better that we stay without."

His father said, "The king's bodyguard and I will stay here in Ayr castle." Although I thought it was a mistake, I said nothing. The steward needed his young king well protected but the men he had brought with him were good horsemen.

The earl said, "If we use your oathsworn, father, we will still have more than two hundred horsemen. With Sir Henry to advise us we can pick off the smaller bands who raid."

I nodded my acceptance of the implied command, "Then we must leave now before they land in numbers and they know what we are about. Let them think we are trapped in Ayr's walls."

Jack was happier to be with me once more. We brought the archers' horses as they would be spares for us and, as the earl had said, there was no fodder for them in the castle. We rode out and headed south and east to the hills that overlooked the beaches. Even as we did so we saw the longships draw up and disgorge the wild men of Norway. I knew these were but a shadow of the men who had come hundreds of years earlier but history had taught us that handfuls of these men had terrorised and ruled huge swathes of land and, until the coming of King William of Normandy, there was little to stop their privations. I would not take anything for granted.

The earl knew the land and the two of us left our horses to climb the tiny mound that was the highest vantage point we could find. The earl had taken us to Dalrymple which had a wooden wall we could use as a place to rest our heads. Just four miles from the fortress of Ayr, it could be defended and still allow us to hurt the Norsemen. We saw the Vikings swarm ashore and then watched as smoke rose from the empty dwellings they had found. Every animal had been taken to safety and this was just malicious mischief. The wooden homes could be rebuilt. The rest of the day saw the Norsemen begin to surround the town, its walls and the castle. Thanks to the raising of the levy there were many men on the walls.

"So now we wait for them to move and to raid."

"Perhaps not, my lord. They will make camps and surround the walls. What if we were to move close and attack their camps while they sleep? It would, at the very least, make them lose sleep as well as make them defend from behind as well as before. A man does not fight well if he is looking over his shoulder all the time."

"How many men would you need?"

I smiled, "So the advisor becomes the leader now, Earl?"

He shook his head, "We are all new to this, Sir Henry. We do not expect you to fight all our battles for us but teach us. If the stories are true was this not how King William the Lion was captured by one of your grandsires?"

"It was. Just fifty men then, my lord. My men at arms and just knights. We leave the squires behind. If we take long spears, we can wreak such damage that none will sleep. Tomorrow, we let the rest of the knights hunt down the warbands who raid."

"Then let us do this."

We walked our horses through the dark. A local knight led us and he used hedges and buildings to disguise our approach. We could hear the noise from the Norsemen who encircled the castle and the town. The people had fled their houses and taken their animals but the food and ale

26

that remained gave sustenance to Vikings who had sailed all the way from Orkney. As far as they were concerned and until we attacked, all their enemies lay within Ayr and that was where their gaze lingered. Noise travels at night and as we drew closer to the walls of Ayr the sounds lessened.

When the local knight held his hand up, we stopped. The earl was with him and when he mounted his horse we all did the same. We had long spears but it would be our animals that would do the most harm to the Norsemen. When we mounted, I could see the glow from their fires. We had seen the sparks rising into the air for some time but now we could see the fires around which they lay. Some slept for it was getting late but others were still carousing. The ones who were awake and talking were close to their fires. Their night vision would be gone. Once mounted I pulled up my coif as did Dick and my four men at arms. They were close to me and we would ride as one. The earl waved his spear to the left and right. We all spread out into a long line. We would not be stirrup to stirrup. We wanted to cause as much devastation as we could. The Vikings had no tents and few had even bothered with hovels. Compared with their native Norway this was a balmy night.

We moved forward at the trot and the sound of the hooves began to thunder, alerting the Norsemen. When the warlord and de Vescy had taken King William the Lion it had been a foggy night. This was a clear one and when we were just forty paces from the camp we were seen and the alarm sounded. By then it was too little and too late. The handful of sentries were easily speared and then we were close to the sleeping bodies lying around the fires. Raven's hooves crunched the skull of a Norseman who sleepily rose and I speared the man next to him who was reaching for his sword. Our horses trampled and crushed men who were, at best, rising to their feet. The ones by the fires stood and some even had weapons. The six of us charged a knot of men with swords and shields standing before a fire. There were just two shields between the eight of them and they huddled together making a small shield wall. It was Dick and I whose spears struck them and the weight of horses, riders and the thrusting of our spears knocked them back to fall into the fire. We wheeled around the screaming men whose beards and hair flared with flames. My men at arms gave four of them a merciful death but one ran screaming like a fiery wraith until the flames and death consumed him.

The horn sounded and it was the signal from the earl to wheel and head back. We had done enough. This was not a battle and I still do not know how many men were killed in the attack for it was night and our horses did most of the work. What I did know was that the smell of

burning flesh filled my nostrils and I counted but one empty saddle. It
had been a success.

Back at Dalrymple, the earl was in a good mood for we had done
better than planned. The knight who had fallen had been unlucky or,
perhaps a poor rider. I was not yet ready for sleep and I groomed
Raven. It allowed me to empty my mind of the horrors I had seen. The
next raid was due that night and I wanted to be awake in case we were
needed. I forced myself to lie down and sleep. It was daylight and I
never slept well in the daylight, however, what woke me was not the
light but almost the lack of it. I was woken by a wind howling to the
west of us and when I opened my eyes I wondered if it was the night
already for the sky was dark. It was a storm. I had been warned by the
steward that the weather could change in a heartbeat and the seas to the
west would brew up a witch's cauldron of a storm. This was one such
storm. Tents were blown into the air. Luckily few men were in them.
The horses began to pull at their tethers and we were forced to calm
them. It meant that the raid did not take place and we spent the night
enduring the rain and the wind. We were all soaked to the skin and
when dawn finally came it was hard to tell for there was no clear
demarcation between sky and land. The clouds were still black.

The earl came over to me, "We are blind here, Sir Henry. I would
know how Ayr fares. Have the Vikings taken advantage of this storm to
attack the walls? I intend to take all our men and view their camp. At
the very least our banners will give hope to those within its walls."

I nodded my agreement, "And better that our horses do something
than endure this buffeting."

All of us were in agreement and I had the men at arms bring our
archers' horses. The last thing we needed was to lose their mounts.

When we reached the camp it was empty. The Vikings had gone and
as we neared the town the gates opened. We rode directly to the castle
which had the best view of the sea. Leaving Dick and my men to see to
the horses I joined the earl as we hurried to the donjon. The king and
the steward were there already and a triumphant steward pointed to the
ten or so longships that lay wrecked along the beach. "As I told you, Sir
Henry, nature has come to our aid. The enemy ships have fled north to
escape the storm."

His son saw that which his father did not, "Then we have merely
shifted the enemy. They are still there."

The king asked, "Why? Surely this is over now."

"No, King Alexander. North of here are two islands, the Cumbraes.
They lie close to the coast and the fleet can shelter there in their lee. It is

a safe haven for ships caught in a storm to the west. The men of the isles will know this. The danger has merely shifted from Ayr to Largs."

His words told us that we had to march north and face the Vikings before they could gain a toe hold on the land. We had thirty miles to march and while the horses would normally have made the journey quickly the storm had weakened them. Leaving the king safe behind Ayr's walls we marched the rest of the men north with the wind still blowing and the rain still slashing down. It was late in the afternoon when we spied the Vikings. Almost a thousand were on the beach. There they were repairing some of their longships. A local knight, Sir William Boyd, rode in to tell us that there were a further two hundred on a mound some way inland. They were led by a chieftain called Ogmund Crouchback.

We halted. It was partly to rest the horses and also to allow the men on foot to catch us up. The three of us held a council of war. The earl and the steward had come to include me in all such discussions. "So, father, do we drive the ones from the mound or charge those on the beach?"

He shook his head, "We use our horsemen and drive a wedge between the two forces. I would not risk charging uphill on a wet and slippery slope nor would I bog us down in wet sand."

I concurred and my nod gave encouragement to the steward. "Form up the horsemen and we will lead the advance. Have the Sherriff of Lanark form two bodies of men on foot and they can flank us. Have those with shields at the fore and the slingers and the archers can shelter behind. We shall see if the training your archers have given us, Sir Henry, has paid off."

This time we wore helmets over coifs. I wished that I had brought a caparison for Raven. It afforded some protection from blades and arrows. I did not wish to be unhorsed. As soon as our advancing line was spied from the mound, the Vikings there, obviously thinking they were going to be cut off, began to move towards the much larger army on the beach.

Sir Walter shouted, "Now, let us charge them while they are spread out and are not in a shield wall."

It was the right decision and, couching my lance, I galloped after the earl. What had been an orderly retreat from the mound became a flight as the line of a hundred horses, those closest to the Vikings, thundered towards them. A Viking shield wall is hard to defeat for the men lock shields and present a solid line of spears. Although their shields were on their left side and faced us we were mounted and could stab down at them. We were in a looser line than normal but that gave us the freedom to pick and choose our targets. By the time the survivors reached the beached ships more than eighty had perished. It was then that their weight of numbers began to tell. The ones on the beach, led by the Viking king himself, had formed a massive shield wall. They were using their ships as forts and men on their decks began to loose arrows at us. I think that we could have held them but when the steward arrived he ordered us to fall back to the mound which had been occupied by Ogmund Crouchback. He had ordered the foot soldiers there already and so we began a fighting retreat. We stabbed with our spears and when the Vikings fell, turned our horses and moved back a dozen or so paces. In this way, we slowed their attack and that allowed the men on foot to ring the bottom of the mound. Our horses were weary and as we neared the bottom the Earl of Menteith ordered us to form up to the east of it. There we could provide a threat to the Vikings.

Neither Alfred nor Matthew had been in danger. They had been protected by a double line of mounted horsemen but Jack and the others had been in close combat. All had lost their spears and their shields showed that they had been in the thick of the fighting. Jack nodded, "These are hard lads and no mistake, my lord. They seemed to shrug off wounds that would have felled another warrior."

I nodded, "This day is not over yet. Their ships are filled with warriors. They will outnumber us."

The steward dismounted and joined the men on the mound. There were less than eight hundred of them and by my reckoning, the Norsemen were in their thousands. They chanted as they marched in a line of wedges. The steward had placed his mailed men in the front line.

The earl nudged his horse next to me, "When the horses are rested, we will charge their flanks. That is where they are vulnerable."

King Alexander was lucky in his steward. He and his family were brave men who were undaunted by the sea of metal that hurled themselves at the mound.

This was a more even battle than the one on the beach. Here the archers and slingers kept up a rain of stones and arrows that thinned the Vikings who wore no mail. At the battle of the swords and axes, however, the Vikings were winning. The Scots were brave but the Norsemen were reckless and cared not if their arms were laid open to the bone. They fought just as hard. As the Vikings neared us, whittling away at the edges of the men on foot, the earl shouted, "Horsemen, charge."

We spurred our horses forward and slammed into the side of the Norse wedge that was about to break through the line of Scots at the foot of the mound. The Vikings who had shields held them in their left arms and we struck on their right. My spear went through the shoulder of a huge, mailed warrior. It drove into his body but even in his dying, he tried to wrench the spear from his body. He was a powerful man and although he failed his dying body dragged my spear to the side and with it Raven's head. Dick had also encountered a Viking who was unwilling to go quietly to his Valhalla and although the spear had hit the Viking in the chest he had fallen back clutching it and tearing it from Dick's arms. The warrior with the two handed axe seemed to appear from my left as though a ghost. A bear's head and skin hung over his helmet and naked back. He swung the axe not at me but at Raven's head. My poor horse stood no chance. He had a quick death as the Danish axe smashed into his skull. As he fell, I was thrown from his back. Even as I sailed through the air I dropped my spear and used my right hand to hold the shield. Ahead of me, I saw the Vikings I would hit. The shield smashed into the skull of one of them and then I was lying on the ground, winded.

I heard Dick's voice in the distance, it seemed, "Sir Henry is down!"

I would soon be fighting for my life. I held up my shield as the Viking sword came down and the sword smashed into it hard. I tried to rise and as I did so, saw the Viking as he was speared by Dick. Four Vikings ran at Dick with their shields held before them and they smashed into Dick and his horse. He too tumbled from its back. The distraction enabled me to rise to my feet and draw my sword. As I hurried to stop the four Vikings who were keen to butcher the knight I saw Alfred and Matthew skewer the bearskin-covered Viking. They were coming to our aid but all it meant was that four of the Warlord's descendants would die on this Scottish mound. My grandfather had taught me that a battle was never over until the end and no matter what the odds you fought on.

I brought my sword over my head to split the back of one Viking in twain. I pushed another, already overbalancing because of the swing of his axe and he fell over Dick's body. Dick's sword was waiting and he stabbed a third Viking in the groin. The Norseman's scream sounded like a vixen in the night. The fourth thought he had Dick until Alfred's spear appeared through his chest. Jack and my men at arms had fought their way through Vikings and they rode behind us with their spears over us.

I reached out with my shield arm, "Come cuz, we have chanced enough this day."

I pulled him to his feet. His horse, Ajax, had already headed back to the field where they had been grazing. Side by side and with our shields before us we backed towards the safety of the other horsemen. The

Vikings were determined to take our lives. Alfred and Matthew, along with our men at arms, backed their horses behind us and their spears jabbed over our heads to poke into the faces of the Vikings that escaped our swords. We still had forty paces to go and a group of Vikings made a determined attempt to get at us. The twenty arrows that came in two flurries from our right smacked into them. When I saw arrows enter mail then I knew it was our archers and that they were using bodkins. They must have emptied their sheaths for none of the Vikings reached us and we made the safety of the squires and horses.

Dick sheathed his sword and shook his head, "I thought we had both fought our last there, cuz."

"Thank you for coming to my aid."

He lifted his helmet from his head and I saw him smile, "You repaid the favour and more."

I turned to my son and squire, "And you two, what were you thinking?"

Matthew shrugged, "If you both died then we could never go back to Stockton and being a Scottish sword for hire did not appeal."

The battle did not end there but the crisis had passed. The horsemen who had survived reformed and the battle carried on until dark. The Vikings ended their attack and went back to the beach. We waited on the mound and in the fields behind it. Waterskins were emptied and we waited all night for a sneak attack. As dawn broke the Bishop of Glasgow prayed for salvation and we all prepared to do battle once more.

It was the smell of burning that told us the battle was over. The high tide had stranded some ships and the storm had completed the work. The Vikings had put their dead in them and set them alight. The rest of the ships were heading north and home by the time the steward led us to the beach. We had lost men but the Vikings had to have lost more. The smell of burning flesh in the ships made us retreat back to the mound. I went to find Raven but all I found were the remains that had not been butchered for meat. My brave horse would ride to battle no more.

While light horsemen followed the Viking fleet up the coast we returned to Ayr. I rode one of the sumpters my archers had used to carry our war gear and we rode together. I had been thanked by the earl and the steward for I had exceeded their expectations. Our attack and the death of the bear-skinned leader had broken their attack and the steward was grateful.

It was dark by the time we reached the fortress and we had not eaten for more than a day. Riders had warned the king and those in the town of our plight and the smell of cooking food greeted us. While our men at arms and archers headed for the camp the four of us, with bloodied surcoats and dented helmets entered the castle. We were greeted by the king. The steward and his son had been the ones who had told of the battle and the three of them waited for us in the Great Hall.

"Sir Henry Samuel, you have done all that was asked of you and more."

I bowed, "I am a knight, King Alexander, and when men are dying I cannot simply sit and watch."

"We have word that the Scottish fleet continued to head north. The threat is over and the Vikings have returned to the islands. Winter is coming and they will not return again. The steward assures me that we can take Arran and the islands off the coast here. I shall send ships to King Magnus of Man and King Dugald of the isles. With their ally gone, they will be more willing to negotiate. Your service here is done. You may return to your valley with the thanks of the King of Scotland and his queen."

I was relieved and it showed on my face as I smiled, "Thank you, King Alexander, I am pleased that we were of service."

"And you should not suffer for our victory." I was not sure it was a victory as the Vikings had not been beaten but I said nothing. "I have a war horse for you, Duncan, he can replace the one you lost and two hackneys. There will be a chest of coins for you too."

"Thank you, King Alexander."

"Now rid yourselves of those bloody raiments. This night we hold a victory feast and then you can accompany me back to Edinburgh on your way home."

I did not mind the detour for we would be comfortably housed but I knew it would add a week to our return to Stockton.

It was November and the ground was icily hard as we rode down the Durham Road and saw the sturdy wooden walls of Stockton. I reined in and watched the smoke from the tannery drift across the river. "Remember, Alfred and Matthew, we do not speak of Raven's death nor the near death of Dick and me. I would not have your mothers worry the next time we go to war. We advised and the Vikings were beaten. That will be enough."

The two squires were just happy that they had been rewarded. Dick and I had shared out the treasure between all of us, archers and men at arms included. I knew that the men at arms and archers would speak of the battle but so long as word did not reach either my wife or my sister-in-law I would be happy.

"Now let us go home and enjoy a Christmas in Elton and Stockton."

Chapter 4

Sir Henry Samuel

The Perilous Ride

My hall at Elton felt warm and cosy after the fortresses of Edinburgh and Ayr. What was hard was living there without Alfred who now served my cousin in Stockton. Samuel wasted no time in asking for his training as a squire and, ultimately, a knight to begin. Jack and I began in the first week of December. We exercised in the walled yard before the house. I had seen, through Alfred's actions, that our training worked and with Matthew aiding us we began to make Samuel become a warrior. His body had already filled out in the time we had been away and he heeded every piece of advice. Perhaps there was something to be said about the blood of the warlord for he had natural reactions. It was Jack who recognised them.

As Matthew sparred with my youngest son, Jack said, "I have trained many men, my lord, but your sons take to the work more naturally than any men. The things we normally have to teach are there in every move and stroke. All that we need to do is to sharpen them. They are like a blade, fresh from the weaponsmith. We know that it is true and all that it needs is to be sharpened."

"I pray that we have enough time to do so before we go to war again."

"Again, my lord?"

"King Henry is now planning on retaking his land back from the rebels."

"Rebels, my lord? Has there been a war I knew nothing about?"

I laughed. Jack was typical of the ones below the rank of knight. They heard little of the political manoeuvrings of the ones who ruled England. "Aye, but one not fought with swords but words and alliances. The pope and the King of France now support King Henry. Simon de Montfort is back in England, his supporters are busy persecuting and murdering Jews to take their money. It is a way to make King Henry poorer and more reliant on Parliament which is controlled by London and Simon de Montfort."

I saw understanding on Jack's face, "So we will draw sword again."

I nodded, "And the war will not be fought here in the north, thank God. It will be the midlands and the south that will be fought over.

There will be no fighting until the next campaigning season, we have time. Samuel apart, how are we for men who can fight under my banner?"

He put his sword down so that he could use his fingers to count, "There are eight of us with mail and another ten who can ride, have a sword and a helmet." I knew that most of those were farmers from my manor. They would all have a jack or brigandine as well as a shield but none would have a warhorse. "There are twenty bill and spearmen as well as eight archers."

I shook my head, "When we are mustered, they will guard Elton."

"Then you will only wish those archers who are mounted?" I nodded. "There will be ten."

"That is satisfactory. There will be a larger contingent from Stockton as well as men from Norton, Redmarshal, Hartburn and Thornaby."

He looked up at me, "Redmarshal?" He knew as the whole valley did of the unwillingness of Sir Robert of Redmarshal to go to war.

"There are men there who will fight. Do not forget that Sir William will not be going to war either. Men will fight beneath my banner and that of Stockton. We may not have the numbers of lords like Lord Mortimer but what we have will be solid enough."

We visited Stockton a week before Christmas. We usually celebrated Christmas as a family in the Great Hall there and so the early summons was unexpected. I had, of course, told my uncle all that had happened in Scotland. He was a warrior and he understood what we did. Whatever the reason was for the summons it was something which had occurred since our return. Dick and my son greeted me at the door to the donjon. Alfred could not contain himself, "We had a visitor here at the castle, Lord Henry Almain."

I sighed, "As a squire, Alfred, you need to learn discretion." I now knew the reason for my summons. "The earl has sent for me and it is he who will tell me the reason."

"Sorry."

I smiled and ruffled his hair, "Do not worry, I made such errors until I was chastised enough."

The other knights of the valley were there too and I wondered what had prompted such an impromptu gathering. Sir Robert was not in good humour. He snorted, "Why it takes some knights longer to reach Stockton than those with manors further afield I shall never know."

My uncle glared at Sir Robert. They had been friends once but those days were gone, I wondered if having to defer to the earl had made the difference. When I became the Lord of Cleveland would I have the same problem with Dick, Richard and Thomas? I did not think so. Sir Robert and I had different characters.

"Now that we are all gathered, I can give each of you the news brought by the king's nephew." I sat at my normal place, on the earl's right hand and his squire poured me some mulled wine. Its warmth drove the chill of the short ride from my body. "The king has summoned me to Oxford. He is gathering his loyal lords around him. The meeting will be on the twelfth night."

My brother William was there, of course, with the inevitable wax tablet. He commented, "An interesting journey, my lord, through England in the depths of winter."

"Just so." He looked at me, "I will not be going." I nodded. He added, "I am afraid that my old wound suffers in the cold. Sir Henry Samuel will be my deputy."

"I do not mind, uncle." I knew it made no difference if I minded or not. A representative from the most powerful family in the north had to be there.

Sir Robert of Redmarshal said, "Why on earth would the king summon knights in the middle of winter? It makes no sense."

"It does, Robert, for the de Montforts are back in England and they are not only persecuting Jews and depriving the king of his due but they are also fortifying their strongholds. The Earl of Leicester has tried to reimpose the provisions of Oxford but there is not the will to do so. London has rebelled against the king and The Lord Edward makes war in the Welsh Marches. We have a civil war already and it is only the cold of winter that keeps it at bay. The king needs our advice and support. Henry Samuel is the best placed to do so."

My brother, William, looked up, "And yet if he has to travel through the midlands then he passes through the heartland of de Montfort. It will be a perilous journey."

My uncle nodded, "I know."

My cousins, Thomas, Dick and Alfred all clamoured and offered their services. I saw my uncle and Sir Geoffrey Fitzurse smile. My uncle held up his hands, "The smaller the number who travel the better. I will let Henry Samuel take men from his manor."

I nodded for I was happier with that. I had done the reverse of the journey when I had returned from Wales and I knew the places to avoid.

Sir Geoffrey Fitzurse, the most senior knight in the room, my uncle apart, nodded too, "It is the right decision but you need to take care, Henry Samuel. Your success in France, Italy, Gascony and now Scotland, not to mention Wales makes you a target for Simon de Montfort, his brother and his sons. They will have spies who will report

36

to them that Lord Henry Almain left for the north. They will be watching for you."

"I know but I also know that whatever they try it will be clandestine. They will try to catch me and execute me so that none knows the true story." I was in brother William's eye line and I saw his mouth drop open. "I will just have to be sneakier and more cunning than they."

My uncle continued, "For the rest of us it will be a time to prepare young men to fight for this land. The three old men, myself, Sir Geoffrey and Sir Robert will have to be guardians of the north when the men of the valley ride to war."

My conversation with Jack came to mind, "And to that end, uncle, I would take only mounted men. I have eight archers who have horses and can ride. They will be the only others I will take. I would rather take fewer men but ones who are more mobile, than a slow worm of foot soldiers to slow us up." I looked at Sir Robert, Thomas' father, "I expect every lord of the manor to provide some mounted archers."

"The expense!"

As I had expected it was Sir Robert who reacted and Sir Geoffrey who responded, "If we are to squat safely in our halls while our young men shed their blood then the least we can do is give them the best that we can."

My uncle waved a hand to my brother with the wax tablet, "William here will act as quartermaster. You will send him a weekly update about numbers of men, horses, weapons, arrows, spears and lances so that he can let me know which lords need the goad." Again, he looked at Sir Robert who was now squirming a little under the scrutiny. I had never really known Sir Robert and, thinking back, I realised why. He had rarely fought alongside my grandfather and I could not remember the last time he had ridden to war. Worse, he had mistreated his son, Thomas and almost destroyed the young man. Had he not come to Gascony with us then he might not be the fine knight he was. I felt sorry for his wife Isabelle and his daughter, Isabelle. They had to live with him.

We spent until noon, when food was fetched in, discussing matters martial. When I looked around the table as hands took the cold meats, cheese and bread I realised that the knights who would ride forth were now all my cousins. I wondered if King Henry would demand that all the knights of the manor obey his muster. I dismissed the idea immediately for King Henry knew that the bastion that was Stockton needed to be defended and he would need young blood on the battlefield.

37

It was, surprisingly, my brother William who brought up the matter of battle, "Will there be a battle?" We all looked at him and he said, "As you know I have read about our family's history and it seems to me that even in the time of Stephen and Matilda there were few battles. The largest one, the Battle of the Standards, was fought against the Scots and thanks to my brother we know that cannot happen. Will this be a war of sieges and holding strategic towns and castles?"

My uncle stared at my brother, "Perhaps the only one who is not a warrior has seen the heart of the matter."

Everyone looked at me and I shook my head, "The king needs a battle. He has to defeat Simon de Montfort decisively and when the earl is defeated to hold him." I looked at William, "There will be a battle but before that battle is fought there will be manoeuvring and marches until we have the right place to fight and to win."

William smiled, "As you say, uncle, I am the writer and not the warrior. I am glad that it is my brother that leads us to war."

Sir Robert left as soon as it was convenient, that is to say when the food had been devoured and the jugs emptied. Poor Thomas looked embarrassed. I went over to him, "You are a true knight and when we were in Gascony, no one was braver. Hold your head up. The blood of the warlord is in your veins and you will lead the men of Norton and Redmarshal in this war against anarchy. Your father is… well your father but you have the blood of the Warlord in your veins."

The others drifted off during the afternoon until there was just William, my brother and the earl. "I have maps for you, brother. The Warlord kept such things and he travelled around Oxford and the land to the west."

"Thank you, William."

"I would be at your side but my quill is not as mighty as your swords and I would be a hindrance to you."

"Never." I looked at my uncle, "I think that Sir Thomas should lead his father's men and, perhaps, they should train at Norton rather than Redmarshal."

"No, Henry Samuel, they shall train here. I may be too old to go to war but I know how to train men. When we have the Christmas feast then every warrior in the valley will train here under our eye and when you travel to Oxford it will be under my steely gaze."

I smiled, Sir Robert was in for a shock if he thought he would avoid having to do any work.

Knowing that it would take up to ten days to make the journey surreptitiously we left on St Stephen's Day. It was the time with the shortest days of the year and, especially in the north it was the coldest of times. We would be invisible. We wore no surcoats and I took the same eight who had come to Scotland with me. They were unmarried and had proved their worth to me.

Eirwen was unhappy at my departure. She understood the need but, understandably fretted about my safety in the depths of winter and travelling through a land filled with my enemies. "Listen, my love, I am not a fool. I know I am safe as far as Lincoln. That is still a royal castle and it is loyal to the king. We will travel without marks upon us. When we leave Lincoln then I will take the road west and pass to the north of Nottingham. That will allow us to pass to the west of Leicester. The earl is in London as are his brother and his sons. Few fools will venture beyond their doors at this time of year."

"Yet the fool I married will hazard the cold and the deadly knives."

"All will be well. De Montfort has made it quite clear that not only is he my enemy he has sworn to have my life. This is a battle to the death. Either he dies or...."

She kissed me, "Come back safe!"

In high summer we could have ridden to York in one long day but the short days of late December meant it took two days and we did not stay with either the archbishop or the Sherriff. Instead, we took a room in the inn by the river, 'The Saddle'. It was in many ways a rough hostelry but grandfather had used it and when we stayed in the castle my men at arms and archers slept there. There was another reason, my father had been murdered when he had stayed with the Sherriff. I felt safer. The innkeeper was a discreet and loyal man. My secretive arrival evoked no questions and we were given a table in a side room. Ralph kept it for the smugglers who used his inn and for friends. We fell into the latter category.

While we ate the delicious stew, washed down with dark beer, I went over our plans. Each day saw a slight modification of them as some idea or other entered my head. "Robert and Alan, I am trusting in your local knowledge to help us navigate a way through the forests north of Nottingham."

They nodded, "There are bandits there, my lord, but Robert and I know them. All will be well."

Jack said, "It is still Leicester that worries me, my lord. When Lord Henry Almain came north to visit the earl his man told us that the Earl of Leicester keeps a good watch on the road north. Simon de Montfort keeps patrols seeking to bar a passage north or south. He holds the Midlands in a death-like grip. The forest helps us avoid Nottingham but not Leicester."

"There are forests there, Jack. Matthew and I used them when we fled Leicester the last time."

"Yes, my lord, but they lie to the north of the city. We would stick out like landed fish south of the city. We are too great a number to hide and questions would be asked."

I smiled, "Are you saying, Jack son of Oswald, that you think just Matthew and I ought to travel alone and that way we might have more success?"

He shook his head and frowned, "My lord, do not put words in my mouth for it is full of stew in any case." I smiled. Jack had wit, "I am just saying that we need a plan in case the road is barred."

Alan nodded and said, "The Fens."

Matthew asked, "The Fens, Alan?"

I said, "The place where King John lost his treasure. It is a boggy, stream-riven land and everyone avoids it."

"Except, my lord, that this is winter and the water and land will be frozen. We might be able to use that route."

"Yet we have no maps. A good suggestion and it might satisfy Jack the doubter. If we cannot go south then we go south and east."

Our journey was without incident as far as Lincoln. The weather was cold and the land was frozen but we wore woollen hats and thick, oiled cloaks. We paid for grain for our animals when we stopped and we did not push them beyond their limits. There was no need for we had time enough to make the journey. Lincoln was a royal burgh and the sentries on the gates alerted the captain of the guard. We were the last to enter before the gates were closed and barred for the night. Any secrecy we might have enjoyed was gone and we had to visit the castellan. That he was a friend and would not betray us was immaterial for there would be Montfortian spies in the city and even without livery I would be recognised. You cannot hurl a skull in a hessian sack into Leicester Great Hall and expect anonymity. My grand gesture might have been a mistake.

I learned much in that meeting. The Lord Edward was still causing havoc, along with Lord Mortimer, in the lands to the west. Simon de Montfort's men had attacked Winchester. It was not yet full war but the sparring had begun. The Jews had been the first to suffer. Simon de Montfort's son had driven out the Winchester Jews while Peter de Montfort and John Ferars had killed many Jews in Worcester, prompting the raids of The Lord Edward. In London, it had been even worse. Isaac fil Aaron and Cok fil Abraham were killed by John Fitz John, a leading Montfortian, with his bare hands. Five hundred Jews perished in the frenzied attack. When we had been in York the Jews there were safe. If Simon de Montfort ever took control of the land then it did not bode well for the Jews.

"If you are riding south, my lord, then I believe that you will be heading to Oxford." I stopped mid-drink. "It is common knowledge that King Henry has summoned his lords to a meeting there. You are the only one who has come from the north but then again yours is the only family that dared to challenge the de Montforts. I would offer men to escort you but…"

"No, castellan, this is a royal castle and must be defended, for the king. You bar the road to York. Thus far de Montfort has not cast his covetous gaze there but he might do." I finished my drink, "What you could do, my lord, is allow us to leave at Lauds and delay the opening of the gates. Any Montfortian spies who are in Lincoln will be behind us and word will not reach our enemies directly."

"Of course."

We also took food from the royal larder. For the next few days, we could not guarantee either a roof or food on our journey. We slipped out of the gates before anyone else. The castellan would risk the ire of the merchants by preventing anyone from leaving until well after dawn. Our early start meant that we covered more miles than we had previously. It was getting on to dark when we left the great road north to head into the forests north of Nottingham. We chose a place where we could do so unseen and Robert and Alan led us along a little used trail to a small clearing with water. We made a camp but, despite the cold did not light a fire. We ate a cold meal. We tethered the horses together and hobbled them. They would have mutual warmth and we did the same. The ground was hard and cold but we all managed some sleep. Most importantly we were hidden. The next day we worked our way through the forest and emerged, just before dark to the south and west of Nottingham. Once again, we took to the road but we were seeking a wood once more. We were all suffering. We could endure the cold but the cold with just cold food was not good for a man. We found a wood but it was less than a mile from a small nameless hamlet. This time we had two of us on watch. We each did a two-hour session.

It was as we headed south that we were seen. We were rounding a bend and a farmer and a youth I took to be his son were using a horse to drag a log towards their farm. Flight would have alerted them and so we rode down the road and passed them. They both recognised me as a knight and took off their woollen hats as we passed. We were no longer hidden. We did not deviate from the road until we were well out of sight.

"Well, cuz, the carrot is out of the ground. What next?"

I nodded to Alan, "We take Alan's advice. We head east and find sanctuary in the fens. It means that we will need to head for Northampton and I do not know the political affiliations of that city. Let us ride."

We took the next small road that led east. It eventually came to the great road that headed south to London. We crossed it and found a small road, little more than a track that headed south and east. The path took us across solid islands while between them was a crunchy frost-covered wetland. Alan had been right. The ground was frozen. Despite the mail that I wore we did not sink beneath the mud. There were places that rose above the flatlands and as darkness came, we headed for one. We had not seen any settlement and as we unsaddled our horses, none of us detected woodsmoke. I took a decision, "We will risk a fire. We have endured two nights of hard, frozen ground and cold rations. Let us cast the bones, eh?"

The hot hunter's stew we made ensured that we all felt warmer. Our isolation meant we did not need to lose sleep and the embers of the fire kept both the animals and us a little warmer than we had been for some nights.

The next day we rose before dawn and headed south and west. I knew that we had travelled twenty miles through the fens and if there were pursuers we had to have lost them. When the skies darkened and sleety snow fell then I felt that God was on our side for whilst it was uncomfortable it hid us from view. Only fools would be on the road.

As we neared Northampton it was clear that we had no convenient wood in which to hide. Worse, there were others on the road and we had been seen. I did not know if Northampton was Montfortian and I decided that we would try to gain entry and see the reaction. The sentry at the north gate was surprised to see so many of us entering but did not seem concerned. He even offered us advice about which inn to use. I suspect he was paid by the innkeeper to do so.

Sometimes Fate intervenes. I had seen it many times and my grandfather had told me how a chance meeting in the holy land led to a crusade to the Baltic. As we passed the entrance to St Andrew's Priory the Prior and some of his priests were entering the gates. He reined in and said, "Riders from the north? This is rare in winter."

"Needs must, my lord."

He nudged his horse next to mine and said, "I am Prior Robert of Poitou and I believe I know you. You are Sir Henry Samuel of Elton, are you not?"

I was shocked and did not deny it, "I am, but how do you know?"

"My brother is Sir Guillaume of Saint Severin. When last I was in Gascony he told me of knights from the north of England who saved him and his family. He described you well."

"Even so, my lord, I am hooded and cowled."

"And your journey has been noted. I have just come from the castle. The Earl of Leicester's son, Simon de Montfort, arrived this morning. He is to command the town."

My heart sank. All of our efforts to escape were now in tatters.

"He told everyone to be on the look out for Sir Henry Samuel who would be travelling south with retainers. You had best enter my priory." I hesitated, "I trust my people and you can trust me although in truth you have little choice." The bell sounded for the closing of the gates.

I nodded, "Thank you, Prior."

As the gates of the priory closed behind us he said, "I am not popular with the Montfortians for I am Poitevin. They hate us. My hope lies with King Henry. I am your friend."

As we were taken to the cells kept for visitors, I realised that having the Prior as a friend would keep us safe for the night but when we left we had gates to negotiate and guards who were looking for Sir Henry Samuel. Thanks to my great-grandmother we all had features which marked us as slightly different. To a Montfortian who hated all things Jewish then I would be identified. We would be trapped in the walled town of Northampton.

Matthew did not have to serve at the table and he sat with the Prior and me. We were questioned closely about our time in Saint Severin. I could tell that we had made a real impression, "And how are Eleanor and Louis? Is she with child yet?"

Alfred had married Eleanor, Sir Guillaume's daughter and Louis, one of his sons, was Sir Thomas' squire. I shook my head, "Not when I had left but they are young and there is time." He nodded and I ventured, "Thank you for your hospitality but we will have to leave your priory at some point. How do we do that without being apprehended?"

He smiled, "There is a way. The wall to the west of our priory is old and the mortar from the stones has been eroded. It would not take much for men such as yourselves to push down the stones, perhaps before dawn tomorrow. All you have to do is to slip down the bank and cross the meadows and the River Nene. You would have to swim your horses but then you would be clear of Northampton and de Montfort, even if he saw you, would have a long ride to catch you. It is a long fifty miles to Oxford but only the first ten are in Montfortian land. Towcester is held for the king."

"I cannot thank you enough for this knowledge but will you not be harmed if de Montfort discovers what you have done?"

"If you work silently and only remove enough stones to facilitate your escape then it is unlikely that any will hear of this. I trust my people. I trust that you are as skilful as my brother said."

We were up at lauds and led our animals to the wall. We had been given food and our ale skins filled. Robert of Poitou, cowled and hooded, led us to the wall. He was right. A once substantial wall, some stones had already fallen. Jack and the others knew what to do and they began to remove a section of wall just wide enough for a man and horse to walk through. They made it look as though the stones had fallen naturally so that it was wider at the top than the bottom and the stones were spread on both sides of the wall. It did not take long. I clasped Prior Robert's arm, "I thank you."

"I am repaying a family debt. Go with God." He made the sign of the cross over our heads and we mounted.

The bank was steep but I trusted in the advice we had been given and, leaning back, we slithered down to the meadow. The ground was frozen hard. We made our way to the river and the edges were frozen. We said nothing as we approached for it was still dark and noise carried a long way. I led for I was the one wearing the mail. I stepped my horse, Blackie, into the water. I had been told that we would not need to swim far. It was icily cold. The current was sluggish and the river was narrow. I was soaked and I was cold but the crossing was far easier than I had anticipated. When his feet found purchase on the other side I sat on the saddle. I was soaked through and as cold as I had ever been but as it was still dark it meant we had escaped de Montfort and had, I hoped, a clear ride to Towcester and thence Oxford.

We reached the motte and bailey castle at Towcester by terce. Sir John Wallingham knew me from the Welsh wars and we were made welcome. He insisted that we stay the night and enjoy a night in a bed when he heard that we had crossed the icy Nene.

"We have endured a few brushes with the younger de Montfort. We keep patrols of mounted men out and when they come across de Montfort's men there is always the clash of blades. Thus far it has only resulted in wounds but when war comes…"

Chapter 5

Henry Samuel

King's Council

We arrived at Oxford Castle earlier than might have been hoped and I was relieved when the gates of the castle were closed behind us. We arrived on the morning of the appointed date. We had enjoyed more than our fair share of good fortune. I went to the chapel as soon as we arrived to thank God for I was sure he had watched over us. The men were taken to the warrior hall. Oxford was a royal castle and they would be comfortable there. Matthew and I were taken to a bed chamber. It was not large, indeed the small bed almost filled it and Matthew would have to move the palliasse into position once I was abed but it was ours and we had to share with no one. We would be cosy and in mid-winter that was no bad thing. My cousin helped me to dress. The clothes in which we had ridden stank of horse and sweat. We had brought dried rosemary with us and I rubbed it along my body. When we had been in Northampton, we had enjoyed more space and I had bathed the upper part of my body. We would not offend the king.

I lay on the bed while Matthew changed, "So cuz, we have managed to reach here safely. Can we get home safely when this is over?"

"We will attend to that problem when we know the time and date we are leaving and the king's plans."

Our talks with the prior had been most illuminating. It was clear that the north was considered neutral by both the Earl of Leicester and the king. I was the only northern magnate who had been summoned south. The de Vescy family had been deprived of Northumberland and were now rebels siding with the earl but they lived on their manors in the south. When the muster came it would only be the men from the valley who would have to march south and I now knew of the ring of castles held by Simon de Montfort. They would be a barrier and as well as working out a way to get home I needed to discover a way to join the king when the time came.

We headed down to the Great Hall. I recognised John de Warenne. The Warenne family had ever been loyal and the first Earl of Surrey, William de Warenne, had been one of William the Conqueror's companions. Our family was well known and I was greeted with a welcoming smile. "So you have made the perilous journey from the north, Sir Henry. You have shown more loyalty to the king by making such a journey in winter."

"I know better than most, my lord, the perfidy of de Montfort. I would journey through hell itself if it meant that Simon de Montfort would be defeated."

"Would that more men in the north felt as you do."

I felt I had to defend the rest of the north, "My lord, we still have cross-border raids from Scotland. As you said, it is a long way from the Roman Wall to Oxford. When we leave our homes, we do not know what will remain when we return."

"You are right and I apologise. We southern lords seem to think that England ends at Lincoln."

There were a few other nobles and they joined the two of us. I was the most junior but my exploits in Wales and Gascony meant I was accorded great respect.

The servants came in to lay the tables for the feast and we headed for the fire where we drank wine brought by our squires and watched as the tables and chairs were laid out. I counted just twenty chairs and that meant a small and somewhat intimate feast. I deduced, from the faces, that the men here were the most loyal and dependable in the land as well as being the most senior.

When the king and his brother, Richard of Cornwall, arrived then all talk ceased and we bowed. They were accompanied by the Bishop of Oxford. When they took their places we were shepherded to our seats. We were ranked according to seniority. Had my uncle been there he would have been seated with the earls of Surrey and Pembroke. I was a mere baron and was the furthest from the king. That said there were so few of us that we were all as close as I would have been in Stockton Castle. The Grace was a long one for the bishop invoked God's help to defeat the rebels. The food was then fetched in. It was, as one might expect at a royal feast, of the highest quality as was the wine. I drank sparingly.

There were fewer courses than normal and when the steward emptied the hall of any other than the lords and their squires then I knew the king would speak. He was now more than fifty years old and he looked it. His younger brother looked far healthier. King Henry's voice, however, was firm when he spoke.

"My lords, you are here so that you, my most loyal of leaders, may know our plans. We have suffered at the hands of a pernicious Parliament led by a corrupt and evil man. We now have the blessing of the pope and the support of the French. We can end this." He paused and we dutifully banged the table in support. "As you can see my son is not at my side. He is in the west securing that border for us. Thanks to the efforts of Baron Elton our northern border is also safe." Eyes swivelled to me. "I intend to order all those who hold to me to assemble here, at Oxford by Quadragesima. By then my son will have secured allies in the west and, once more, thanks to Baron Elton, we shall have allies from Scotland who will come to join us. King Alexander is grateful that England supported him in his battle with the Norse and there will be a host larger than the men of the Tees Valley coming to join us."

That was news to me and welcome news at that. The Earl of Surrey had told me that King Hakon had died. The circumstances of his death were still shrouded in mystery but the result was that the King of the Isles, Dugald mac Ruari and the King of Man and the Outer Isles, Magnus, had all sworn fealty to the Scottish king. King Henry's son-in-law was now secure. If we had Scots fighting alongside us then that might be the edge that would win us this war. I also saw the plotting and planning that had necessitated my journey to Scotland. My uncle was right, the king was still using them as his pawns.

"You are all here as my counsellors. You have been chosen by me and not some rebellious Parliament that seeks to undermine me. You should all know what is in my mind. When we are mustered, we will march north and take Northampton. The Sherriff of Nottingham is now a loyal servant to the crown and that is held for us. It means that Leicester will be isolated. We are making Rochester Castle stronger and when the Midlands are ours, we shall march to the Cinque Ports and make those ours too." He sat back as though he was done.

The Earl of Pembroke said, "A good plan, my lord, but it presupposes that the rebels allow us to do all of this."

He smiled and gestured to his brother who spoke, "You are right, Sir William. The Earl of Leicester will come to fight us but we will determine where that shall be. It may well be that it is at Northampton which, as it is held by his son, is a prize he will not choose to lose. If he does not take the bait then we shall take Leicester."

The two of them went on to explain all their plans and I confess that they seemed, to me, to be sound ones. I realised that we would have a mobile army while the rebels would be reliant upon the mob that was the London men. Our foot would be the Scots and those from the south of England. We had a chance and, that night, as I retired, I felt more confident than when I had left Northampton.

The king and his brother sought me out the next day for a conversation away from others. "You did well, Sir Henry. King Alexander was fulsome in his praise of you. You understand we had to be circumspect when speaking of the help you afforded but King Alexander told our ambassador that you did more than my nephew asked of you. You should know that I concur with your uncle's view that you should be the next Earl of Cleveland. You sat easily with Surrey and Pembroke but I would know if this might cause discord with Sir William's sons?"

I shook my head, "Sir Richard was my squire and Matthew is my current one. They are like sons to me and both are happy with the arrangement. I saw when I went to Scotland that it was only the strong hand of my grandfather and uncle that have kept us safe for these many years."

The king nodded, "I owe my throne to your grandfather and I was just sad that he could not be rewarded more. My son knows your worth, Sir Henry, you and all your clan. Fear not, you will not be forgotten when de Montfort is an unpleasant memory."

The afternoon was spent detailing the number of men who might be summoned. It was far fewer than I had expected. The number of knights, even the most optimistic of them, was barely a thousand. While some men, like the Earl of Surrey, might bring almost five hundred men, knights such as my uncle could field a bare one hundred and fifty warriors from the valley. How many would de Montfort bring?

We spent a week in Oxford and I was satisfied I understood all that was asked of me. I would be the figurehead behind which the men from Durham and Scotland would march. I would not lead them in battle but I would command them south. My knights and I would fight beneath King Henry's banner.

The council over we headed north and this time we would head, first towards Tamworth and then to Nottingham. Leicester would be to the west of us and now I knew that the Sherriff of Nottingham had been replaced then I was happier about the risk of passing close to Leicester. We would rely upon speed to evade any danger. It was more than ninety miles but we now had a list of castles and holy houses where we could stay. With a royal warrant in my hand, we would not need to risk inns and, travelling home, we could be more open.

The last time we had ridden this road there had been just Jack and Matthew with me. I had ridden to Leicester and confronted Simon de Montfort. Even without my surcoat, I would be quickly identified. Robert and Alan also had bad memories of the treatment of their family at the hands of the de Montforts. It had cost them their mother. They also knew the land and when we neared Ashby de la Zouche, they took over our direction. Our last stop would be in St Mary's Priory in Coventry. Half owned by the Earl of Chester the priory was as safe a

48

dwelling as we could hope to find. We hoped to make the journey to the priory in one day.

This time Fate decided to throw danger into our path. Our route was discovered and when Robert and Alan galloped urgently back towards us then we drew swords in anticipation of danger. The two would not have ridden back if the passage ahead was clear.

Reining in, I shouted, "Draw swords and shields. Ned and Leofwine, string your bows and take position behind us."

"Aye, my lord."

"Leicester men, my lord." Alan's shouted warning confirmed what I had suspected. I had my shield pulled up and my sword drawn as Robert and Alan rode behind us. I saw a hundred paces up the hedge-lined road ten men in the livery of the Earl of Leicester. I recognised the leader. He had been the captain of the guard when we had visited the castle and now, from his spurs, he was a knight. They reined in and waited.

Jack shook his head, "I do not like this, my lord. Why are they waiting and why so few of them?"

I turned and looked behind. We had passed a large oak that overhung the road a hundred paces back and there the road bent. "One of two things: either there are men coming up behind or men with crossbows and bows waiting in the hedgerow." Sometimes you have to make quick decisions and this was one of them. "Archers, dismount and give your horses to Matthew. Head into the fields. If there are men waiting there then kill them and if not then loose bodkins at the horsemen."

"Aye, my lord."

"Matthew, when our men are in position, we will charge these men, if they bar our progress. They outnumber us but they will not be expecting it."

"Aye, my lord." There was not a sign of hesitation in their voices. I often wondered about our success in combat. I think it was because I knew that my men would do the right thing at the right time. That gave me more confidence when I went into battle which others might not have. The captain of Simon de Montfort's guard might not have the luxury of confidence. They might have planned this ambush but how would they react if I did not do what they expected?

I spurred my horse and he leapt forward. The others were slightly echeloned behind me making us into an arrow formation. It meant that Matthew could tuck closely behind my horse. A bolt clanked into my helmet. Inside my helmet, it sounded like a bell but the helm was well made and it held. My eyes were focused on the horsemen ahead who were, somewhat belatedly, reacting to our attack. The shout from my right told me that the crossbowman was dead. Neither arrow nor bolt came at us and I knew that my archers had eliminated that threat. The captain of the guard and his sergeants were armed like us and had just swords. The captain had reacted first and he was a horse's length ahead of the rest. I chose to take him sword to sword. I held my sword behind and below me. He had his raised. He was going for my head. Even as I swung my sword to slash across his middle, I was raising my shield. Both of us were gambling that our blow would strike first and would win the deadly duel. It was my rising shield that bore the brunt of the sword's strike at my head although the tip did scratch down the helmet. My sword struck his mail for he had not even tried to bring his shield over. The cantle behind his back held him firmly while the speed of his horse helped my sword to break mail, tear through his gambeson and, as his horse took him down the road, to rip into flesh. John was on my right and it was his strike that unhorsed and, I dare say, killed the captain.

Jack took on one of the sergeants charging towards us while I raised my sword to combat the one who followed the captain. This time I was shield to shield and our horses had slowed. It meant I was able to stand in my stirrups and bring my sword down while punching at his shield with mine. He tried to reel out of the way but his companion, fighting Jack, was there. My sword struck his mailed coif. He might have worn an arming cap below it but the sword severed the links and his skull. When two riders were felled by arrows and their leader died, the survivors of the ambush fled.

I whirled in my saddle. Matthew was grinning at me and my other men were also unharmed. Ned led my archers towards us. They held purses in their hands. I looked and saw that just five of the men who had ambushed us were dead. The wounded had fled with the rest. There were four horses wandering around and I said, "Put the dead on the horses and we will take them with us to Nottingham Castle."

We had to bang on the gate of the castle to gain entry, for they had been closed at sunset. My name afforded us entry and the High Sherriff of Nottinghamshire and Derbyshire came from the hall to greet us. I had been told his name in Oxford but I did not know him. He bowed, "Peter Marc at your service, my lord. I can see that there is a tale here."

I nodded, "We were ambushed. These men are from Leicester Castle, I recognised the captain of the guard."

He went to the draped corpse of the captain and lifted his head. He nodded, "Aye, that is Guy of Gainsborough. You did well to survive such an ambush. He is a treacherous man."

"You have come into contact with him then?"

"Aye, my lord. I was brought here to replace the former Sherriff. He was a Montfortian and the cousin of Guy of Gainsborough. We have learned to send out patrols of twenty men for this Guy of Gainsborough ambushed and killed when we sent three or four. It meant we were blind to many of the privations of the men of Leicester. We are an island here and at Derby. We hold for the king but we are like the farmer constantly repairing a dyke. The moment we stop then the enemy will flood the land."

"We would spend the night here."

"And you are most welcome, Sir Henry. I served in the Welsh Wars and was at Dyserth. You would not remember me but I was always glad when the knights of the north were in the fray, it meant that we would win."

It was a cosy affair, as we dined with the bachelor Sherriff. Matthew ate with us as did my sergeants and archers. Peter Marc was not a knight, he was a gentleman. "So, my lord, you will be privy to the state of the land. When will this uneasy conflict burst into battle?"

I smiled for he was the kind of man I liked, a blunt and honest soldier. "Hold firm and when it is Easter be vigilant for the war will begin then."

"The best that we can do here is to hold firm. I have a garrison of less than thirty and the majority of those are crossbowmen and archers. I now have just ten sergeants. Our cemetery has fresh graves and that is down to Simon de Montfort."

"And the people of Nottingham?"

He shrugged, "Much the same as people everywhere, my lord. They wish for peace. We both know that wars are fought by those who seek to hold the power. God gave that power to King Henry but Simon de Montfort seeks the crown. The people here are loyal to the king but we are not strong enough to withstand a long siege. We have Leicester to the southeast and Kenilworth to the southwest. Both are held by Montfort and if he chose, he could bring his army and take Nottingham."

"But thus far he has not."

"No." He leaned forward, "We have many merchants who travel this road and they are full of useful information. De Montfort is busy emptying London of the funds of the Jews. He is using their money to buy the loyalty of London. It is the largest city in the land. The rumour is that they can field fifteen thousand men. Now that seems to me more men than King Henry could raise."

"But their quality…?"

"As you know, my lord, he has quality in men like Guy of Gainsborough, his brothers and his sons as well as lords like Hugh le Despenser, Gilbert de Clare and Nicholas de Segrave."

"You are an astute man, Peter Marc."

"I have chosen my side and that, I hope, is the one favoured by God. When the bodies have been cleared I hope that we are victorious and that I am duly rewarded. I am an honest Sherriff and do not line my purse. I hope the king knows that."

"I am sure he does." I was not but I would ensure that when the muster came, I would let the king know of the loyalty of his Sherriff.

Chapter 6

Henry Samuel

The Maiden's Plight

It was neither a quick nor comfortable journey home but it was one without further incident. We left half of the captured horses with the Sherriff as thanks for our stay as well as the mail and weapons of two of the dead. The rest we took with us. Our weaponsmiths would be busy reusing the damaged equipment. It was close to the end of January when we wearily rode into Elton. I would give my news to my uncle the next day but all I wanted was to see Eirwen and my family, to be safe behind the walls of my manor and enjoy a little peace.

Eirwen and I were eminently well-suited to one another. She knew when to chatter like a magpie and when to be silent. This was a time for the magpie and she spent the whole meal telling me what had happened in the valley in our absence. It was all wonderfully trivial. It had nothing to do with who wore the crown or who was in favour or out. My daughters had both grown and were both chatterboxes who vied for my attention and their cousin Matthew's. It made me smile. Not for the first time I felt the weight of responsibility. I was doomed to leave my hearth and home and wield my sword for King Henry and his family. That was my duty but that evening, as I ate in the bosom of my family, I wished I could be an ordinary knight or even a farmer.

As I lay in bed, that night, with Eirwen in my arms I sighed and she said, "What ails you, my love? Was the food too spicy for you?"

"No, the food was perfect but I know that this time of peace here in Elton will not last. Come Easter we will have to ride forth and battle our enemies once more. I will have to leave."

She kissed me, "And I do not wish you to leave either but we both know de Montfort and his clan are evil. They have hurt both you and my family. Enough is enough. I hoped when he fled to Gascony that he would stay there but it is clear he will not. You and your family will be the sword that severs his fetters and stop him from taking the crown. When that is done you can return here to Elton, hang up your sword and I will fatten you up so that you will not be able to ride to war."

"And I look forward to that day as much as you."

The land was a white blanket when I rode to Stockton. Once we had passed Osmotherley on the road north we had entered a world of white.

I was lucky that the snow had not drifted. Enough people had used the road through Hartburn to Stockton that whilst it was a little slushy we were not held up. I took my sons with me and that annoyed my daughters who, not for the first time, felt left out.

Dick and Alfred were in the castle and the two of them, along with William, my brother, were eager to learn what had been said in Oxford. My uncle, since he had ceased going to war, appeared to have less interest in such belligerent matters but he listened and commented as I spoke.

When I had finished my brothers and cousin were intrigued by the Scottish connection. "It seems, cuz, that our intervention north of the border has reaped a benefit."

"Aye, Dick, and now that I am back, I wonder if the king planned this all along. It means he has more men at his disposal and he does not risk being rejected by summoning knights who might refuse to serve."

William brought out his wax tablet, "I have been keeping a record of each knight and his mesne." He looked at our uncle, "I have assumed that you, my lord, Sir Geoffrey and Sir Robert will be staying here in the valley."

"Yes, William, although it goes against the grain to let Sir Robert off so lightly. Once more, others will go to war on his behalf. Sir Geoffrey has done more than enough for any knight and deserves, as I do, a time of peace."

I shook my head, "I would rather that we only took those who are willing to war. When we go to battle, my lord, I want to know that every sword and lance that are behind me will do their duty. Make no mistake, de Montfort is a worthy adversary. He has won more battles than King Henry and his men are very loyal."

"What of The Lord Edward?"

I turned to Alfred, "I have high hopes for him, brother, but this might be his first major battle. He has not enjoyed great success in the Welsh Marches. I pray that he has learned from the mistakes he has made there." They all nodded and I turned to William, "So, little brother, how many men will I lead?"

He took out a parchment. I saw that there were scratchings out and I smiled. Someone had changed their numbers and that would not suit my brother. He liked things to be neat. "I have included the men from Stockton in your total, brother." I nodded. "There will be five knights, forty sergeants, thirty-four archers and thirty-eight armed with other weapons." I was disappointed, I had hoped for more but I knew that my uncle would want some men left to watch his walls and protect the valley.

"And mounted?"

"Half."

"Then we will have to leave at least ten days before the muster to make it on time. That means I must ride to Durham and tell the Prince Bishop. He has the names of the Scottish men who will follow our banner."

"Knights?"

I shook my head, "We did good service in Scotland but not that good. The knights will send their levies to war. If I am to be truthful, I think the Scots will be there to make up numbers. If they are not led by their masters then I would not be certain of their reliability. I only lead them south. Once we form our battles then they will be commanded by another."

"Do we fight with The Lord Edward?"

I shook my head, "I fear not. King Henry wants the men of the valley to fight beneath his banner."

My uncle snorted, "He wants a victory and you are the surest way of ensuring that he does."

"Perhaps but I believe my grandfather would approve. He saved the crown for King Henry and he would want us to be close at hand and protect it."

My uncle sighed, "You are right and that is why I am happy that when I pass on you shall be a better leader. I am too cynical and mistrustful of this royal family."

I took Dick and Alfred with me when I rode to Durham a month later. The Bishop of Durham was Robert Stitchill. He had been the illegitimate son of a priest and it was remarkable that the pope had sanctioned his election to the most prestigious post in England. He was a devout man who did good work. He had recently invested in a hospital not far from Herterpol, at Greatham. What he was not was a warrior. He would not be leading his knights to war.

When we reached Durham I was surprised at the lack of knights in the hall. This was the first time I had visited Durham since the bishop had been invested. The previous incumbent had often had ten or more knights staying in the castle. We were each given our own chamber and that was a rarity.

"The bishop is busy with church matters but he will dine with you, Sir Henry. He knows why you have come."

I nodded and waved an arm around the castle, "I am surprised there are not more visitors."

"The bishop is unlike his predecessors, my lord. Apart from yourself, there is just Sir Robert de Neville and his granddaughter. They are from Raby. You will see them when we dine."

We went to our chambers. I reflected that I could have brought Samuel too. I had not because I had expected a crowded castle. When we had changed, I joined the others in the Great Hall. Servants brought us wine and freshly baked scones topped with cheese. The bishop might be a monk at heart but he knew how to entertain his guests. We had barely made inroads into the delicious morsels when a grey-haired knight, his squire and a pretty maiden entered. We all stood while they entered.

"I am Sir Henry Samuel of Elton, my lord. This is my cousin Sir Richard of Stockton and my brother Sir Alfred of Stockton."

He smiled, "I recognise your livery and your name is well known to me, my lord. I am honoured to meet one of the heirs of the Warlord. You have kept this part of England safe for us all. I am Sir Robert de Neville of Raby and this is my eldest granddaughter, Margery de Neville. I pray you to sit and not stand on ceremony."

We all waited until the maid, I took her to be less than twenty summers old, sat. She was decidedly pretty and I saw Dick react with a smile as wide as the mouth of the Tees.

"What brings you three knights here, Sir Henry?"

"The king has asked me to lead the knights of Durham to the Easter muster at Oxford. Such things take time to organise and as I will be leading Scots too, I want no delays for the campaign against the rebels will need every warrior."

He nodded and sipped some of the wine his squire had poured for him. "Margery's father, my son, would have been with those men but sadly he died. Her younger brother is but three years old and has the weight of duty upon his shoulders already. That is why we are here, Margery and I need to know that when I die the bishop will support my grandson's claim to the manor."

Alfred said, "Surely he will."

The old knight nodded, "In a perfect world he would but stranger things have happened. When the de Vescy family were denied their manors by King Henry then that drove them into the Montfortian camp. Who knows what will happen when I die." He nodded to me, "Your family is no stranger to the whims of those who make such decisions. Your grandfather had to go on a Baltic crusade to win back Stockton and that was despite being the hero of Arsuf. No, the visit is necessary, Sir Henry. I want my granddaughter acknowledged as young Robert's guardian should anything happen to me."

Margery de Neville spoke for the first time and her voice was musical, like a songbird trilling, "Grandfather, you will not die. You are hale and hearty."

"As was your father, Margery, before God took him. This visit will do no harm. We shall visit the crypt of St Cuthbert and I will pray there for the souls of your father and mother." He smiled sadly, "My son married well. Margery's mother, Mary Fitz Ranulf was the joint heiress to Middleham Castle. I fear that fortune is now lost to Margery and all she has left is the hope of marriage to a knight with land."

"Grandfather!"

"I speak the truth and these knights know that." He popped a scone in his mouth and ate.

There was a silence which while not awkward needed to be filled and it was Dick who did so, "You should have no difficulty finding a husband, Mistress Margery."

"And who said I was looking for one? It is my grandfather who seems to think I need the protection of a man, I do not." Her voice changed to a shrill one.

Dick was flustered, "I am sorry, I meant no harm." He shrank back before her words and glare.

I felt honour bound to defend him, "You must forgive my cousin. My brother and I are both married and Richard is a warrior first and foremost. He knows little of the ways of ladies."

Her grandfather had washed down the scone with wine, "Aye, especially, those with tongues like adders. Sir Richard meant no harm with his words, indeed, they were courteous and flattering."

The young woman looked around our faces. It was as though she had just realised what she had said. She put her hand across the table to touch Dick's and she said, "My grandfather is right, Sir Richard. Forgive me for my outburst. It is just that I do not wish to be seen as a helpless maiden."

Dick beamed, "And there is nothing to forgive. My cousin is right. I know little of the ways of the world. I should learn to keep my mouth closed, eh, my lady?"

She smiled and I noticed that she did not take her hand away. "Do not do so on my account. Indeed, I would like to hear your tales."

"What say we don cloaks and take a turn around the cloister? I have filled up on scones and the exercise would be welcome." He looked at Sir Robert, "With your permission, of course, my lord."

He smiled, "Of course. Ralph, fetch my granddaughter's cloak for her."

My son had already raced up the stairs to bring Dick's. I forced myself to keep a straight face for it was clear to me that my cousin was smitten and would woo the maid. His father had not ceased in his efforts to make his son find a bride. Dick had not found one he liked until this moment and I had seen his eyes when Margery had touched his hand.

Once they were cloaked and had departed, we all burst out laughing. Sir Robert shook his head, "It was almost as though my words were prophetic, eh Sir Henry?"

I nodded, "You saw it too?"

"She has a temper and does not like her spinsterhood being brought up."

Alfred said, "But she is not that old, is she?"

"Raby has few eligible young men close by and those that there are have married maidens younger than Margery. While her parents lived, I did not see the problem. When they died then all the attention went to her young brother. Her two sisters are young and Margery, now that her mother has died, finds herself thrust into the position of mother to three siblings. It is why I brought her with me. If Sir Richard's intentions are honourable then this will solve a problem for me."

"Surely, it creates one for you."

He shook his head, "Sir Richard is the son of an earl. His cousin is the most powerful knight in the north. If anything this secures Raby for my grandson. I cannot see the family of the warlord allowing his claims to be overridden by any," he lowered his voice, "the king included."

He was a wise man.

I do not know if the steward was privy to our conversation but that evening he seated Dick and Margery together. Sir Robert and I flanked the bishop. Thus it was that I did not hear the conversation between Margery and Dick for I was too busy speaking to the bishop. He might have been a very holy man but he was practical too and understood the needs of the king.

"These demands from the rebels are abominable, Sir Henry, and as much as I do not approve of Jews, the way the Montfortians abuse them is unchristian. I am not a warrior but I will happily do all that I can to supply the men that King Henry needs. He has already told me of the Scottish lords who have promised men." He paused, "You know that few of the lords will march with their men and that I do not expect a prompt muster?"

I nodded, "I expect just their men and, to speak truthfully, I do not see their worth without leaders but the king…"

"Aye. I will ensure that any who arrive on time reach Stockton in plenty of time for you to make the muster. It will mean, of course, that the men of the north give the king a longer service than those from lands closer to Oxford."

"The men of the valley know that but what of the knights of the Palatinate?"

"Let us hope that the king succeeds in his endeavours the first time. The worst event would be a long protracted war. We do not need another anarchy."

He was right. The Warlord had finally triumphed but it took sixteen years for him to put Empress Matilda's son Henry on the English throne.

I did not get a chance to speak to Dick until the next morning. My brother Alfred teased my cousin, "Héloïse and Abelard, eh, cuz?"

Dick blushed and then smiled, "Was it so obvious?"

I nodded, "From the moment she touched your hand I saw the effect she had on you but tell me, does the lady reciprocate?"

He smiled, "Aye, she does. I told her, almost as soon as we left the hall, that I found her beautiful beyond words and she said that she had reacted the way she had out of a feeling that I was too lofty a lord for her." He shook his head, "Can you imagine anything more ridiculous?"

"It is understandable," I told him what her grandfather had told me.

"Ah, now I see. I would wed her, Henry Samuel."

"Is this not hasty?"

"Perhaps, but my father has made me acutely aware that I need to wed."

"Take time, Dick."

Dick turned to my brother, "As you did in Gascony?" Alfred realised that our cousin was right. "I will speak to her grandfather. With your permission, Henry Samuel, I will offer to escort them back to Raby. You may be right and this might be hasty. Let me spend as long with her as I can and if she decides that it is too sudden and too rash then I will back away." He looked earnestly at me.

"But you do not think that she will?"

"No, last night when we dined I looked into her eyes and I saw love but I will not ruin two lives by acting rashly."

"That is sensible. We shall leave this day and I will tell your father that you are delayed."

Chapter 7

Henry Samuel

The road to war

The wedding of my cousin to Lady Margery de Neville took place in Raby Castle a month after they met. While it might have been prudent to wait, the Easter muster dictated haste. In truth, no one objected. Dick's family, all of us, were happy and Sir Robert was delighted for the alliance with our family secured his grandson's inheritance and like Alfred and me, he had witnessed the magic of love in Durham's Castle. There was no manor yet for Dick, he would have to wait until I vacated Elton, but they were both happy to be given chambers, like Alfred, in Stockton. When we went to war the women would have mutual comfort. As Mary, Alfred's wife, was with child once more then Margery would be as a sister to the Gascon. Eirwen was pleased for Dick. She had come to know him well when he had been my squire and like all women felt that a man when he married, was complete.

The only shadows on the wedding were Sir Robert and his daughter Isabelle. Both seemed out of sorts. In Sir Robert's case, I think it was because he did not like his manor nor the family but Isabelle looked, to me, like a frightened young deer, lost and alone. While the other young women of the family fluttered their eyelashes at the relatives of Margery who attended the ceremony, Isabelle sat apart. I went to her mother and asked what was amiss.

Lady Isabelle looked unhappy too, "She is a young woman, cousin, and perhaps the sight of one of her cousins marrying is upsetting."

"I know not why. Dick is not a boy anymore."

Glancing at her husband, who was busy doing his best to consume as much wine as he could, she said, "Speak to her. I know she values you above any of the other knights in the valley."

I nodded and sat next to her, "Why the sad face, Isabelle? Are you not happy for Dick?"

She forced a smile, "Of course, and I am sorry about my face. It is the one I was born with, Henry Samuel. Margery seems a delightful young lady and the family are lucky to have her." She sighed.

"Then what is it?"

She leaned in, "My brother is lucky, Henry Samuel. You took him from our home and gave him a life. He is clearly happy now. If I had been born a boy then you might have taken me to war."

I understood her. My daughters resented the fact that my sons had more of my attention. I wondered why her father did not lavish more attention on her. I knew that Myfanwy and Eleanor could wind me around their little finger. I might take my sons to war but I adored my girls. "I am afraid that we cannot change our lives that much. Remember our Aunt Rebekah?"

She shook her head, "She was before my time."

I nodded, "She was an old lady even when I was young. Her husband was taken from her but she did not let that ruin her life. She did good works in the valley. One day you will find a young man and you will wish to be married. Until then do as Aunt Rebekah did, try to make the world around you a better place. There will be poor in Redmarshal who need such care."

For some reason, she brightened, "Henry Samuel you are wise beyond words. Of course, there are things I can do!" She kissed me on the cheek and then went to join my daughters. I felt proud of myself. This was not about war or fighting and yet I appeared to have made a difference.

The wedding out of the way, I could concentrate all my attention on the muster. Jack and John of Parr were my leading sergeants. They both knew the strengths and weaknesses of every man who would be marching beneath our banners. I held a meeting with the two of them and Ned and Robbie, my centenars, to plan for the campaign.

"It goes without saying that the four of you will organise and lead the men on the march south." I nodded to John and Jack, "That means one of you will be needed to lead the men on foot. They will be the largest contingent we take."

Jack said, "John and I have discussed this and I will whip them into shape. It is my view, my lord, that if there are men without lords it will need sharp discipline to keep them in line."

"Aye, but not too much, eh? The last thing we need is for so many desertions that the king does not have the number of men that he wishes." He nodded. "Ned, we will need bodkins and in great numbers. It is my intention to use a wagon to carry them. Do we have enough spare bow staves?"

"Aye, my lord. Robbie procured them while we were in Scotland."

I looked at the archer we had found hiding from Simon de Montfort, "Yes, my lord, I knew that war was coming and we had unfinished business with the Snake of Leicester. We can never have too many bows and there is a good stand of yew towards Coatham. We have spent the winter shaping them."

"Good. In a perfect world, every man would have a helmet."

Jack shook his head, "Not even all the sergeants have those, my lord. We have more here than most mesne but that is because we took them from the dead. We have some old ones, ancient helmets from the time of the Warlord. They might suffice."

John of Parr said, "Better than nothing."

I turned to Matthew, "I would have the squires mailed."

"Expensive, cuz."

"As most of the squires are either blood of the warlord or kin then it will be coins well spent. See the weaponsmiths and have them begin work on the hauberks. That is a priority. John and Jack ride on the morrow to the armoury in Stockton Castle. We will strip it of its weapons."

The planning took all day and I was grateful to my brother for his immaculate lists. We were not dealing with vagaries but actual numbers and that helped.

It was that night when Samuel approached me, "Father, you have not yet said if I will be going to war with you."

"Are you ready for war and all that it entails?"

"I believe so but until I have been to war how will I know?"

I smiled, "Very clever." I studied my youngest son. He had grown and whilst not as tall as his brother was not far behind. "You know that I cannot watch out for you when we leave this manor?" He nodded. "You will be tasked with holding horses, fetching food and preparing beds. You will not be a squire but a pueros."

"Pueros?"

"When the conqueror came, they were young men who went to war but were neither sergeants nor squires,"

He laughed, "Neither fish nor fowl then."

"Exactly and that would be you."

"I know but I also know from Matthew and Alfred that there will also be opportunities for me to see if I have courage and fortitude. It will not all be easy. Many are talking as though we have already won and defeated Simon de Montfort. I am not so sure. We do not know what awaits us and I am content. I have a good leather jack and one of Matthew's old coifs. I have my sword and I intend to make a shield before we go. I do not expect to have to fight but if I am called upon then I will be able to defend myself."

"Take a couple of javelins too."

He nodded and then took in what I had said. His face broke into a smile, "Then I can come with you?"

"You have the right attitude and as I recall I rode behind my grandfather when I was about your age. I just hope that you enjoy as much luck as I did. No matter what a warrior's skills are if he is without luck then he is doomed to die."

Eirwen was philosophical about our son's decision to ride behind us but she was a mother and so she fussed about what he would take. She knitted hats for him to wear as well as socce for his feet. She was right to do so. It could be as cold in March as in the depths of winter and we had a long journey to reach Oxford. I had my new horse, of course, but I would also take White Sock, a good hackney. Blackie was simply too old. One advantage that Samuel would have would be a good horse. I gave him one of those taken from our ambushers. Whilst not a war horse, it was almost as big and had endurance. Both would serve my son well. Alfred and Samuel were excellent riders and neither had ever fallen from their mounts. I remembered my cousin Thomas when he had been learning to ride. He had fallen off more than enough. The Gascon war made him a better horseman.

The Scottish contingent and the palatinate warriors left it as late as possible to arrive. Worse, not all of them made the muster and there would be just a couple of hundred Scotsmen for me to lead. Luckily the bishop had warned me that they would be tardy. The exceptions were the men from Raby. Sir Robert might not be coming to war and there was no knight but Captain Ralph led the ten sergeants and twelve mounted archers who arrived a week before the date we were due to begin our march. That they got on well with my men bode well and I decided that regardless of the king's dispositions, the men from Raby would fight alongside my men. The green area around St John's Well was where my uncle placed the men. It would only be for one night but his contribution to this campaign was to feed them.

In all, I led almost five hundred men south towards York. The number was an estimate. I knew that even without the men from Raby, I personally led almost a hundred and eighty men. The only knights were mine. The Palatinate sent gentlemen, archers but mainly bill and spearmen. I rode at the fore with my old friend, Sir Richard of Hartburn. I remembered when we had been the young pups of war and now we felt like grizzled old hounds compared with the younger knights, Dick, Alfred and Thomas. My sons and my squire rode with them leaving Richard and me at the fore and able to discuss what lay ahead.

"This will not be like fighting the Scots, old friend."

Richard smiled, "Is that a good thing or a bad one? I remember some close run fights up by Otterburn."

"De Montfort has been fighting wars longer than we have. When I travelled through the Cathar country I saw and heard evidence of his savagery. He has skills and it would not do to underestimate him."

He lowered his voice, "And you worry about the king."

I nodded, "Poitou and Gascony were not his finest hour. He needed one to advise him, the Earl Marshal or my grandfather perhaps."

"And The Lord Edward? You know him better than I do."

"A better soldier than his father but untried yet. We shall see. I am just glad that Richard of Cornwall fights with us. The King of the Romans has a good retinue."

The journey seemed interminable for we moved at the pace of walking men. On a good day, we might make thirty miles and on a bad one twenty-five. We were like a giant slug slithering down the road. It took five days to reach Nottingham. The weather could have been worse, we might have had snow and we did not but the cold and the showers resulted in twenty desertions, mainly amongst the Scottish continent. There might have been more but for the leadership of Jack. He caught and punished four men after the first twenty had fled and promised the rest of the army that he would hunt down and hang any who fled. It worked. I spoke to the whole contingent outside Nottingham, as we prepared to head south.

"Men, we face our first challenge now. We will be riding through the lands of the Earl of Leicester. He may choose to attack us. I want no laggards. That is for your safety as much as anything. The men I led from Stockton, the men of the valley and Raby, will act as outriders to warn us of danger. We march armed and ready to fight if we must."

In the end, we were untroubled and reached the ancient town of Coventry unharmed. We were now within forty-five miles of Oxford and halfway through the next day were greeted by a patrol of riders sent by the Earl of Cornwall. It was they who escorted us, first to Banbury and thence to Oxford. I was a relieved man when I was able to hand the men from Scotland and Durham over to King Henry. Leaving my knights and men to Sir Richard of Hartburn, Matthew and I were taken into the castle. The other leaders were there already and The Lord Edward was keen to speak to me.

I had not seen him since the meeting with de Clare before my rescue of Eirwen's family and he had changed. He now looked like a leader. He greeted me as an old friend and his cousin, Lord Henry Almain, beamed behind him. "Sir Henry Samuel, it is good to see you. Our family is forever indebted to the knights of the north but none more so than your good self. With your family riding to war with us then there is nothing we cannot achieve. When we have defeated de Montfort then we will right the wrongs done to us and this country by de Montfort and his rebels."

"We are always loyal, my lord." I looked over to the Earl of Surrey, "And the plan is still the same one we made when last I was in Oxford?"

"It is. De Montfort is in London and his son is in Northampton. That is where we strike first."

The Lord Edward nodded, "You will not have long in Oxford for we leave on the third of April."

Sir John de Warenne said, "And that is a good thing. The town cannot support such a large army as ours. Better we take from our enemies, eh, Sir Henry?"

The Lord Edward added, "While my father heads north I will be taking my retinue towards Derby and Staffordshire. Lord Ferrers is a threat and I intend to take from him what we need to fight and to prevent de Montfort from having a refuge to which he can flee."

That had not been discussed when I had been here the last time. It showed me that the next King of England was already flexing his muscles. His chevauchée would let him be a leader and he would not have to endure the sieges of Northampton and Leicester. He would garner glory, treasure and notoriety.

The Lord Edward left the day before we did. The Earl of Surrey was sent south to ensure that Tonbridge, Kingston and Rochester were defended. King Henry had my men riding just behind his as we headed up the road, first to Bicester and thence to Towcester. It would take just two days to reach Northampton and, as we rode from Towcester to Northampton, I discussed the attack.

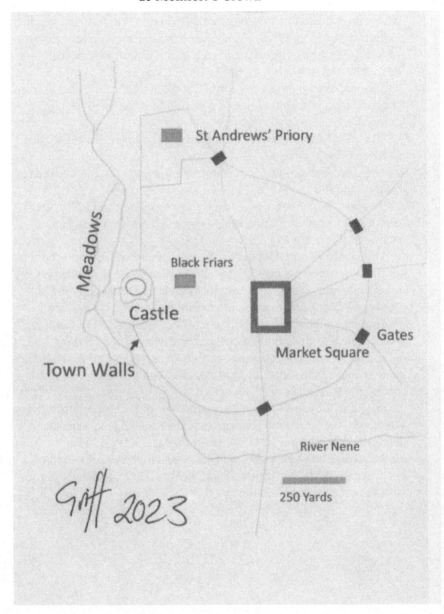

St Andrews' Priory

Meadows

Black Friars

Castle

Town Walls

Market Square

Gates

River Nene

250 Yards

Griff 2023

Northampton 1264

"It is good that you show interest, Sir Henry. Your grandfather was a great advisor to me and I hope that you will give me the advice I need.

The south gate will be assaulted. My men have ladders at the ready. Once we take the gatehouse we can besiege the castle from within."

"King Henry, there is another way."

"You intrigue me. Go on."

I explained how we had escaped from the city through the priory wall.

"Surely they will have repaired the wall by now."

"The prior is a Poitevin, my lord, and he is an ally."

"Yet it was only wide enough for you and a handful of men. How can we get enough men through the broken walls?"

"Let me try with my men and the men of Durham. If nothing else it will distract the attention of the defenders from your assault."

He could see that he had nothing to lose. "Very well, make it so."

We camped south of the town and rose at Lauds. The king would not lead the attack himself but he had some of his senior leaders ready to do so. I led my men, now augmented by the bishop's men, up the river to the meadowlands. I saw that the breach had not been repaired. As the bells from the priory rang for prime I heard the cheers from the south as the assault on the gates began.

Jack knew the wall well having begun the breach. I would use him to lead the attack, "Jack, take twenty men and enlarge the breach. Ned, have the archers ready to discourage the defenders. As soon as the breach is big enough then we will attack." None of my knights wore their helmets. They hung from our cantles but we could don them in a moment. Jack and his chosen men waded their horses across the narrow river and then approached the breach. With my archers at the river, I led the rest of the mounted men to cross the river and we were ready to exploit the breach. The castle jutted out from the town walls and it was an eagle-eyed watcher who shouted the alarm. I drew my sword as the shouts rang out. "Be ready to defend our men. Jack, work quicker."

"Aye, my lord." While it had been relatively easy for us to get out of the priory by moving a few stones, the steep bank meant that we had to make a sort of ramp to let us get in and to widen the breach. We needed it to be at least twenty or thirty paces wide.

The first to arrive were some men on foot with crossbows, spears and pikes. Our archers sent a flurry of missiles over the water and they took shelter. Their bolts made Jack's task harder. They had made a breach ten paces wide when the three mounted men arrived. I recognised the livery of the son of Simon de Montfort, Simon. He and the other men had courage. Their mail and shields protected them and they rode at the breach.

Jack's shout made his workers take cover as the three men tried to jump over the breach. Two of the horses refused and wheeled away but the earl's son made the jump. Unfortunately for him, he landed on a slippery stone and he was thrown from his saddle. My young brother, Alfred, was on him in an instant, "Your sword, my lord, for you are now our prisoner."

He nodded and handed his sword over. I said, "Well done, Alfred, collect his horse and take him back across the river. Guard him well."

I decided that the breach, now twenty paces wide, would have to do. Raising my sword I shouted, "Forward!" I had chosen White Sock because I would not risk Duncan becoming injured at the breach. He proved to be a good climber and he scrambled up the improvised stone ramp. Reaching the top I rode directly at the men who had followed the young de Montfort. My knights and sergeants were behind me and the rebels fled before us. We left the priory and headed past the Black Friars towards the castle. Some men tried to take shelter in the Black Friars but the gates were barred and they were slain. I saw Peter de Montfort trying to rally men but when he saw my conroi charging down the road he fled into the castle leaving many of his men stranded outside. They wisely surrendered. I did not halt at the castle. We endured bolts sent from above but they did little damage for we were riding quickly. As we neared the gates the defenders gave a wail and then threw down their weapons. They were attacked both before and behind.

"Get those gates opened."

The gates opened and The Earl of Pembroke led the men into Northampton. We did not have the castle yet but we had the town. It was not even sext and we had taken the town.

The taking of a town is never a pleasant thing. These were rebels and as men ringed the castle so others began the systematic looting of the town. Men drew swords to defend their homes and it was they who died. My men and I chose the grounds of the priory for our camp as arrows were sent at the walls of Northampton Castle and the task of grinding down the willingness of the defenders began. We had done our part and there were more than enough men with the king to send arrows and stones at the defenders.

Peter de Montfort knew that the situation was hopeless and he surrendered the next day. Thus far this war was a civilised one. Although not one of de Montfort's sons, he was proud of his name and it was galling for him to have to surrender. Only one knight died, Henry de Eyville refused to surrender and died with his sword in his hand. We had captives and they were held for ransom. Even some of King

68

Henry's crossbowmen managed to take prisoners. The knight, Henry of Isham, brought them forty marks in ransom. As the prisoners were taken back to Oxford we took the supplies we would need for the rest of the campaign. Jack ensured that when we took the armoury he gathered as many helmets and weapons as he could for our men. We also managed to take another twenty horses from the stables.

The march to Lewes 1264

When we left Northampton, we were laden with booty and we headed north. We heard that the Earl of Leicester had led a relief column towards Northampton from London but stopped at St Albans when he heard that the town had fallen. The word was that he was making London into a fortress.

We reached Leicester less than a week after the fall of Northampton and the earl's castle and town surrendered without a blow being struck. The Lord Edward had taken Tutbury and captured Lord Ferrers. Other towns happily paid him not to raid them. Our coffers were filling. At Nottingham we found more men waiting to join us. Robert Bruce and John Comyn led more Scots, sent by their king to aid his father in law. At least the Scottish soldiers now had their own leaders. Our army grew while the enemy's diminished. By the time we reached Grantham then the whole of the land north of London was in the king's hands. We had fought just one battle and, it seemed to all of us, that victory was in sight but Rochester was under siege from Simon de Montfort. If that fell then the whole of the south would be in the hands of the rebels. We headed back south towards London.

The king, now reunited with his son, intended to threaten London. Whilst a good idea, it was our first failure for the citizens of London were Simon de Montfort's closest allies and the mob that barred our way across the river ensured that we would not seek to take London. We could not win by defeating the men of London for de Montfort would be safe inside the Tower. Instead, we headed for Kingston upon Thames. We took the castle without a fight and headed for Rochester. That was held by the Earl of Warenne's men and de Montfort was besieging it. We might yet have our battle.

As we headed towards the mighty castle that had defied King John for so long, The Lord Edward was in a most confident mood. "We have de Montfort just where we want him. With our men holding Rochester and the river behind him he will have to fight us and as we have lost nary a man then we shall win."

Lord Mortimer was an old adversary of Simon de Montfort and he shook his head, "My lord, de Montfort is a cunning and tricky enemy. I would wager that while we might find his army at Rochester, he will have fled back to London or, perhaps, his lands in France."

The Lord Edward dismissed that immediately, "If he flees to France then he has lost. My father has secured King Louis as an ally. If he flees from this island then we have our victory. He will fight us and I hope that it is at Rochester."

Sir Roger was proved right. When we reached the river, we found a rearguard of rebels left to continue the siege. The Lord Edward personally launched an attack that ended the siege on one glorious charge of mounted knights and sergeants. The score of knights and one hundred sergeants had held Rochester against an army numbered in their thousands. We had another victory. The Lord Edward had grown since I had met him all those years ago.

There was a council of war in the Great Hall of Rochester and I was invited, once again. I saw at that council the real leader was The Lord Edward. The confident king of Northampton seemed unsure of how to retake his kingdom. Many of the earls and lords who were gathered wanted to march to London and take it.

While King Henry frowned and fiddled with the cross that hung around his neck, his son was decisive, "If we try to march on London and to take it then we would lose. They can supply the city by the river and as the Cinque Ports are still loyal to de Montfort we would be powerless to stop them. We would have to feed our army and desertions would begin."

"Then what do we do, my son?"

"We head for the coast and make the Cinque Ports bend to our will."

Such was the force of his personality that none disagreed but I had misgivings. Until we faced Simon de Montfort on a battlefield then this civil war would drag on. We had taken the earl's son and his ally, Peter de Montfort but the earl still had his other sons as well as Gilbert de Clare and the rest of the rebel lords. I kept my doubts hidden and we rode to the Cinque Ports.

Although the ports acknowledged King Henry as their leader the most senior burghers took flight in their ships and fled to the islands off France. It was not a defeat but nor was it the victory that we had hoped. Then began the worst days for as we headed north we began to leak men. Food was scarce and the people of Kent chose not to welcome their king. Some of those who had been sent from Scotland decided that enough was enough and deserted. At the start of May, men were ambushed by Kentish archers. The king's cook was amongst those slain.

I was summoned by The Lord Edward who was as angry as I had ever seen him, "Sir Henry, you have mounted archers and good sergeants. Take your men into the woods and bring these archers to me. We shall see them punished."

I would have tried to argue with him but there was no use for he was angry. I gathered my men, "Ned, you will have to find these archers for me. You will ride ahead of us. John of Parr, ride with them and when you find them sound your horn. We will ride and surround them. Hopefully, they will surrender for I do not relish an archery duel in lands that they know well."

"We will find them, my lord." He turned, "String your bows and when I give the command dismount. Worry not about holding your horses for Sir Henry will gather any that flee."

They headed into the huge forest. Ned and his archers were excellent trackers. I knew how to spot tracks but they were able to read more into a broken twig than I could. We rode with coifs upon our heads and not helmets. We needed to be able to hear well. The forest was full of shadows and shade. A rebel archer could have been just paces away from me and I would not have seen him. We rode in a column of twos. Sir Richard of Hartburn rode next to me. As soon as we heard the horn I waved the right-hand line to follow me and we headed through the trees. Sir Richard took the other half to the left. I heard shouts and cries from my left. I was riding White Sock again and he was sure-footed. When the sounds of shouts to my left faded, I led my line of sergeants and knights towards the sound. I was gambling that we would have surrounded the archers. We were lucky. We caught the fleeing archers as they ran from both Sir Richard and my archers. Seeing mailed knights and sergeants before them they threw down their weapons and surrendered. Some escaped but they were a handful only. The sorry lines of rebel archers were flanked by horsemen as we headed to Hastings and the Conqueror's Battle Abbey.

I do not know what I was expecting but it was not the draconian punishment imposed by The Lord Edward. He and his father ordered every archer to be beheaded. It was a low point for all of us. My archers and sergeants were unhappy with the punishment and my knights also felt that their honour had been betrayed.

"Cousin, you must speak to The Lord Edward. This was badly done."

"I know, Dick, but we cannot undo the executions, can we?" I recognised the anger and I nodded, "I will speak with him."

I found him with his uncle and father as well as Lord Henry Almain. While my men were unhappy with the executions the four men I approached were the opposite. They were laughing and appeared in good humour.

"Ah, Sir Henry, you have done well once more."

I shook my head and spoke to The Lord Edward, "No my lord, we did not. Had I known that the archers were to be executed then I would not have captured them."

"They killed my father's cook."

"One of them did so. Why execute them all?"

He frowned, "Sir Henry, are you a rebel too? Do you question a king?"

"If a king does not show compassion and justice then aye."

72

"We do not need you and your men. You are dismissed. Skulk back to Stockton and when we have dealt with Simon de Montfort, we shall deal with you."

I looked at the king, "Is this your command, my lord?"

He looked from me to his son and shook his head, "My son, you are angry. We need the men of the north. We have heard that the Earl of Leicester leads fifteen thousand men from London. His sons have joined him and we will have to fight a battle."

"I do not need rebels but you are the king. Just so long as I do not have to fight alongside Sir Henry then all is well."

The king gave a weak smile, "There, we have concord once more, Sir Henry. You shall fight close to me when we discover where de Montfort wishes to give battle."

As I headed back to my men, I thought about the king's last words to me. He was allowing Simon de Montfort to choose the battlefield and that was not a good thing. I had also made an enemy of The Lord Edward. I could not go back in time and undo my words for they had been the right ones. The Lord Edward was in the wrong. Perhaps he had not changed as much as I had thought.

Chapter 8

Henry Samuel

The Battle of Lewes

None of us was happy with the attitude of our leader. The sergeants from Raby were as incensed at my treatment as the rest of my men. Dick said, "If the ungrateful pup does not want us here, Henry Samuel, then let us obey his command and depart for home."

I shook my head, "The king wishes us to fight at his side and we owe it to him to stand by him."

Sir Richard of Harburn said, "And where do we fight?"

"I know not but it will not be here. I believe that The Lord Edward favours a battle closer to London but who knows?"

I was now an outcast from the councils. I was like the rest of the army and waited for an earl to tell me what we would be doing. That night as we prepared our beds I took my sons to one side, "Whenever and wherever this battle is fought you should listen for my command. If I tell you to flee then do so."

Alfred was appalled, "Flee? We have the upper hand and have not lost yet. Where is the honour in fleeing?"

"Where is the honour in the beheading of so many archers? That single act may result in repercussions during the battle. I would have you both safe. My cousin is right in one respect. We could leave the army now and do so with heads held high. We were the ones that won Northampton and no one would blame us if we left The Lord Edward. I do not intend to do so but, Alfred, there is no honour in anything that we do. It is like two wolves fighting over the carcass of a sheep. The only difference is that one of the wolves, in my view, is crueller than the other but today I saw a side to the future King of England that I did not like."

The word came to us the next day that twenty banners, perhaps four hundred mounted men, were to be left at Tonbridge to guard our rear. I now saw why the king was loath to lose me. He had sacrificed almost a quarter of our mounted men and he needed my men. We headed for Lewes Castle. In one respect that made sense to me for Lewes Castle could be defended. With a double motte and the river if things went awry the king would have a refuge. On the other hand, when we reached Lewes I saw that the slope before the town and castle would suit a mounted charge. The rebels had forced our hand and they lay just nine miles north of us in the woods close to Fletching. We had a choice, march to force a battle and leave our sanctuary of Lewes or wait for Simon de Montfort to choose his moment to attack. The king and his son chose the latter.

The Lord Edward and those closest to him stayed in the large castle built by the first Earl of Surrey, John de Warenne. King Henry and his brother stayed in the priory. My men and I camped close to the Winterbourne, a stream that would give us water and good grazing for our horses. It was Richard of Cornwall who supplied the sentries for Mount Harry. The highest point around, it was almost eight hundred paces from the town of Lewes. It was they who reported the arrival of the rebel army at Hamsey on the twelfth of May. As soon as they were sighted we stood to but, as was usual in such matters negotiations took place. Once more since I had been dismissed from the council, I was not privy to the discussions but I heard from Lord Mortimer that the rebels demanded that the Oxford Provisions be put back in place and that the rebels would pay the king thirty-three thousand pounds in compensation. It was, of course, rejected and both Richard of Cornwall and The Lord Edward offered dire threats if the rebels did not surrender. We were going to fight.

I was summoned, along with other leaders like Robert de Brus and Lord Mortimer, to receive my orders. The king's battle would occupy the left side of our lines. Richard of Cornwall would have the centre and The Lord Edward the right. We had little room to manoeuvre and no reserves. Any reserves we did have were now at Tonbridge. The next day the rebels arrayed for battle but the king was not willing to advance up a slope to fight them. Whilst a sensible decision it did not help us for food and grazing were scarce. Warhorses need grazing. My camp meant we were not in danger but others were.

Jack and Ned came to see my knights and me at the end of the day when it was clear that there would be no battle that day. "My lord, this is a bad place to fight a battle. My archers will be loosing uphill and we have nowhere to fall back. Our archers have horses but what of those who fight with us?"

Jack nodded, "The stream has been a godsend, my lord, but if we are pressed then it becomes a barrier. Men in mail would drown."

Sir Richard of Hartburn shook his head, "This is not like you, Jack. You are normally the most optimistic of men."

"I am, my lord, but this battle is commanded by the king and not Sir Henry."

I was flattered by my sergeant at arms' words but we had to show that we supported the king, "King Henry will do all that needs to be done but I will have Samuel take the battle horn. Know that I will give orders should the battle not be going the way that the king envisages. We will keep the spare horses tethered by the wagon. That can be a fort if we need to defend and your archers, Ned, could use it as a raised platform."

That seemed to satisfy them. Sir Richard of Hartburn shook his head, "It is a sad thing when men like Jack lose faith in their leaders."

I nodded, "Then we must restore that faith. When we do battle, whenever that may be, I want our squires as close to us as our skin and to have spare lances. I will keep Samuel next to Matthew so that any orders I give will be swiftly carried out."

Thomas said, "You would disobey the king?"

"I have yet to hear our orders and so I cannot say that I will."

That night I went over my plans with Matthew and Samuel. They needed to know my mind better than any."

When I had finished Samuel said, "This is not the way I saw the war going, father. After Northampton I pictured us riding through London and receiving the accolades of all."

"That is war, Samuel. As my grandmother used to say, it is not over until the carrot is cooked."

He frowned and Matthew explained, "Carrots take a long time to cook. You only know that the food is ready when the carrot is done. We will wait and see, Samuel. Like Jack, I trust your father. We will prevail."

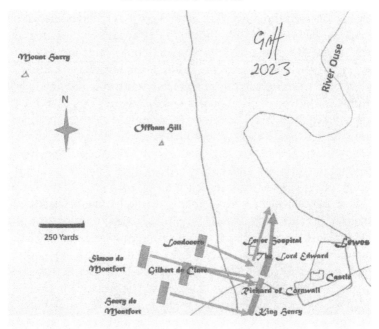

The Battle of Lewes 1264

In the end, it was Simon de Montfort who directed the course of the battle. We awoke to find him and his army arrayed in four battles above us. We were already in place but it still took time to dress in mail and prepare our horses. With shaffron and caparison, they would need protection this day. The bulk of King Henry's battle was with him in the priory and it seemed to take forever for them to filter out of the narrow priory gates. Richard of Cornwall, the former King of the Romans was in position first and then The Lord Edward, leading more knights than the rest of us, formed up his line.

As we were in position already on the far left of the line, I had a good view of the enemy dispositions. Henry Montfort led the enemy on the right with Gilbert de Clare in the centre. The London contingent, by far the most numerous one, was on their left and Simon de Montfort was a reserve. It was clear that once they had passed Mount Harry they would swing around to attack us frontally as the leper hospital determined the anchor point on the right. That day both leaders seemed to want the battle to be fought as equitably as possible. The rebels did not take advantage of the tardy arrival of the king. The king stayed at prayers as long as possible. He waited until all our men were in position before he ordered the advance. Our archers would have little to do until the mounted men had fought their battle. It would be the same for the rebel archers and crossbows, not to mention the huge numbers of foot soldiers. Whichever side lost the battle of the horsemen would then have to rely on archers and foot soldiers. Our battle and that of Richard of Cornwall moved at a steady pace up the slight slope that threatened to sap energy from our mounts whilst aiding the rebels. The Lord Edward had a slightly flatter approach and, once he passed the leper hospital, his line began to get ahead of ours. He was still young and, perhaps, thought to win the battle for his father. His line struck the Londoners before the order came for us to 'Spur on'.

The crash, when it came, seemed to me to be like the crack of thunder or perhaps the noise of a thousand weaponsmiths all beating metal at the same time. The crack of splintering lances and the bang of metal on metal were augmented by the screams of the dying as the knights of the heir to the throne and John de Warenne destroyed the Londoners. The effect was instantaneous. The men of London fled and headed to the north and east, towards the London Road. All that The Lord Edward needed to do was to wheel his men around and attack Gilbert de Clare in the flank and the battle would be won. He did not. He and his men charged after the Londoners slashing at unprotected backs.

It was then the order came to 'Spur on' and lowering my lance I led my handful of knights towards the knights of Henry de Montfort. The five of us were in a perfect line. Jack and twenty sergeants in two lines were on our left and John of Parr, leading another two lines were on our right. Behind us, our five squires and Samuel were as close to our war horses as they could get. My conroi had trained together for months and none raced ahead. The gift of a king, Duncan was the best horse but I controlled his eagerness for battle and with Sir Richard on one side of me and Dick on the other we headed up the slight slope to the wall of metal and brightly clothed horses and men who galloped down the slope. The only differences between the knights and the sergeants were the horses that they rode. Some sergeants had no helmets and rode coifed but as my sergeants all wore helmets, as far as the knights led by Henry de Montfort, the earl's son, were concerned, they could have been facing knights.

I could hear the clash further to my right as Richard of Cornwall's men collided with Gilbert de Clare's but I concentrated, as I had been taught by my grandfather, on the battle before me. I was dimly aware of the king riding just forty paces from me. Two men guarded him and his horse and Hamo Lestrange carried his banner. The king was not hiding behind others this time. He was charging to battle to fight for his crown before it was stolen from him. It was when I was within just ten lengths of the enemy that our five horses, eager to get to war, pulled slightly ahead of our sergeants. I pulled back my lance and made sure that my shield covered the left side of my body. I aimed my lance at the yellow shield with the three red diamonds and I punched hard. The spear smashed into the shield with such force that it shattered but threw the knight to the ground. His lance hit my shield but a heartbeat after I had struck him. I held my right arm out and Matthew urged his horse to close with me and handed me a long spear. It was just in time for a sergeant faced me. I barely had time to thrust my spear at him. The slightly uneven ground meant that Duncan's head dropped a little and my spear went into the sergeant's horse. It fell and the sergeant was hurled towards me. I just managed to move my warhorse out of the way. The hooves of our squires would end his life. It was sergeants that we faced. The knights who had led them were either unhorsed or had headed towards the greater prize, the king. My men would have their ransoms but only when the battle was fought and won. Duncan was a most powerful horse and the sergeants I faced had smaller ones. They were brave enough but I had more skill than they and I speared with impunity. We had long since stopped our charge and were fighting at a standstill. Suddenly there were no horsemen before me. We were through their horsemen and all that I could see were the archers and foot soldiers.

Despite The Lord Edward's reckless pursuit of the Londoners, we could still win and I reined Duncan a little to allow my knights and sergeants to form a line once more and I awaited the command to charge the foot soldiers. It did not come, instead, I heard my cousin Thomas, on the right of me shout, "The Earl of Cornwall has broken. De Clare has him on the run."

Walter of Bishopton shouted, "Ware right, my lord, the Earl of Leicester brings his horsemen."

I turned and saw the disaster that was about to unfold as Simon de Montfort and his son brought their battles to charge into the king's men. We were outnumbered by more than two to one. We had a static line and we faced, not the charging horsemen but foot soldiers.

"Wheel right." I hoped that the king would have the wit to also turn his men and face the charging horsemen.

We turned our horses and as I looked along my line, I saw that we had lost at least fifteen of our forty sergeants. My knights were intact but our sergeants had paid a price already. It was then that the king's nerve broke and turning his horse he began to gallop back down the hill.

I heard his voice as he shouted, "All is lost! Sauve qui peut! We have been undone." The standard followed and that was the signal for retreat. He was ordering us all to run for our lives and join him to seek sanctuary in the priory. Only knights would survive. They would be ransomed while the sergeants, archers and foot soldiers would be slaughtered. That was not what I intended for the men I had led from the north. The Scots were fleeing for their lives. Had this been Scotland they would have fought to the end. It had been a mistake for the king to rely on them and they had contributed to his flight.

The battle was lost in that instant for I saw Gilbert de Clare's men charging after Richard of Cornwall's men and Henry and Simon de Montfort were hurtling after a fleeing king. They wished to get him before he reached the priory. All was lost but in that moment of despair, I spied a kind of hope. We were almost unnoticed. There were men on foot coming towards us but they were streaming down the hill. What I could not do was abandon the men on foot.

"Squires, ride down the hill and bring our men on foot and archers, take any horse you can. Samuel, sound the horn. Knights and sergeants, we need to buy our squires the time to save as many men as we can. Form line and follow me."

Samuel sounded the horn and lowering my spear I urged Duncan to ride diagonally across the field. The dismounted sergeants, billmen and spearmen who raced down the hill thought that the battle was theirs and that they would have the luxury of spearing men in the backs. They had a real shock as we rode through them carving a swathe of death. We did not face knights or mounted sergeants. They were already down the slope and approaching Snelling's Mill and Lewes. I reined in and shouted, "Hold." I turned in my saddle. Samuel was still there, his javelins were gone and his sword was bloody. "Where are the squires?"

He turned and pointed, "They have the archers and some of the men on foot. They are coming."

I looked down the hill and saw Matthew leading the squires and the remnants of our archers and men who fought on foot. There should have been seventy of them but less than forty galloped up the hill. At least all were mounted. I turned my attention back to the field before us. There were men gathered around the rebel's baggage but the road north, towards Fletching, was open. We could do nothing about the slaughter below us. The Lord Edward's flight had begun the trickle of stones that resulted in this avalanche of death. I saw that we had less than twenty sergeants. If all made it home then we would be lucky.

Standing in my stirrups I shouted, "Men of the valley, this battle is lost but we are not. When our friends reach us, we will carve a path north. We will not stop until I am sure we are not pursued. Knights, we will lead." I saw that John of Parr and Jack were still alive, "Sergeants, you will be the rearguard."

Matthew neared us. I saw his helmet was gone and his surcoat was spattered with blood. Ned, Robbie and his two sons as well as Leofwine had survived too. I saw not a sign of the men from Raby. Perhaps they had died, or fled, I knew not. I saw men being pursued across the boggy ground beyond the Winterbourne. It may have seemed like salvation but it was not for they would be hunted down and either captured for ransom if they were a knight or slaughtered if they were a commoner.

"We ride north!"

It was not even noon and the battle was almost over. As we passed Offham Hill and the rebel baggage the men there took shelter behind their wagons. They were safe from us and we would not waste a moment ransacking the baggage train. I just wanted to be as far from Lewes before nightfall as I could. Sir Richard of Hartburn and I led. We kept a steady pace up the hill so as not to irreparably damage our horses. Had the king not shouted what he had I knew that honour would have forced me to continue to fight. Surrender was never an option for me and I knew that if he had not given the command then I would now be lying dead. The rest of my family would also be dead and the line of the Warlord would be ended. I did not like the ignominy of a retreat but it was necessary. When we had crested the rise and made the road that led to Fletching I halted and turned in my saddle. I saw that The Lord Edward had returned to the battlefield but the field was de Montfort's. I saw riderless horses wandering the field and dismounted knights being gathered for ransom. Simon de Montfort had won. He had the king and soon would have his heir. England and the crown were his and all because The Lord Edward had chosen glory over all.

Chapter 9

Henry Samuel

The road to recrimination

It was as Richard of Hartburn and I rode north that I worked out where we would find sanctuary. The king had left a garrison at Kingston upon Thames. There was a castle there and we would find food and safety. We would be the harbingers who would tell the north that the king had lost. Pursuit would come but I was too small a fish for Simon de Montfort to worry about. He would want to get to London and have his heartland acknowledge his victory first. I knew enough about the man to know that he would secure the crown before he did anything else. The king and his son, as well as the Earl of Cornwall and the other lost leaders, would be ransomed. That gave us a week to get back to Stockton. Then we would be on a war footing. I could not see Simon de Montfort allowing the men who had plagued his royal progress for years to survive. We would not surrender. That was not my uncle's way. We had lost men in the misery of Lewes but there were others we had left in the valley and young men who would wish to be trained and follow in their father's footsteps.

First, we had a hard ride to Kingston and the castle there. We stopped at the Augustine priory at Raygate. It had been founded by William de Warenne and both the manor and the priory were loyal to the Earl of Surrey. He would be a prisoner now. The wounds suffered by our men were healed and we were fed. The rest enabled us to push on to the castle at Kingston which we reached just after dark. We had delivered bad news at the priory and there was disbelief in the castle when we told the sorry and tragic tale. We had left the castle in such confidence and with our victories at Northampton and Leicester seemingly guaranteeing our victory. Fate is a cruel mistress.

We spent the next days outrunning pursuit. I was grateful for the maps that William had shown me. He had patiently explained which priories would be safe to use. It was almost as though he had anticipated disaster for his maps, planted in my mind, helped me to steer a course that was safe from enemies. We used royal priories and not the ones endowed by de Montfort and his Lusignans. We did not know for certain that we would be pursued but as de Montfort would be sending men to claim Surrey and its rich manors then they would discover our route.

When we stopped, sometimes at priories and, if we were certain of the loyalty of the men, in castles, we spoke of the battle. The archers and the billmen had been able to view what was happening. Ned said, "As soon as The Lord Edward left to follow the Londoners, it allowed the enemy to outflank the earl. His archers tried to stem the tide but they did not have enough bodkins. The knights broke through and slaughtered them. When they reached us, they found that the men of the valley were better prepared. Their sergeants fell in great numbers but once the king and the earl fled then it was like trying to stem a stampeding herd of cattle. That was when we lost men, my lord."

I nodded, "You did all that could be asked of you, Ned, and I am just sorry that we lost so many of our archers."

He waved a hand, "There are just five of your archers left my lord. There will be widows back in Elton, Stockton and Hartburn."

My brother Alfred asked, "Is this the end of King Henry then, brother? Will we be punished like we were in the time of King John?"

Every eye was on me. My uncle was the earl but they knew it was me who understood the politics of our land better, "I will not lie, that is possible. This time, however, the Bishop of Durham is not a corrupt man and he is loyal to King Henry. Even if King Henry becomes a prisoner for life he will still be king."

"What if he is killed?"

I looked at Matthew, "Regicide is an unforgivable sin. King Henry was anointed and his life cannot be taken. Even de Montfort would not do that but he could be held in the Tower and Simon de Montfort rule as a regent. It is The Lord Edward who is in the greatest danger. If he is killed then all hope for the kingdom dies with him." I saw the downcast faces and smiled, "We are in no worse a position than the Warlord was. Then he held the north against Stephen the Usurper and while it took him many years, he was able to put Empress Matilda's son Henry upon the throne. We can do no less."

My words seemed to fill them with hope.

It was north of Leicester, as we neared Nottingham, that pursuers caught up with us. Mounted men barred the road and the progress to the royal castle of Nottingham. Fast riders using the best of horses could easily outstrip the sumpters ridden by my billmen. They must have reached Leicester and men were waiting to take us prisoner. I recognised the knight who led them, Sir Aubrey de Ferars had lands south of Leicester and was a loyal servant of the earl. The men who faced us had clearly not fought at Lewes but they had heard of the

83

victory. Perhaps they thought we were so dispirited that we would surrender without a fight. That was not our way.

As soon as they were seen my sergeants and knights formed a line so that unseen by our enemies my archers and billmen could dismount and fight on foot. Our squires took arms too. There would be no bystanders this time. More to give my men the time to string their bows I spoke to their leader. The knight led twenty sergeants and behind him were twenty crossbowmen as well as forty men from the fyrd. The crossbowmen were all mounted and that was a mistake.

"Sir Aubrey, give us the road. We have shed enough blood."

He laughed, "You think to fight? I am here to accept your surrender and for your archers to suffer the same fate as the men of the Weald. Throw down your weapons and yield."

Knowing that our archers would be beheaded was confirmation that the decision to fight was the right one. Behind me, Samuel said, quietly, "The archers have their bows strung and bodkins nocked." We had eighteen archers who could pull a bow. Alan of Sadberge was wounded but would fight with a spear.

"I beg you to yield us the road for if I give the command then men will die here and for what? A ransom that will never be paid."

He turned, "Crossbowmen, dismount."

The Battle of Lewes had been one where I had little control, here I did, "Charge them."

My archers were already drawing as we spurred our horses to cover the forty paces to the men of Leicester. The crossbowmen were dismounting and their weapons were not armed. More importantly, the knights and sergeants I led wanted to rid themselves of the taste of defeat. We slammed into the knight, his squire and his sergeants as the arrows fell amongst the crossbowmen and the levy. The brigandines worn by the crossbowmen were not enough to stop the bodkins from penetrating. Some of my archers had a clear sight of the sergeants too and the bodkins came as a total surprise to them. I rode at Sir Aubrey and vented my frustration on him. I was unused to losing and I did not like it. Sir Aubrey could have ridden away and declined the fight but he had not. He had chosen to fight me and take the consequences of that combat.

The speed of our attack meant that his sergeants were not ready to fight. They should have had swords already drawn but they did not. Even Thomas, our most inexperienced knight had slain men and our swords slashed across mailed men's middles. Some of them brought their shields around in time but a couple did not. Sir Aubrey was one of them and I heard the rasping of metal as my sword sawed through links

84

and his gambeson. I drew blood but the wound would just be an irritant.
Alfred slapped his sword against the squire's helmet and he fell from
his saddle. Jack and John showed no mercy and the sergeants they
fought died. As we passed through them we were greeted by a half
dozen crossbowmen trying to load their weapons. We did not falter as
we rode at them. They hurled their weapons away and tried to mount
their horses. The levy just ran. It was one thing to fight a demoralised
and weakened band of warriors but quite another to cross swords with
battle-hardened veterans. As they ran and I reined in I reflected that this
could have been the outcome at Lewes but for The Lord Edward's rash
charge.

The skirmish was over. I turned and saw half a dozen sergeants
galloping south. The knight was leaning over his horse's mane. He was
clearly in some discomfort. Two crossbowmen had not managed to
mount their horses and they cowered before me.

"We will not harm you. Take your master and the squire and the
wounded men. You are free to go but we shall take the horses for I
spoke fairly and gave Sir Aubrey the chance to decline battle. He did
not. If he wishes revenge then tell him I will await him at my home in
the north but if I fight him again, it will be to the death." I knew the
knight had heard me but by speaking to his crossbowman I was
ensuring that others would hear the tale. His men hurried away and I
spoke to my men, "Take the horses and any weapons and purses you
wish from the dead. They cast the bones and they lost."

I wanted nothing from them. We entered Nottingham after dark.
Word had reached the castle of the disaster and the High Sherriff was
full of trepidation. "What do I do if the earl comes north?"

"That is between you and your conscience, my friend. We will fight
de Montfort. Even if he has the king killed we shall uphold the rights of
his son, The Lord Edward. That is our decision. Every man must make
his own choice."

Once we passed Nottingham then we were beyond the lands that
owed fealty to Simon De Montfort. Lincoln was a royal castle.
Doncaster and Pontefract were also loyal. York would not support de
Montfort. The Jews of York had not been harmed and many refugees
had fled there when de Montfort and his allies had raided the Jewish
community.

We crossed the Tees and rode into Stockton Castle on the first of
June. Word had reached my uncle and the walls bristled with men. We
rode in so that all could see that the men from the valley had done their
duty and paid the price. We rode in with heads held high but our hearts
were in our boots. Defeat comes hard to those who have never tasted it.

There was relief from the mothers, wives and sisters of those who had returned. Sir Richard, Sir Thomas and I would ride to our homes but only after I had spoken to my uncle. We had ridden in his stead and he needed to know that we had done our duty. I knew that some men would say that we fled but I knew that we had obeyed the last order given to me by my king. Had he stayed and fought then our bodies would lie around him and his oath sworn.

My uncle surveyed the remains of my command and shook his head, "The war is over?"

I shook my head, "No, uncle, but the battle was lost and the king was taken. Simon de Montfort has the crown within his grasp."

He looked as though he was going to say something and then shook his head, "Your families will be anxious to see and to speak with you. Go home and tomorrow bring your families back to Stockton, we shall hold a feast to celebrate your return."

Dick shook his head, "Father, we return safely only because of my cousin's sharp mind. It will take more than that to keep us safe in the months to come."

I said, "Dick, we escaped and lost fewer men than we might have expected, given the scale of the disaster. Let us celebrate that. God watched over us and it is my belief that he will continue to do so. Your father is right, Richard, Thomas and I need to return to our homes and sleep this night in our own beds. Tomorrow is time enough to pick over the bones of this defeat and plan how to rise from the ashes of the bone fire. We will be stronger."

Thomas took his men through one gate while Richard and I headed west along the river road to our homes. We passed the Oxbridge and Richard and I parted at his fortified manor. We headed to Elton, the western outpost of my uncle's land. It was as I neared it that I realised just how vulnerable we were to an attack. There was a ditch and a wall but the tower that had been begun years earlier was unfinished. I could not think of the reason until I remembered that I had been sent to Rome by King Henry. I had returned and forgotten it. That was a priority. I hoped that the rebels would give me until the harvest to prepare our defences.

As we clattered through the gates, the men I had left to work my grange and to protect my family looked up. Some were old warriors and they saw that some of their friends were not with us. Sons looked for fathers. The women would be in the kitchens or their homes. Wails would rise when they were told the news.

I dismounted as did my men. They formed a circle around me. I nodded, "Aye, you all heard the words I said to the earl. I meant them. This is not over but it is a setback such as I have never experienced."

Samuel said, "Father, when you were thrown into the dungeon in Rome then all appeared lost. You returned from that stronger did you not?"

Jack grinned, "Aye, my lord, young Master Samuel has the right of it. I saw nothing at Lewes to suggest that the enemy is stronger than us. We just need to be better led."

Jack of Parr was equally optimistic, "And if these southerners come north then they will find that we know how to defend our land and they will be given a bloody coxcomb for their trouble."

My wife emerged and frowned. I spoke, "I thank you all, now return to your families and I appreciate your service. None of you let England down. That was down to others." I turned to Samuel, "Go and greet your mother and tell her that Alfred is safe. Matthew and I will see to the horses." He looked like he was going to object and I said, "A good squire obeys all orders."

He nodded and ran off.

Matthew said, "Squire?"

"Aye, Matthew, he acquitted himself well at Lewes. He threw javelins and used his sword, besides, you are ready for your spurs. I will speak to your father tomorrow but we will need every knight that we can if we are to defeat de Montfort."

"You think I am ready?"

"I know that you are but it is you who needs to believe that you are. Rome, Gascony, Wales and Scotland have all tempered the steel that is Matthew of Stockton. I can teach you no more and Samuel is ready. This is meant to be. Tonight will be your last one in Elton."

We groomed our horses, aided by Osgar the old ostler who looked after my horses. I needed to bathe for I stank of horses. We had ridden almost every day since we had left in March. It was now June and our pungent aroma would be offensive to ladies.

Eirwen had anticipated me for, after hugging and kissing me when I entered the hall, said, "Samuel is filling a bath for you and your daughters are choosing clothes. You will bathe and dress in clean raiment. Samuel told me that the battle was lost. Let us begin anew this night for I know my husband. He is already planning ways to defeat our enemy. The bath will wash away not only the smell but will clear your mind."

"You are the best of wives."

87

She was right, the hot bath filled with aromatic herbs and flower petals eased my body and the wine Matthew brought for me soothed my mind. The problem I faced was like my unfinished tower. It needed to be completed and made stronger. My manor needed much attention as did the whole valley. As I lay with my eyes closed and the sweat and detritus of the last months soaked away I put myself into the mind of our enemies. The valley of the Tees was not a priority. Simon de Montfort needed London under his hand. He was not only a warrior, but he was also a politician and he would seek to do as he had at Oxford and put provisions in place to chain King Henry. We would be safe until de Montfort had put restrictions to control King Henry and his son. He would need to call a Parliament and that took time. I hoped we had until after the harvest. As the water cooled and I contemplated dressing I realised that it would take until September to do all that he intended and only then would he be able to address the issue of the north. He also had the west and Wales to consider. I could not see the Welsh king, Llewellyn, letting slip the chance to steal pieces of England. As I stepped out of the bath and Matthew placed the towel cloth around me I worked out that we had until the New Year. Six months was a lifetime if a man was determined.

I smiled and Matthew said, "You have a plan then, Sir Henry?"

"I have the beginnings of one but more importantly, I have hope. The skies look dark but winds can shift clouds and behind them, there will be sunshine. Despair is for those who have no true faith that what they do is right. I know that we are in the right."

There was a cheerier buzz around my table that night than one might have expected. I was in more positive humour and my wife and daughters were just glad to have their men back. As we sat back to enjoy the pudding that Alice the cook had made I nodded to Samuel, "You normally have such sharp hearing Samuel."

He looked confused, "I do, why, what did I miss?"

Matthew said, "I heard it, Samuel, and wondered why you did not."

"Do not tease, Matthew. What did you hear that I did not? Is there someone outside with the horses?"

"When your father and I took the horses to the stable what did your father say?"

I smiled as I saw him thinking, "He said a good squire obeys all orders... well I did..." realisation set in and a broad smile appeared on his face, "Squire?"

I nodded, "I think you are ready and Matthew here deserves his spurs. We need knights. Perhaps Louis is ready too."

Matthew smiled, "Aye, the Gascon is ready. He slew two sergeants at Lewes."

"Good, then how do you feel Samuel?"

"If you think I am ready then…"

"Tomorrow your training begins and before we leave for the feast, I will give orders for work on the manor. We are not a castle but we must become like a hedgehog which, whilst small, discourages predators from feasting on him."

That night, as Eirwen lay in my arms we spoke. "We have widows now, husband, and fatherless children."

"All will be provided for. We throw no one from our land."

"We could build a hall for them and mutual comfort would give them succour. I can find employment for them."

I had not thought of the idea yet it was a good one. "There will need to be changes to the manor. I intend to finish the tower. The walls will need a fighting platform and there needs to be a gatehouse. If we use the new building to go from the warrior hall to the kitchens then we will create an inner bailey of sorts. Aye, that would work. I have given you much to do, my love."

"No, husband, others who led the warriors did that. I know from Samuel's words that you did all in your power to try to save the battle but mistakes were made by others. If Simon de Montfort comes north with men then it will be you that he faces on our ground and that will make all the difference."

I rose after but three hours of sleep. The days were as long as they were going to be and I intended to use every moment of daylight. After a hot breakfast, I summoned every man on the manor. It took some time for men like Ralph lived almost a mile and a half from the hall. I gathered them near to the gates. From there we could see the unfinished tower and the walls.

"You all know by now of the disaster that was Lewes?" All nodded, even those who had not been there. Word had already spread. "We begin work today to make this a bastion. You will all work your own fields but I need you to work each day here, at the manor. If trouble comes then all will be housed here. When Ralph hears my bell tolling he will fetch his family and animals to shelter behind Elton's walls." I pointed to the walls. "At the moment they are not substantial enough. They need to be four feet higher with a fighting platform. We need a strong gatehouse with two wooden towers for archers. We finish the tower." Everyone nodded, even Jack and John of Parr who would normally be above such labours. "We lost men and there are widows now. Some have bairns who still toddle. I will not abandon them. We also build a home for them." I looked around at the faces. There was a determined look on all of them. "We search the fields for rocks. We hew trees and we dig ditches. I will wield a shovel with the rest of you. Can we do this?"

The roar of "Aye!" could have been heard in Hartburn. I had my answer.

Chapter 10

Henry Samuel

The rising of the phoenix

I spent the rest of the morning explaining to Jack, John and Ned what was needed. The first day of work would be an easy one. They would collect stones and cut down trees. The trees would need work to be made into usable timber. In a perfect world, the wood would be seasoned. As we had discovered at Lewes our world was far from perfect. While they began the preparatory work we rode to Stockton. Eirwen and my daughters knew how to ride and the journey was not a long one. We rode first to Hartburn where we could join with Sir Richard, my aunt Rebeka and their three children. Stockton Castle would be filled. As we neared the walls I saw that work was already started. The ditch around the castle was being cleaned and the sluice gates that led to the river were being repaired. My uncle was also preparing. We were not the last to arrive but I saw that Sir Robert was not present. Sir Geoffrey was in the hall and my cousin Thomas had yet to arrive but the absence of Sir Robert was ominous.

My uncle smiled as we entered the hall and he waved an expansive hand, "Welcome, heroes of Lewes. Make yourselves comfortable and I will join you when I have spoken to my nephew. Come, Henry Samuel."

We headed to his solar. Edgar the steward had already placed a jug of wine and goblets there. He closed the door after we were seated. "Dick told me all." He shook his head, "I had thought, from your words, that the hope of England lay with Edward."

"I believe it still does but he is young and he made a mistake."

"A mistake that gave the crown to de Montfort and he will not relinquish it easily." My uncle sounded pessimistic.

I sighed, "One step at a time, uncle. He cannot kill the king and while the king lives then there is hope. As strange as it seems our two old enemies may prove to be his salvation. King Alexander of Scotland and King Louis of France are both allies. They will be a refuge for those who do not wish to bear the yoke of the Lusignans."

"I pray that you are right. You saw that I am improving our defences?"

"As am I. I pray that the other knights do so too. Sir Robert?"

"He declined my invitation. I fear that he is the weak link in the defences of the valley."

"Redmarshal is isolated somewhat in any case. Thornaby, Norton, Elton and Hartburn are the ring that will keep the enemy at bay. Thornaby is the one most at risk."

"Aye, and Sir Geoffrey knows that. Our biggest problem is the men we lost." He held up his hand, "I know that you saved more than might have been expected but the loss of almost half of our best men cannot be borne easily."

I went through my plans and my thoughts. When I had finished, I said, "We have six months at most, uncle. We are not poor and what better use for our gold than to make our walls stronger?" He nodded and emptied his goblet. "And one thing more. I would give Matthew his spurs. He has earned them and another knight guarding Stockton is not a bad thing is it?"

I could see that he was pleased, "Thank you, Henry Samuel. I hoped I would see him dubbed. His mother will be happy to have her sons within these walls once more."

We spoke for an hour or more about the problems that we would face and how we would deal with them. The thorny issue of Sir Robert was ignored. He had been summoned by my uncle and we both hoped he would attend, if he did not then he would need to be spoken to.

"The bishop will need to be informed. I shall ride there as soon as I am able."

My uncle shook his head. "I have shirked my responsibilities long enough. It is not far to ride and perhaps a visit to the shrine of St Cuthbert might aid me. I will take Matthew with me and have his knighthood confirmed by the bishop. We will dub him this night, it seems an appropriate time."

"You have spurs?"

"I have my father's. I think he would have liked the gesture."

"As will Matthew."

We had talked so long that the whole family, Sir Robert excepted, were worried. Sir William spoke to Edgar when we entered and the steward scurried off. My Aunt Isabelle was there and I could see that she was uncomfortable. I was going to ask her about Sir Robert when my mother caught my eye and shook her head. I nodded. I saw that young Isabelle was looking like a frightened hind once more.

My uncle beamed. He was not at all discomfited by the absence of the sour-faced Sir Robert. He spread his arms. "Welcome back to the knights of the valley who have once more upheld the honour of the family. You might not have been fighting a border war but you all acquitted yourself well." He turned to me, "Henry Samuel, your sword has earned the most honour. May I use it?"

"Of course."

Samuel was doing his best to hide his grin for only he, along with Eirwen and Matthew knew what was to take place.

"Matthew, my son, take a knee." Lady Mary put her hand to her mouth and my mother put a protective arm around her. Dick, Alfred and Thomas looked delighted. He knelt and my uncle said, "Matthew, do you swear to be a true and faithful knight, to serve the king and the realm?"

"I so swear."

"Do you swear to protect all women and those in need?"

"I so swear."

"Do you swear to treat all vanquished enemies as you would wish to be treated?"

"I so swear."

"As Earl of Cleveland I dub thee, Sir Matthew of Stockton." He nodded to Edgar who stepped forward and handed the spurs to the earl. "Rise, Sir Matthew and take these, the spurs of Sir Thomas of Stockton, the hero of Arsuf."

I was not sure if Matthew would break down for his face was filled with emotion. I put my arm around him, "You deserve this and grandfather will be happy knowing that one of his blood is wearing them."

The decision to knight my cousin before we ate was an inspired one as the mood was not one of doom and gloom as it might have been but joy. Another part of that joy was the absence of Sir Robert whose glowering face and brooding manner seemed to put a damper on any celebration. We spoke of a new hope that this would be the start of better fortune. Not to have spoken of the Battle of Lewes would have been a mistake but, as we spoke to Sir Geoffrey and Sir William, not to mention my studious brother, we spoke of the positives. We had come within a hair's breadth of victory and the battle had shown us how a warrior had to fight cold. I knew that my mother had discovered the reason for Sir Robert's absence. She lived in the castle and would tell my uncle when there was time for privacy.

I told Sir Richard of my plans for Elton. He nodded, "I too, have plans. Had King Henry allowed it I would have built a castle but that cannot be and so I will make the manor a fortified one. I have becks to the north and south of my manor. Hartburn Beck and the swampy land around it might be reclaimed one day but for the moment I will leave it as a barrier. I shall have some of Hartwell Wood copsed to provide palisades and I will do as you are doing and make my walls higher. I confess, old friend, that I am grateful that your manor is the west of us. If any come from that direction then you will be able to give us a warning." He nodded towards Sir Geoffrey. "It is Sir Geoffrey who is in the greatest danger for his manor is south of the river. He has the river on one side and that is all."

I nodded, "He is another who should have had a castle. That Stockton is the only one is a weakness."

"Perhaps when Edward becomes king, he might allow us to build castles."

"No, my friend, The Lord Edward fears us and he would keep us vulnerable. Stockton is enough to keep the northern enemies from the south. I believe that the next King of England will be a ruthless man. The archers of the Weald have made me lose sleep at night. I was the one who took them."

"You could not have refused."

"Perhaps but apart from the second King Henry, we have been ill-served by our kings."

He lowered his voice, "You would not side with de Montfort would you?"

"How little you know me. Better to lie in a bed of snakes than take up with the Lusignans. I now know what the Warlord did for us. He moulded Henry to make a good king." I pointed the bone I was gnawing at William my brother who was listening to Alfred's account of the battle. "William knows such things. My little brother is a wise man and, tomorrow, before I leave for Elton, I will pick his brains. If we do not learn from our past then we are destined to make the same mistakes in the future."

The noise in the hall grew and I saw my uncle frown as the squeals and laughter echoed around the hall. My mother saw it too and she clapped her hands. My mother was the matriarch of the family and all obeyed, "I remember," she said, "when Henry Samuel was a squire and aspiring to be a knight that he could sing a pretty song. Matthew did not have to learn such skills but I would ask my son to indulge me and sing a song for his mother. Perhaps its melodious refrains will bring calm at the end of this wonderful evening."

My uncle nodded, "I agree."

"I have no rote!" I hated the attention my mother was heaping on me but I understood why she did it.

My brother, William, grinned, "I have one." He raced off.

Eirwen put her hand on mine, "And as I only met you when you were a knight then I would like to hear you sing."

94

Alfred and Samuel both clapped the table with glee, "Yes father."

"I think I shall revive this custom for the next squires in our family. Listen to the song well, Alfred, for the next time it is sung shall be by you."

I searched my memory for one that I could remember. One came to mind. William had kept the rote well-tuned and he winked as he handed it to me, "This bodes well, brother for you were the last knight who sang for our grandfather. His spurs go to Matthew and the song you will sing goes to all."

I chose to sing the Song of Roland. I sang it in its original form as I felt it was more beautiful than the translations I had heard.

> ***Desuz un pin, delez un eglanter***
> ***Un faldestoed i unt, fait tout d'or mer:***
> ***La siet li reis ki dulce France tient.***
> ***Blanche ad la barbe et tut flurit le chef,***
> ***Gent ad le cors et le cuntenant fier.***
> ***S'est kil demandet, ne l'estoet enseigner***

It was a very long song and I did not sing all of it but enough to make the ladies smile. When I had finished there was applause and William said in my ear, "It was like Taillefer was reborn. You must let me copy the words down."

"I did not remember them all."

"You remembered enough."

That night Eirwen cuddled into me, "You have a lovely singing voice. Why have you not sung for me before?"

"Embarrassment, I suppose."

"You have nothing to be embarrassed about." She was silent for a while and then said, "Your Aunt Isabelle told your mother the reason for Sir Robert's absence. He said that he was indisposed."

"That sounds like a lie."

"Of course it is. When your uncle hears there will be recriminations."

"My uncle travels to Durham so the chastisement will have to wait."

My father took Dick and Matthew with him the next day and I went to the hermit's cell which was my brother's room. "I need to pick your brains, brother. How do we defend our castles against de Montfort or whoever he sends against us?"

He nodded and went to a rack of parchments. He searched through and found one. "The valley has rarely been attacked from any direction except the north. Norton has often been ravaged and the eastern end of the town has always suffered. That is why our grandfather had the stronger gates put there. You need beacons."

"Beacons?"

"You could light them when danger approaches. That way the other knights of the valley could ride to whichever manor was in danger. All that you would need to do would be to ensure that your manors cannot be taken quickly. Any attacker coming from the south either has to use the ferry, which we can keep moored here, or use the old Roman Bridge at Piercebridge. A wise man would ask the lord of Piercebridge to send warning of danger."

"The Balliol family."

"I know, they were enemies but now you are the favoured one of King Alexander. Use that friendship to our advantage. The real problem comes if they take Thornaby. There is a river between it and help."

I nodded, "And how do we defend our walls?"

"There are weapons that can be used by any. I am not a warrior but a weighted dart could be thrown by me. A man climbing a wall cannot defend himself. Lustrum, Green and Hartburn Becks are filled with stones. Smaller ones can be used by slingers and boys love to hurl stones while larger ones can be dropped. The Warlord used lillia, sharpened stakes in the bottom of his ditches. Use those to make the crossing of those obstacles impossible. I doubt that they would take the time to build siege weapons for manors. They would hope to surprise us. Our advantage lies in the proximity of the manors to one another. Fast horses can reach Hartburn from Stockton and Elton in less than a quarter of an hour. We are divided for defence but united for an attack."

"But if he brings all the men at his disposal…"

"Then we will lose." I nodded. He leaned forward, "From what I have heard the last thing he would do would be to bring his whole force. It would be like taking a giant hammer to break a walnut and if he did not succeed immediately then it would be seen as a failure. It would also accord you more respect than I think he wishes. He thinks that you ran at Lewes. He will send one of his lords who is eager to take the standard of Cleveland and, perhaps, be rewarded with the land."

Everything that William said made sense and when we left for home I had a much better idea of how best to prepare for whatever the Lusignans threw at us.

When my uncle returned, after four days away, it was with news. The bishop was still loyal to the king but The Lord Edward and the king were now prisoners and held separately as was the King of the Romans, Richard of Cornwall. The supporters of the king were exiled and their lands confiscated. The Prior of St Andrews had also been punished for our entry to Northampton and he had been removed from office. The only opposition to Simon de Montfort now lay north of the Tees. I told him what William had said and he thought it was all a good idea.

"I must now ride again, this time to Redmarshal. I need to beard Sir Robert. I think it a good idea if you speak to Balliol."

Lord Balliol was not at Piercebridge but at Barnard Castle. For one who never left Stockton Castle my brother was remarkably knowledgeable. The lord of Barnard Castle was more than happy to send word if the Lusignans came north. I rode into Stockton Castle in remarkably good humour. We would have warning of an attack from the west and our defences were improving day by day. I had only been away for three days but things had changed. I was taken by Edgar to my uncle's solar and the earl's face told me that there was bad news.

"Sir Robert has deserted both his manor and his family. I told him that we would oppose the Earl of Leicester and yesterday my sister came to tell me that he had fled south. He is joining the enemy."

I nodded, "It could be worse."

"How?"

"He does not know that the Scots will aid us and is not privy to our plans for mutual help. It is not a disaster, not for us but for poor Aunt Isabelle…"

"She fell in love but with the wrong man. I have asked her to come here and live with us. Redmarshal will seem empty without her son and her husband. I thought to ask Matthew to live there and see to the defences. Sir Robert had done nothing."

"A good idea, uncle, although I think that if de Montfort sends men to extract retribution it will not be Redmarshal that is attacked first."

"We know nothing yet, Henry Samuel. The bishop will do his duty and remain loyal but for the rest? Who knows? We do what we must do to protect our families."

I was still there when Aunt Isabelle arrived with her two companions, and her daughter, Isabelle. It was then I realised that she had been lonely for her husband, it was now clear, valued the manor more than the marriage. I had thought back to Sir Robert's time with us and I knew, although I did not give voice to my thoughts, that he had married my aunt for the manor. We had confirmation of that when she told her brother the last of her news.

"I fear that my husband must have been planning this for some time, brother. The coins we had collected for the king and the bishop's taxes, not to mention yours, have been taken along with all the money we had accrued. Redmarshal is now worthless and Sir Robert has fled."

I looked at my uncle, "And we know where he will go."

My uncle nodded but Aunt Isabelle looked confused, "How can you know, Henry Samuel? He was my husband and I know not where he will go."

"We are the king's men and he knows it. He will go to the enemy of the king. He will seek sanctuary with Simon de Montfort. He will buy a place at the high table not with his gold but with knowledge. He will give them all our secrets. He will sell us to the Lusignans."

Her eyes widened, "I wish I had never married him."

I put my arm around her, "Thomas and Isabelle came from the marriage and that is a good thing. Take comfort from that."

She smiled, "Aye, you are right."

"And we, Henry Samuel, will have to work even harder now to undo the damage that will be done by Sir Robert."

I gave young Isabelle a warm smile. She gave a half-hearted one in return and I saw her fingering the cross around her neck. Her eyes looked to be shadowed. She was still an unhappy child. Worse, she was even more fearful now than the last time I had seen her. I saw that when a man came near her she moved back and her eyes widened in fear. How had such a happy young girl become so sad?

The longer days of summer allowed us to work much longer. Of course, it wearied us but, my manor especially, all knew of the threat. We had lost men. We finished the tower first. I was annoyed that I had neglected it for so long. It was attached to the main hall by a single door and inside had ladders to ascend the floors. Arrow slits were placed on each floor of the three-storied building and the top had crenulations and a wooden roof. It could hold four archers on each floor and the top, whilst the lowest story, the largest, could hold fifteen people. It would be a refuge in case the hall fell.

That done we began work on the women's hall. We had to await the completion of the tower first as the scaffolding we had used to finish the top covered the ground where the hall would be. It would be at right angles to the tower. The two wings of the hall and the kitchens meant that we just had to build a wall and a gate to join the women's hall to the rest of the manor.

It was the last day in July when one of the men working on the roof at the top of the tower shouted that he could see men approaching. This was not the time to take chances. As soon as I was informed, I shouted, "Women and children into the hall. Men, arm yourselves."

We were stripped to the waist for we were labouring but our weapons were close to hand. The archers strung their bows and the rest of us grabbed swords. I waved the archers to the tower, although the command was unnecessary as Ned was leading them there. I waved

John of Parr to head to the recently built fighting platform and I led the rest to the gap between the construction and the kitchens. We formed a double line.

The men who approached on foot were clearly warriors. They wore brigandines and carried short swords. By their physique, at least four of them were archers. I could see that they posed no threat for two were bootless and had bloody bandages about their feet. I sheathed my sword as did the others. If this was a trick then my archers would still have nocked arrows and a good view of any danger.

"Thank God, we have found you, Sir Henry Samuel."

I frowned, "Do I know you?"

The man who spoke, clearly the leader, shook his head, "But we know you. We fought close by your men at the wretched battle of Lewes. We heard the same call as you did when the king gave his command. Old Sir Eustace, our lord was slain and we fled. There were fifteen of us who survived the battle but wounds, hunger and de Montfort's hunters took the rest. We nine are the last. We have walked and hidden all the way from Lewes."

"This is no place to speak. Samuel, go and tell your mother we have men who need food and their hurts healed. Jack, prepare palliasses in the warrior hall. Come let us get out of the sun." We led the weary and almost skeletal men to the shade of the kitchens. Alice, our cook would already be preparing food. John of Parr went to fetch coistrels and ale for them. Eight of the nine slumped to the ground. The leader stood erect and addressed me. He was a warrior and a leader through and through.

Eirwen emerged and I said, "These have walked from the battle of Lewes to seek our help."

She nodded, "Ladies, daughters, let us find bandages and salve for their hurts. Alice, food."

The voice came from the kitchen, "It will be ready soon, my lady."

The leader smiled his gratitude, "Thank you, my lady. We have been eating unripe fruit and the leavings of carrion washed down with rainwater this past fortnight."

She looked at him and asked, "Did you not ask for help before?"

"We made that mistake north of Nottingham and my son and nephew paid the price. We were attacked. Since then we have disappeared."

John of Parr and his men handed out the beakers and the ale. The leader did what all good leaders do, he waited until all of his men were served before he drank. I saw him close his eyes and savour every drop. My daughters had brought bandages and some of the widows, water and salve. They began to gently unwrap the bandaged feet. Eirwen went into the kitchen to hurry the work on.

I shouted, "The rest of you, back to work." I turned to the leader, "You have the advantage of me, tell me all and why you have sought me out."

He nodded his thanks as Samuel, who had taken the ale skin from John of Parr, refilled his beaker, "I am sorry, my lord, our plight has driven courtesy from me. I am Joseph of Aylesbury and a sergeant at arms. I led Sir Eustace's men. I am a sorry sight now but I had a mail hauberk, coif and fine helmet once. I rode a good horse and hoped that if we won the battle Sir Eustace would have made me a knight." He shook his head and I saw despair fill his face.

"You have done all that you could. If you have guided these eight here then Sir Eustace would be proud of you."

He smiled, "He was too old a knight to go to war but he was loyal to the king. He had no family and now some Lusignan will rule his manor." He shook his head as though to clear the image from it, "You ask why we sought you out? It is easy, my lord. We saw how you evaded the pursuers and kept your men together. We have all heard of your prowess and we want to have vengeance on Simon de Montfort. We saw his men butcher archers, billmen and sergeants who tried to surrender. The Scots who fought for King Henry were all slain. There is a massive grave now close by the leper hospital. We hid by Mount Harry while we tended to our wounded and they pursued the others south. We saw what they had done. When we were rested we made our way north. When we reached our manor we saw it was occupied already and we took a wide berth west. We thought we were safe until we were attacked by those loyal to de Montfort. We left the roads and took to the woods. We used the handful of arrows we had left to hunt game. They ran out when we reached the Vale of York. The last days have been the worst."

"And you wish to serve me?"

His eyes became fiery, "Aye, my lord, if you will have us, sorry though we look. Five of us were sergeants but we will wield a bill if that is all there is. We want to fight." He nodded to the men as he spoke their names, "This is Ralph of Banbury, William of Stroud, James Poleaxe and Hugh de Varaville." They all knuckled their foreheads when their names were spoken. "The other four are archers, Seth, Walter, Garth and David the Welshman."

I spread my arm, "As you can see, Joseph of Aylesbury, we are preparing for a fight. He has not sent men yet but we believe that Simon Montfort will not allow us to live in peace. If you seek a fight then you shall have one but not yet. You all need to bathe and we shall dress you so that you do not look like scarecrows. There may not be hauberks for you but we have brigandines and jacks. There are coifs and helmets. My archers have arrows. Rest until my wife says you are fit to work and then you can join us in our labours."

"We are ready now, my lord."

I smiled and shook my head, "You will learn that I am merely the lord of the manor, the one whose voice we all heed is Lady Eirwen and she will determine when you are ready."

I do not know if she had been listening in the kitchen but she emerged and said, "Come with me, Joseph of Aylesbury, and you shall eat in the hall. When you are satiated, water will be readied for you and you can bathe and then change. We have clothes." She gave him a sad smile, "Men did not return from the battle so they will be dead men's clothes."

"They died in battle, my lady, and we will be honoured to wear them but we are too dirty to eat in the hall."

She put her hands on her hips, "You will all learn that this hall is one where everyone is treated well. Dirt can be cleaned and you men deserve to sit and eat in comfort."

They all stood and chorused, "Yes, my lady."

After they had gone Jack and Ned joined Samuel and me, "Well, my lord, they are scarecrows now but they are men and can fight behind your walls."

I nodded, "Aye, Jack, and I wonder how many more are there?"

Ned said, "More, my lord?"

"I am not talking about the billmen and levy who turned up because their lords demanded it but how many soldiers like these? Some will join de Montfort but there will be others, like Joseph. They may not make it to the north but they will find men such as we. There is hope."

Ned nodded, "And when they have eaten and rested for a few days we have nine more men to put on the walls."

.

Chapter 11

Henry Samuel

The lull before the storm

The new men recovered far quicker than I would have expected. They were given much attention by my wife and the widows. I think the widows saw their dead husbands in the skeletons who sought sanctuary with us. Their own men were dead but they would make a better life for these survivors. Ned was right in that the extra men made the work much easier and by September the new buildings, walls and ditches were in place. Joseph was a good leader and he seemed determined that he would make Elton as strong as he could. Already a widower before the battle, the loss of his son and nephew on the road north had not made him retreat into himself but stronger. His men had become his family and I saw that as a good thing. I now had three senior sergeants and that boded well for when we fought.

My uncle kept us well-informed about the events beyond our sphere of influence. Ships still came to Herterpol and Stockton and the captains had news from the kingdom. The pope maintained his support for King Henry and Simon de Montfort had been castigated for his actions. The Welsh attacks had threatened to weaken the marches and so the Marcher Lords were released to fight them. The best news of all was that Gilbert de Clare had fallen out with Simon de Montfort. There was, as yet, no split, but there was a crack in the alliance that had undone the king. To counter it de Montfort had called for a Parliament to be held in January. It was not just the lords who were summoned but every knight and burgher. De Montfort intended to buy the crown by enfranchising more people. It was clever and I knew it might work. He would take more power from the king and give it to Parliament which he controlled.

Matthew had gone to Redmarshal and did that which Sir Robert had manifestly failed to do, he inspired the men of the manor. He had them improve the defences and made them train whenever they could. He even chose his squire from the young men of the village. He was Edward, son of Edmund, who had died at Lewes. The boy was an orphan for his mother had died whilst we campaigned in Gascony. It was not only a Christian act but a wise one. It gave the young man purpose in his life and an instant family, Matthew.

It was Sir Geoffrey who had the hardest task for Thornaby was still a wooden manor. When the north had been ravaged by William the Conqueror, the original castle was destroyed. Sir Edward, a former sergeant of the Warlord had built it. No one had improved it. There would be no time to build in stone and so Sir Geoffrey just deepened ditches and added embrasures to protect the men on his walls.

We had a real shortage of war horses. We had been lucky to have taken a few from Sir Aubrey but if we were to be mobile and go to the aid of Thornaby or Stockton then we needed more. It was November when I decided to take Jack and Samuel along with Joseph, to ride to Malton where there was a horse breeder. They would not be cheap but the price did not matter. If we could not ride to war then we would become helpless targets. We now had enough men to watch the walls and most of the work in the fields was done. John of Parr and Ned could continue to train and spend a little time each day digging a ditch from one of the nearby becks so that we could fit a sluice gate and flood the ditch if danger came. It would take at least a month to dig and so we did a little each day.

I took Joseph so that the man from Oxfordshire would have a better picture of the land. We had an old hauberk that he now wore and I had given him one of the horses taken from Sir Aubrey. He was a different man and eager to be of service. Had it been summer then I might have tried to swim the Tees closer to Elton but it was icy so we headed for the ferry. We spoke to Dick and Alfred as we passed through the castle. Like us, they were all busy making the castle and town defensible.

"Any news of de Montfort?"

Dick shook his head, "There is dissension amongst the victors of Lewes it seems. De Clare, from what we hear, does not like de Montfort's ambitions."

I laughed, "I know not why for he has always made it clear what he wants."

Dick shrugged, "De Clare is a fiery man in every sense of the word, cuz, who knows what spurs him. I am just glad that there is no longer a united front and any chink in their armour helps us."

"The king, his brother and The Lord Edward are still prisoners?"

"Aye."

"Then we cannot even contemplate taking back the land. With the Poitevins and the king's allies exiled, then he is helpless. We are the burr that will annoy de Montfort. I am convinced that he will send someone, sometime. He has to. If he can defeat us then he can cow the bishop."

"Where are you off to?"

"Malton to buy horses."

"Abel the Horse Trader is expensive."

"That is because his horses are the best. We have little choice, cuz."

The ferry added to the length of our journey and so we rode hard once we reached the southern shore. We would need to stay in Whorlton on the way back for it was a long ride and we had high ground to cover. The lord of the manor at Whorlton was descended from one of the Warlord's knights and we would be assured of a welcome by Sir Geoffrey. We reached the horse farm in the middle of the afternoon. Abel made a good profit from all his horses and was a very rich man but he knew his animals.

"Sir Henry Samuel, I have not seen you for some years. How is life treating you?"

Abel was the master of innocuous conversation but he had a mind as sharp as any. He would know we had fought on the losing side at Lewes but he would wish to make a sale and would not jeopardise that in any way. I could play the game too, "As well and as badly as any man. We plough and do our best, eh, Abel?"

"A good philosophy to live by, my lord. Now, what can I do for you, my lord? Another warhorse?"

I shook my head, "No, Abel, the King of Scotland gave me a fine one. No, I need some hackneys, rouncys and a couple of sumpters."

"Sumpters are plentiful, my lord, and I have a few rouncys but I only have four hackneys." I was disappointed but I did not let my disappointment show.

"Let me see them and I will see if they are suitable for my purposes." He had his men lead out the four horses. The four were good animals and I nodded my approval, "They will do. Now the rouncys." This time there were eight but not all were of the best quality. Out of the corner of my eye, I saw a pen with sumpters and some looked to be good ones. I shook my head, "You are slipping, Abel. Only four of these are worth buying. I will take those four, the best ones."

"As you wish, my lord. And sumpters?"

"Oh, those six will do." I made it sound casual but I picked the best ones that he had. "And the price?" He gave me a high price and I nodded. He beamed, "Of course, for that price, you will deliver them to Stockton where you shall be paid."

"My lord!"

"I did not know how much they would be and in these parlous times I did not want to risk robbers."

He snorted, "Who would be so foolish as to try to rob Sir Henry of Elton? You drive a hard bargain, my lord, but folks around here know that they are kept safe by your family. I will bring them by the end of the week. Will you stay the night?"

I knew that would be expensive and so I declined. We reached Whorlton after dark. Sir Geoffrey was an older knight. He was younger than my uncle but, to me, he had been born old. He was a knight, carried a sword and rode a warhorse but he was not a warrior and to my knowledge had never ridden to war. His sons, the eldest four at least, had emulated him and enjoyed farming and hunting. He made us welcome, even though we were not expected. His grandsire had been a sergeant rewarded by the Warlord. Sir Geoffrey would have had nothing but for my family.

Samuel and I paid for our food and accommodation by telling them of Lewes. It was his youngest son, the fifth, Roger, who became animated when I spoke of the desperate fight to escape. Sir Geoffrey shook his head, "Had I not been here when he was born I would have said that my youngest boy, Roger, was a foundling. He cares not for farming and wishes to be a warrior."

"There is nothing wrong with that, father. We are a noble family and not farmers."

"Your brothers and I have chosen farming as a life and it has made us wealthy. We have not paid a ransom and there are none of my sons buried in the churchyard because they were killed in battle." He shook his head. "What can you do, eh, Sir Henry?"

"Roger, is it?" He nodded, "If you wish and your father allows it you can come with me and train with my son, Samuel." I looked at his father.

Sir Geoffrey beamed, "That would suit most splendidly and he can have my warhorse, Caesar, and hackney Cassandra as horses. I will give him a hauberk, coif, helmet and sword." He seemed eager to be rid of him and I wondered why.

Roger leapt to his feet, "I will go and pack my bag now, father, and thank you."

I looked at him in surprise, "I am not sure I would be so willing to let my son go so easily, Sir Geoffrey."

He sighed, "His mother died bringing him into this world and he is a trial. We talk of farming, raising animals, and shearing sheep and he is disinterested. I fear that if I do not give vent to his desires then he may seek action himself and I would not incur the wrath of my neighbours. You would be doing me a favour." He leaned forward, "He is a good lad at heart. He has seen sixteen summers and has trained with Egbert my sergeant at arms. He has sword skills, my lord, but knows not battle."

"He can learn that with us. If you have any others on your manor who wish to be warriors and not farmers then send them to Elton. Billmen, spearmen, archers, they are all welcome."

His face changed, "Then war is coming?"

"Probably but I doubt that Whorlton will be touched by it. You can continue your happy existence, Sir Geoffrey, oblivious to the outside world." I do not think he heard the sarcasm in my voice. He just nodded.

As we rode northwest, the next day, I rode with Joseph and Jack while Samuel and Roger chattered away behind us. We kept our voices low as we spoke, "I do not wish to cause offence, my lord, but why does the earl allow Sir Geoffrey to keep his manor? The manor belongs to your family and we could have used the men at Lewes."

"Would it have made a difference?"

"They might have died and not Hob, Walter and the others."

"You cannot know that. It goes back to my grandfather. He never made a man go to war. Sir Geoffrey was a young man then and my grandfather obviously saw that he was not a warrior. The land is rich and Cleveland profits from the work Sir Geoffrey does. Is it the spurs that annoy you so, Jack?"

"I suppose so. Any of the sergeants who serve you would be honoured to be given their spurs. Should a farmer be given them?"

"Sir Geoffrey will be the last knight at Whorlton, Jack, unless Roger earns his spurs and my uncle gives him Whorlton."

Joseph chuckled, "I should like that, my lord. Nothing against Sir Geoffrey, he seemed like a good and honest man but it is warriors that keep lands safe so that farmers and horse traders can profit. It is good that the young man," he gestured behind him with his thumb, "chooses a life which might be dangerous. Will he be a squire?"

"He will not replace Samuel if that is what you mean but he will train alongside Samuel. He is older than Samuel but Samuel has done what Roger has not. He has used his sword in combat and drawn blood. When we fight de Montfort I shall have the confidence of knowing that my son has the skills to survive. Roger will only discover them then."

We crossed the river and walked our horses through the river gate and into the bailey. I had not had the chance to speak with my uncle before I left and now I would. While the others watered the horses, I entered the hall. Even before I could tell him of the horses and Sir Geoffrey he spoke, "The message has come from London, Henry Samuel, we are all summoned to a Parliament in January." Dick and Alfred had been in the bailey practising and they entered behind me.

"We will not go, will we?"

My uncle shook his head.

Dick said, "I think we should. Let us show de Montfort that we are not afraid of him. If we are not there then he can have the Parliament do whatever he wishes."

My uncle smiled, "Tell him, Henry Samuel, I have tried to explain since the rider left for Durham yesterday."

Edgar brought me some ale warmed with a poker. I took it and nodded my thanks. I was chilled from the road and its heat spread through my body, "First of all our voices would make no difference. Most of the lords who support the king are exiled or prisoners. The ones who attend will be the ones who wish for more land. That will be the bribe offered by de Montfort. The Poitevins he sent back to Poitou will have their land confiscated and he will give it to those who support him. That, however, is not the real reason we shall not go."

Dick frowned, "No?"

I looked at my uncle, "Did a pardon come with the message, my lord?"

He smiled and said, "The messenger was curt and came to the point. He said we were summoned to a Parliament by the Earl of Leicester. Nothing more."

"We would not make London. There would be men waiting, as they were the last time, to ambush us but this time they would make a better job of it and in the unlikely event that we managed through cunning and stealth to reach London, then we would be arrested."

"Arrested?"

"We fought against de Montfort. We slew his men. We would be arrested. That is why we shall not go."

My brother Alfred had been listening, "Then they will not try anything until after January, brother. Until then the men who might be sent to destroy us here will be watching and waiting for us."

"It buys us until at least February and, probably, March. The roads leading to the Tees can be treacherous at that time of year. If it is March then the nights are the same length as the days. I might fear an attack in December or January when they could use the long nights to get close. March also means we could train more men." I went on to tell them about Roger of Whorlton and the horses.

Dick was of the same mind as Jack, "Father, Sir Geoffrey should be made to furnish men. He owes a duty as we all do."

Sir William sighed. His son was a good knight but he had much to learn yet, "And if you went to war with them would you have confidence that they would stand?" I saw the realisation in Dick's eyes. "Sir Robert did not go to war with you at Lewes and there was a reason.

He was young enough to fight but I feared he would have fled at the first sign of trouble. Sir Geoffrey and I are too old but Sir Robert was untroubled with wounds." He shook his head, "There are so many signs that I see now. Why did I not see them then?"

"Because of your sister, uncle. Aunt Isabelle is the sweetest of ladies and we all tolerated Sir Robert because of her. When we took Thomas to Gascony and away from the influence of Sir Robert, look at the change. He has gone, like a thief in the night, but good riddance."

My uncle wagged an admonishing finger, "The adder can still bite, Henry Samuel."

Alfred asked, "Were the horses expensive?"

"They were but I have been frugal with the coins I have accrued and it is better to spend them now, while I can, than not spend them and they benefit my enemies."

Dick looked shocked, "We cannot lose!"

I said, "We can and if we go into this thinking that we cannot lose then we shall. We have to fight as though we are fighting for our lives."

Unbeknown to us, William had entered and was seated with his wax tablet and stylus. His voice made us all turn when he spoke, "The Warlord was in a similar position, Dick. Our grandsire was trapped in Stockton with the enemy at the gates. Only he held out hope for Empress Matilda but, despite the death of his wife Adela, he prevailed and defeated them. The hope I have is that all of you have his blood and that will save us."

I smiled, "You have his blood too, William. You fight not with a sword but with knowledge and words. The maps you showed me before we left for the campaign helped me to plot a way home. You were not there but your maps saved lives."

The smile he gave me spoke as much as the parchments he scoured each day. He was part of the family and wanted to do his part.

The arrival of Roger meant we had to make some changes. Samuel was quite happy to share his chamber with Roger who told my wife that he would sleep in a barn if he had to. He just wanted to be a warrior. Eirwen dismissed that out of hand and from that moment included Roger as an adjunct to the family. My daughters were growing and a handsome new squire who was not a relative made them think that he was an early present for the birth of Christ. Eirwen had to take them to one side and explain how they ought to behave. When she was watching they heeded my wife's words.

The horses arrived as promised. A rider came to say that they were at Stockton. We did not ride to Stockton but walked. It took an hour but meant that we could ride the new animals back. Jack carried the sack of coins to pay for them. It was a chance for Roger to see not only my manor but also Hartburn. We crossed the Green Beck and passed Oxbridge Farm and then descended to the Ox Bridge. There were farms now lining the beck. Stockton had grown since its nadir under King John. Many people had migrated from the north when the Scots had been our enemies and they had been given land beyond the walls of the town. It was less than a mile from the Ox Bridge to the town gates and every farmer and his family knew that they could reach safety before harm came to them.

Whorlton was a village smaller than Elton and Hartburn. To Roger, the walls of Stockton, approached on foot, looked like those of a city. The wooden palisade was imposing but I was under no illusions. If Simon de Montfort chose to bring a sledgehammer, then the walls would fall. He knew sieges from his two crusades.

Abel was waiting patiently. The animals had been well cared for, "I have left on their winter coats, my lord, and they do not look their best but come the spring you will see that you have robbed a poor horse trader."

I nodded to the expensive boots and fine sword that hung from his waist, "I do not think you do badly from your trading, Abel. I thank you for fetching my horses, here is the fair price we agreed."

Jack handed him the bag. He did not count it. That would have been discourteous.

"Thank you, my lord."

"Do you stay the night?"

"No, my lord. I ride to Middleham. There is a stallion there I would buy." He held up the bag of coins, "I now have the funds to negotiate for it."

Abel's world was unknown to me but was necessary. As we rode the hackneys and rouncys bareback to Elton, I began to wonder if we could breed. Duncan was a stallion and a fine war horse. Osgar knew horses. He had a son, Osric, and I wondered if the two of them knew enough to breed animals for me. It would be a longer process than simply buying schooled horses from Abel, but as I had no idea if we would have coins in the future it was something to consider.

By Christmas, another six men had made their way north. All were archers and that did not surprise me. An archer could hunt on his way north and keep himself fed. They joined my men and it meant we had, with the young men from the manor, twenty trained archers. When the archers were not working they were making bow staves and arrows. The young boys of the manor, when they had done for the day went to the three becks that were within a mile or so of us and collected stones.

Our year ended at Christmas. The days were the shortest of the year and we had made our normal preparations. They had begun in November with the bone fire when my wife and the ladies had prepared the meat taken from the old animals and sorted out the fruit to store and the fruit to use. My trip to Italy had been fraught with peril but one piece of good to come from it was that I had been able to buy spices there at a much lower price than even in London. The meat that was in danger of going off and spoiled fruit would be soaked in aquae vitae and spices would be mixed with flour to give us a treat to enjoy when the old geese we ate on Christmas day were consumed.

It was not just in my hall that we would celebrate. My grange was the largest in the manor and the warrior hall would be converted so that the people who farmed for me and served the manor could enjoy their own feast. Eirwen and the girls, augmented by Samuel and Roger would serve the food. I know that my mother, who would dine in Stockton on that most special of days would wish me to be there but she would be happy enough with my brothers under her watchful gaze. I might be her favourite but she understood the needs of duty better than any.

We said Grace and then the six of us tucked into the feast. The old, gnarly vegetables had been cooked long and slow and drizzled with our own honey. The trapped rabbits and the old goose gave us the meat while we began with fish taken from our fishponds. We had manchet as our bread and I could see that Roger was impressed with the fare.

"My family pride themselves as farmers but they will not eat as well as this, my lord."

"I noticed that your father does not have a fishpond and there are no rivers close by. We are lucky that the fishpond was put in during the time of the Warlord and when the manor was unoccupied, the fish population grew. We are able to harvest the pond many times. Those in the warrior hall will dine as well as we. The wine you are enjoying comes from a friend in Gascony, Seigneur Guillaume de Saint-Severin. We are lucky here."

My wife wiped her mouth delicately, "But, Roger of Whorlton, we do not take anything for granted. Sir Henry and the other knights are ever vigilant and watch over this land with the eye of an eagle protecting its young. We enjoy this day because we can and do not know whence the next danger will arrive. We thank God for each day."

"Amen to that." I lifted my goblet, "A toast, to the knights of the valley and the ladies. May God watch over us and protect us so that we can give back the crown to King Henry!"

"The knights of the valley!"

110

Chapter 12

Henry Samuel

Montfort's Revenge

The weather changed at the end of February. It had been a hard winter. Snow had lain for quite a while but the weather, inexplicably, grew warmer in the last week of February and the snow melted. Puddles formed on fields and my farmers had to spend time digging channels to allow it to run off to the becks and the fishpond. That was another advantage of the fishpond. It had been put in the lowest part of the land, the part that normally flooded. My grange was the one that suffered the least of all the farms in the manor.

When men were not working in their fields they practised. The ones who lived close to my grange would try to come for an hour or so each day. Lewes had shown the survivors the need to be the best that they could be. The younger warriors had heeded their advice. Bill and spearmen practised their skills using staffs. It resulted in bruises rather than cuts. The archers listened to the advice of my four senior archers. If we had more archers then they would have been vintenars but, as it was, they commanded less than twenty. We had a good stock of arrows but not enough bodkin tips. Ned favoured the fitting of an arrowhead just before a battle when an archer knew his target. There was little point in wasting bodkins on men without mail. We had wasted arrows when we had been ambushed. The weaponsmith had made darts and we had shown the women how to use them. The only time the women would be risked would be if we were about to be overrun. Women knew their fate if their men died and the manor fell.

I regularly visited Stockton with Roger and Samuel. It did my new squire good to mix with the other squires. When war came and we took the crown from de Montfort's head they would fight alongside one another. I was kept informed about the news that filtered from the south. It confirmed the dissension in the rebellious ranks but the king and his son were still captives and most of the king's allies were in exile. We heard that Gilbert de Clare and Henry de Montfort were planning an Easter tournament. We would not go, of course, but it told us that Simon de Montfort would not have all of his followers at his disposal. I had hoped that the arrival of Roger would bring my cousin

Isabelle from her depression. It did not and she fled to her room when he entered.

It was while I visited that a ship arrived at the quay. She was a Gascon ship.

We all descended to the river gate to greet our visitors. I recognised the lord, it was William de Valence. An incredibly rich knight, he had married Joan de Munchensy one of William Marshal's granddaughters. He had fought at Lewes and been exiled. I wondered what was the purpose of his visit.

He was French and I wondered if we would need Louis. He spoke to us, however, in English. My uncle had his knights gather in the hall for this was a momentous visit. We all knew that and as soon as he had stepped ashore my uncle had sent for the others. While we waited for the rest to arrive, we spoke to Sir William. "I am relieved that you all survived and did not bow the knee to de Montfort."

My uncle shook his head, "We will always be the king's men."

"The right king, of course."

"We heard a rumour, in Poitou, that de Montfort had attacked your castles." He shook his head, "I can clearly see that is wrong." He shrugged, "Or perhaps he plans to attack them."

"Is that why you came, my lord, to warn us?"

He hesitated and then nodded, "I was told to sail to Stockton and if I did not see your banner flying to turn around and sail home. The king's friends need to know that this island of loyalty still holds."

I was intrigued, "There is a plan?"

He smiled, "There is. Would you wish me to speak now before your other knights arrive?"

My uncle shook his head, "We are all united in this and we will wait until they arrive."

Sir William smiled, "It is a longer journey from the sea than I expected. I pray that your knights will not take long. The captain is turning his ship around and I will return on the next tide. I have hours only ashore."

None of them took long. Sir Geoffrey arrived first and he had with him Aunt Rebeka as well as his two squires, his sons, Alfred and Geoffrey and his daughter, Isabelle. The last to arrive was Sir Matthew. The ladies went to my Aunt Mary and my mother. They would catch up on gossip and news. We waited for Sir William to speak.

"The reason why I was worried that you might have succumbed to the men who come to do you harm is that the king's friends and allies plan to land in Pembroke in the west at Easter. Gilbert de Clare has let it be known that he is returning to the king's fold. The war will begin in

113

the west. We have decided to use the strength of the west rather than risk the men of London who are unreliable. If we can draw de Montfort from his supporters we have a better chance of victory."

I saw it all clearly as did my brother William who began to use his stylus on the wax, "The men of the valley are to be the distraction in the north that makes de Montfort look here and not west."

"It is. When I leave here, I sail to Scotland to speak to King Alexander. He is another ally and he has his part to play. De Montfort is so concerned with his Parliament that he gives no thought to those he exiled. The war with the Welsh freed many nobles and all of them wish to expunge the ignominy of Lewes."

My uncle nodded, "So you need us to stay here until... when?"

"Until the end of May. We need him to look over his shoulder for the men of the valley and the Scots. Of course, you will not be marching with the Scots but the men of the Palatinate. The Earl of Leicester does not know this. So you can see why we feared you might have fallen already."

"There is a tangible plot to do us harm?"

"We have spies in London and they speak of meetings held where names such as Sir Henry Samuel and the Earl of Cleveland were spoken. The spies were not privy to the conversations but the secret nature of them alarmed those of us from Poitou enough to send me on a long and perilous journey. If Simon de Montfort is in the west when we land then he could snuff out the threat quickly. We need him looking north as well as west until we land. When he moves to muster and to meet us then we will be able to gather all of our allies and take the fight to him. If we succeed then the war may be over before you even arrive but you will have served your king as well as any."

We spoke while Sir William ate, for Edgar had brought in food and when the messenger came to tell us that the tide was turning, he bade a hasty farewell and left. We were all seated around the table and each of us was lost in our thoughts. The visit of William de Valence had given us hope but also raised the spectre of treachery.

It was William, the scribe, who broke the silence. "We have not yet been attacked and I think it is as Henry Samuel said, de Montfort was waiting to see if we took the bait of the Parliament. We did not and that means the threat is still there."

Dick said, "But we have improved our defences. He cannot hurt us."

The arrival of Sir Geoffrey had illustrated the threat, to me at least, "He can, cuz. Our manors are stronger but we know that any of them can fall if they bring enough men. Only Stockton is strong enough to withstand a siege and de Montfort will not want that. He wants to destroy our ability to help the king. Ten knights and a hundred men could easily take any of our manor houses if he attacked at the right time."

My brother Alfred said, "Then we bring our families here within these walls."

Sir Geoffrey shook his head, "I am surprised at you, Alfred, while we would be safe then our people, all of them, would surely die. It is not the knights only that are the threat to de Montfort, it is our people. The archers, sergeants, billmen and slingers are the threat. We have to defend our manors."

"But Alfred is right in one respect, we cannot allow your families to be threatened. The manors must be defended but Sir Henry Samuel, Sir Richard, you must send your wives and daughters here to Stockton. Sir Geoffrey's family is here already. We keep our families safe and trust to you and your men to keep the manors protected."

It was not a comfortable decision to make but having made it my uncle ensured that we all obeyed. I knew that Eirwen would object. She would wish to face the same danger as the women of the manor. My uncle offered any women sanctuary in the castle but I knew that few would avail themselves of such an offer.

Richard and I left with Matthew and Thomas. They were bachelor knights and had no families yet to worry them. My mother and Lady Mary had already begun to organise the sleeping arrangements as I headed back to Elton. I had arguments from Eirwen but Samuel had been present and he was the one who persuaded her, "Mother, any of the women of the manor can go with you. You are not abandoning them. I have never had to defend the walls of my home, only my father has and then that was many miles from here. He was a bachelor then. Do you think we could fight on the walls without worrying about our families? A warrior with a distracted mind can make mistakes. If father and I fight on Elton's walls knowing that you and my sisters are safe we will fight all the harder."

Eirwen squeezed Samuel's hand, "Our son has grown wise, my lord, and I can see that he is right."

I was relieved and I nodded, "Besides, there will be fewer mouths to feed if there is a siege."

"You think we will all be ringed by enemies?"

"If we are then de Montfort has lost already for it would take a huge army to do so. No, I do not. What I do think is that one manor will be attacked to draw us from our manors where they can beat us piecemeal. It is how I would fight."

Eirwen smiled, "But you would never do anything as dishonourable, would you, my love? I will obey the earl's command but I do so reluctantly. Come girls, we will go to Stockton and skulk with the other women behind Stockton's strong walls."

We escorted them, the next day. As we had all expected none of the women wished to leave their homes. Some of the widows had taken up with some of the new men. Alan and Robert, sons of Robbie, were now married to two widows. They had confidence in their men and, I believe, in me. I hoped it was not misplaced.

There was a subtle change when my wife and daughters left. The manor took on the appearance of a military camp. I had Jack send patrols to the river and to the west each day to see if there were signs of an enemy. It was possible to swim the Tees. We had done it before. As it was now March the river was not quite as cold as it had been a short while earlier but it was not something to be undertaken lightly. The damp ground made it easier to spot the signs of an enemy. The lack of signs did not make us relax our scrutiny. I just hoped that the other manors were as vigilant.

It was the smell of smoke drifting from the southeast when we woke one morning that alerted us to danger. We kept a good watch from the tower. I stood in the yard with my squires as well as Ned, John and Jack. I cupped my hands and shouted, "What can you see?"

"There is a column of smoke. It looks to be coming from Thornaby."

"Did the night watch see anything?"

"There was a fog last night, my lord."

I looked and saw that there was still mist over the fishpond. "I want the sergeants mounted. Have those from the outlying farms brought within. Ned, you take command. I want the gates barred when all are within and send your son to tell the earl that I think Thornaby has been attacked."

Roger asked, "Will he not know, my lord?"

"If there is a mist over the water here then it might still be at Stockton. Fog masks sounds and Thornaby has no bell. There is just a beacon. Fog means you cannot see a signal for help."

It did not take long for us to arm and mount but long enough. The fog had gone. We headed to the river rather than the road to Stockton. We headed towards Preston first, to the east of us. The farmer there, Egbert was already driving his animals to Elton. His family were helping him.

"Did you hear aught in the night?"

"Yes, my lord, we heard the clash of metal and cries in the night but I could not tell the direction. To be truthful I wondered if any were attacking Elton. The smell of burning came later."

I knew then, before we had even crossed the river, what had happened. The river was just thirty paces wide but it was deep and we had to swim our horses. This was Roger's first time and John of Parr and Jack flanked him to keep him safe. Joseph led the rest of the sergeants. The three of them got on well and worked as a team. I saw the pall of smoke rising in the sky just a mile away, that was Thornaby. I only had twenty men in addition to my squires and we were not enough to fight an army. Our purpose was to see what had happened. We had taken spears rather than lances and I waved mine to spread my men out in a line.

"Samuel and Roger, ride behind me. Protect my back." It was a lie, of course, I wanted them safe for as long as possible.

We made our way across the boggy ground and then climbed up the firmer slopes. This side of the manor was not farmed, it flooded too frequently. The land that was fertile was to the east. The smell of burnt wood was augmented by the stench of burning flesh. We approached the walls of Thornaby manor slowly and we were all alert and vigilant. We rode into a charnel house. The walls had burned quickly. There were still glowing timbers but oil had been used and it had flamed quickly. We found the first bodies by the ditch. They had been burned the least and we knew some of them for they had been at Lewes with us. Sir Geoffrey and my two nephews lay together before the gate. None had mail upon them and their bodies had been mutilated after death. The smell of burnt bodies came from the hall.

"John, have these bodies covered. We have to find de Montfort's men."

"Yes, my lord." He dismounted and then waved an arm, "What I cannot see, Sir Henry, are the enemy dead. I cannot believe that none died. They have taken them with them."

John of Parr and some of my sergeants had been searching for survivors, "There are no burnt horses, my lord, they have taken them."

Roger asked, "How could this happen?"

I shrugged but I knew the answer, "There is no watch tower here. Men came at night and climbed the walls. They slew the sentries and that drew the defenders from the hall. Sir Geoffrey made a mistake. He and his sons have paid the ultimate price. After they slew the men, they stole the horses and then fired the walls at their leisure. They took advantage of the fog. The fire was to draw men here."

"Yet, father, we were not ambushed."

I pointed northwest, "They did not expect us to swim the river. They will be waiting at the ferry. Come we ride and I pray we are not too late." My fear was that my uncle might send men across on the ferry. He could not send large numbers and the ones who landed first might be ambushed. Whoever had done this planned well. We had lost one manor and the rest were all under threat. We headed for the ferry. On this side of the river, there were trees and bushes that grew close to the water. The quay for the ferry lay in a cleared area. I saw the laden ferry being loaded on the Stockton side. Samuel grabbed my arm and pointed. Hidden in the trees and bushes were armed men, a large number. I estimated more than one hundred. My eyes had been drawn to the river. I recognised Dick and Sir Alfred aboard the ferry and they were trying to cram as many men at arms as they could.

I turned to Jack, "We need to distract them. Samuel, when I say, sound the horn three times. We must stop the ferry from crossing."

Jack nodded, "Form a line. We make as much noise as we can once the horn sounds and make them think we few are an army." He turned to me, "And then what, my lord?"

"We fall back to Thornaby and if they follow us we cross the river and retreat to Elton."

Jack smiled, "And draw their venomous teeth to us."

"And away from the rest of the valley. We are the best prepared, are we not?"

"That we are, my lord."

I saw that the ferry was loaded and I said, "Now Samuel."

He blew three strident notes and then we all banged our shields with our spears." The ambushers would be hidden but I prayed that my brother and cousin knew there was danger. I saw Dick's hand rise and then the ferry stopped. The men waiting to ambush my cousin were not mounted and it took time for them to do so. As they did, I was able to estimate that there were more men than I had first thought. Many were hiding closer to the river and were armed with crossbows. All the men had horses.

"The slope will slow them. On my command, we wheel and head back to the river."

Samuel said, "What about the dead?"

"We can do nothing for them. We save the living. Sir Geoffrey and your cousins would understand and even if they did not I have a duty to the valley." I saw that the leading riders, the squires and pueros were just fifty paces from us. "Now!"

We wheeled and rode in a long line. It allowed for a faster speed and when we needed a column it would be easy to change. I saw Samuel look over his shoulder. "Face forward. Trust your horse. I do not want either of you falling from your horse. It would mean death if you did so." We neared the burnt-out manor. Already the magpies, carrion crows and jackdaws were pecking at the bodies of those who had fallen and not been burned. We could not maintain the line and I shouted, "Column of twos." I led and my two squires rode behind me. Jack and John of Parr would form the rearguard. They not only knew the land better than any, but they both also had good mail and horses that could outrun almost anything. We wheeled around the ditch and headed down the slope. As we did so I saw that the enemy warriors were not in any kind of order. My surcoat had been recognised and if they could kill me then they would have achieved a great victory. I still did not know who the enemy were. They had plain surcoats with a yellow cross. De Montfort's men had worn the sign at Lewes. That was just the sign of a crusader or one who thought he was serving God. It just proved that they were sent by the Earl of Leicester because such delusions fitted his character.

The boggy ground would slow us all down. The difference was that we were expecting it and they were not. "On my command, we wheel and charge them. Roger and Samuel swim the river and help us when we cross."

The two of them said nothing although the rest of my men said, "Aye, my lord."

"I cannot hear you, boys."

"Yes, my lord."

I waited until the river was just twenty paces from us and shouted, "Wheel!"

As White Sock turned, I lowered my spear to use it like a lance. My men had all wheeled the same way. Our practice had paid off. As I had expected the men without mail had been the ones able to stay close to us. The knights and sergeants were still fifty paces from us. It was clear that they were not expecting us to do what we did. Some men did not have spears and their swords were sheathed. My spear took one warrior with an old pot helmet and leather jack cleanly in the chest. I let my hand drop as he slid, screaming, from the saddle. The next warrior raised his shield but that merely gave me a good target and I knocked him from his saddle. The enemy sergeants were closing and it was time to show discretion.

"Fall back!" I did not turn immediately. Along with Joseph, Jack and John, I waited for a couple of heartbeats to allow the others to enter the water and for the sergeants to aim at us. The lighter-armed horsemen had seen what happened to their comrades and reined in. "Now." The three of us rode hard at the river and all three of us leapt in rather than walked. We had good horses and the jump took us three horse lengths from the bank.

I heard an order from behind, "Crossbows!"

I did not panic. I slipped my feet from my stirrups and lay flat along the back of my horse. It helped him to move more quickly as the water partly supported my weight. It also ensured that I was the smallest of targets. Even so, I had a real shock when the crossbow bolt pinged off my helmet. Had it struck my mail it might have penetrated but the helmet held. Ahead of me, I saw that Samuel and Roger were emerging from the river. The first of my sergeants were nearing the shore too. The cold had not hit me the first time we had crossed but lying horizontally meant I felt the cold of the river bite. When I felt White Sock's hooves gain purchase on the bank I sat in the saddle once more. I turned and surveyed my line. No one was hurt although four had lost their spears.

"Face them and any who manage to cross we either take or kill. I would know the name of the man who leads this warband."

I saw a discussion taking place on the other bank. They did not know the layout of the land, that was clear. An order was barked and twenty light horsemen took to the river. The fifteen crossbowmen knelt and began to send their missiles over the river. They were easy both to see and to stop. We all wore mail and had shields. It would take either a lucky or incredibly accurate bolt to hit us and cause a wound. As with all such weapons they took an age to reload as the crossbowman had to stand and use the hook on his belt to draw back the string, load his bolt and then kneel again. It was also clear that they had little experience of crossing a river. Three of the riders fell close to the other shore. The horses continued to swim across, following the rest. Some turned back, perhaps fearful of a fall. Six of them had more courage and they neared the shore. They obliged by not arriving together and they clearly did not know that the six of them were unsupported. The first to arrive had a javelin and he hurled it towards me. I flicked up my left hand and my shield took it. John of Parr angrily speared the man. A second rode at John of Parr but Jack's sword smashed into the side of his helmet and he fell from the saddle. The other four turned but none made the river. All four were speared in the back.

"Roger, Samuel, bind this man to his horse and take him back to the manor. Rafe, go with them. Godwin, take two men and gather the horses."

We watched as the knight lifted his helmet and began to give orders. His coif hid most of his features but there looked to be something familiar about him. When his men dismounted and went to the stand of willow trees with axes in their hands then I knew what they were about.

"They are making a raft. It will take time and we need to get the manor prepared for the attack." I pointed, not towards Elton, but the Stockton Road and Hartburn. "We will go via Hartburn and warn Sir Richard." The trip would only take a little while longer and as they did not know the land, it might confuse them. Any confusion could only help us. I had to trust in my family. The earl was the best placed to take the offensive. He had at least forty mounted men he could use to seek the enemy and he would still be able to leave the castle well-defended.

When we reached Hartburn I saw that Sir Richard knew of the danger and families were being brought behind his walls. "They are building a raft and they will cross the river. We have hurt them but there are well over a hundred men, Richard. We will have to hold on until help comes."

He nodded, "The earl's decision to take our wives into Stockton was a wise one, old friend. Take care and may God be with you."

When we reached our home, it was like a small fortress. The walls bristled with my archers as well as the boy slingers and the billmen. The smell of baking bread drifted from the bread ovens. We had built them well away from the house and while they could the women were baking bread.

Rafe waited to take our horses, "Your son and master Roger have the prisoner in the hall, my lord. Jack fetched him a heavy blow and I fear he is not long for this world."

As we threw our legs over our cantles Jack said, "Sorry, my lord."

"It cannot be helped but perhaps his person can tell us who he is even if he cannot."

Father Thomas was there. We had no church in Elton but the priest lived in a cell and ministered to the manor. He was more of a monk than anything but he could heal. He shook his head. "He is still unconscious, my lord, I cannot divine what goes on inside his head. There appears to be bruising but no cut." He shrugged, "Wounds I can heal but inside the skull and body is a mystery to me. I shall go and prepare salves and bandages. I fear that I shall need my skills soon enough."

He left us and I looked at the warrior. He was a little older than Roger. He had a crucifix around his neck and the coins in his purse were French. That did not tell me much. I looked at Roger who was staring at the young man. I said, "Do you regret coming here now, Roger?"

He shook his head, "No, my lord, but I was wondering how a blow with the flat of a sword could do this to a man. He was wearing a helmet and arming cap."

"Jack has a powerful arm," I was just about to tell them to go to the walls when the eyes of the wounded man flickered open and he stared at the ceiling.

"Am I dead?"

"No, you are not but you are hurt. Who are you?"

"William of Mansfield, my lord, and I serve Sir Guy de Ferars. Did we lose?"

I smiled, "Not yet. Now lie still. Roger, fetch Father Thomas." Roger hurried off.

"A priest? Then I am dying."

"He is a good man and he will know."

"At least I can confess my sins before I die and perhaps, I will enter heaven."

"Samuel, give him some ale."

Cradling his head in the crook of my arm Samuel poured some ale into his mouth. William of Mansfield smiled his thanks and closed his eyes as I laid down his head. The priest returned and the warrior's eyes flickered open. "Father, I would confess."

Father Thomas nodded and said, "While you do, I shall examine you. Open your eyes as wide as you can."

"Father, I have killed and burned men alive. I did not want to do so but Sir Guy said we had to in vengeance for his brother's slow death. A man has to obey his lord does he not?"

"He does but a man chooses his lord."

William gave a sad smile, "You either choose the earl or the king. I chose the earl for my father said that King Henry was a weak king and …" His eyes just closed and he lay still.

Father Thomas put his ear to William's chest and shook his head, "He is dead." He made the sign of the cross over him, "You confessed your sins and I give you absolution. I pray that you will enter heaven for I can see that you had a good heart."

I looked at Samuel, "Well, we now know who the enemy is. This Guy de Ferars will come for us. Stockton and the other manors are safe. This is personal. Come, let us tell the others. This will be a hard day of dying."

Chapter 13

Richard of Stockton

Family Ties

When the guards on the walls saw the smoke from Thornaby we knew what it meant. Sir Geoffrey had been attacked in the night. The rider from my cousin, Henry Samuel, confirmed it. He did not dismount but, having delivered his news, headed back to Elton. My father ordered men to the walls and Edgar went to tell those in Stockton that we could expect an attack. By the time the walls were manned and we were all armed we could see no sign of an enemy and the pall of smoke diminished.

My father, for once, was being indecisive and I took charge. "We cannot sit idly by and wait. Sir Geoffrey may need help. Let me take forty men and cross the river. You will still have thirty men and more to guard the walls."

"Very well but you will not be able to make the crossing in one go. Be careful."

I smiled, "Fear not, father, Henry Samuel taught me well."

Alfred grinned, "And me."

We went to the gate. The ferryman and his family had a small home by the river. When they were not ferrying, they used a punt to fish. They had good lives.

"Ethelred, we need to cross the river."

He nodded, "I saw the smoke, my lord. It does not bode well."

"Walls might be burned but the hall may well still stand. We need to go to Sir Geoffrey's aid."

As we loaded the first horses, he said, "We heard the clash of steel and shouts, seemingly in the distance during the night and then smelled burning. Since then we have heard nothing."

Alfred said, "Perhaps Sir Geoffrey beat off the attack."

"Perhaps, cousin, but as your brother taught me, speculation gets you nowhere." We had just loaded the ferry and I said to Robert of Tithebarn, the captain of our sergeants, "Bring the rest over as soon as the ferry returns. We will wait in that gap between the willows."

Ethelred and his sons began to pull on the rope. Suddenly the silence of the river was shattered by the sound of a horn. It sounded three times.

I looked up and saw, on the bluffs above the river Henry Samuel and his men. They were beating their shields with their spears.

Raising my sword I shouted, "Stop." I peered across the river and it was then I caught the flash of metal. There were men waiting to ambush us. My cousin had warned us and I had to trust his judgement. "Back, it is a trap." As we began to head back some bolts flew at us. We lifted our shields to protect both ourselves and our horses. Four of them slammed into the wooden hull of the ferry but we and our animals were unharmed.

We disembarked and I saw Robert of Tithebarn point his sword, "My lord, look."

I saw that there were more than a hundred mounted men and they were heading towards the bluffs. Henry Samuel had gone. I looked at Sir Alfred, "I pray that your brother has not paid a heavy price for his warning. Come, this needs my father and your brother."

We headed into the castle and, leaving our squires and sergeants with our horses raced into the Great Hall. The women were there and I saw a distraught Aunt Rebeka comforting my cousin Elizabeth. They looked up as I entered.

"Well?"

"It was an ambush, Henry Samuel warned us and then rode off. He was being pursued."

Every eye went to my aunt. We all knew that all hope for her husband and sons was gone but we said nothing.

William said, "My brother will retire to Elton and that is where the enemy will attack. He has drawn them to him. His messenger said he would investigate what had befallen Thornaby. The ambush confirms it."

"Then instead of crossing the river I will take the men and ride to Elton."

My father shook his head, "I am not sure. What if Henry Samuel has not managed to evade those men who would have ambushed you, my son?"

"We cannot wait and do nothing. Would you have us squat behind these solid walls as craven cowards while our families are slaughtered?"

William nodded, "Your son is quite right, Sir William. If we hide behind these walls then this unknown enemy can pick off the manors one by one." He looked at me, "How many men did you see, Dick?"

"Over a hundred and my cousin has just twenty mailed men. We saw them with him on the heights."

William was not a warrior but no one could deny that he was, probably, the cleverest man in the valley and when he spoke we all listened, "Sir William, let the two knights in the castle take just thirty men. That will be enough to deter wanton mischief and still leave enough men in the castle to defend its walls. Remember, your other son Matthew is alone at Redmarshal and Sir Richard at Hartburn. While Sir Thomas might be safe at Norton, we could lose four manors in the blink of an eye."

Aunt Matilda was the matriarch of the family and she rose to face my father, "William, I have never asked you for anything. I have borne the loss of a husband, stoically. I am begging now, do not abandon my son for surely he is the embodiment not only of his grandfather, Sir Thomas, but also the Warlord. Let Dick and Alfred go to the aid of Elton."

My father had no choice, "Very well, but if Elton has fallen already then return here."

As we headed for our horses Alfred said, "You know my brother as well as any, do you think that we will find blackened walls at Elton?"

I laughed, "I think that you and I will need to draw our swords and go to the aid of Henry Samuel. This will be a first eh, cuz?"

Sir Alfred turned and looked at his namesake, my squire, Alfred. "Do not fear nephew, your father has endured attacks on his walls before. He will be resilient."

My squire was tight-lipped but he nodded.

The gates of the castle slammed ominously behind us. Twenty of the men we led were mailed but the others had metal-studded brigandines. We were all armed with spears as well as our swords. We passed the Oxbridge and headed up the slope to the farm. The grange was abandoned and when we reached Hartburn we saw men on the walls. Sir Richard opened the gates. "Sir Henry Samuel rode by two hours since. He said that he would defend the walls of Elton."

"We have been sent to assess the danger."

My cousin's best friend shouted, "Walter, fetch our horses and bring ten men. The rest watch our walls. I will join the knights of Stockton." Sir Richard was showing a courage my father had not.

It took time to saddle the horses and I was impatient to reach Elton. It was not a long journey but less than half a mile from the manor we heard the clash of metal and the cries of battle. I knew the land as well as any, having been my cousin's squire. When we heard the sounds of battle, we reined in.

Alfred looked at me, "Why do we delay, cuz? My brother needs us."

"And we are few in number. Let us exercise caution. Do you think that an enemy can overcome Elton's walls in a morning?" He shook his head. "There is a dry valley between here and Elton. The woods Henry

125

Samuel left there are below the walls of the hall and will afford us cover. We ride along the dry valley and then filter through the trees. If the enemy is looking to ambush us it will be along the road. We leave the road now and loop around to the dry valley."

Sir Richard nodded, "A good plan and you are right. We can approach unseen that way."

It added half an hour to our journey but when we reached the trees we were unseen and we heard the clash of arms above us. The noise of battle would hide the sound of my voice but I spoke quietly to Sir Richard and Alfred, "We walk our horses through the trees and halt at the edge of the tree line. If I think we can succeed we will charge any enemies that we see but this will be my decision, understand?" I looked directly at Alfred who nodded. "Now tell your men and when they all understand we will move," I spoke to Robert and he and I passed the word.

When all was ready, we headed up the slope. The noise grew as we did so. My cousin had cleared the trees that lay close to the manor's walls. It was now occupied by the raiders who were loosing arrows and bolts at the defenders. I counted just thirty men before us who were thus armed. There were ten sergeants and their horses waiting. There was no gate on this wall. The gate was on the side closest to the Stockton Road and I guessed that was where the main attack would be. I took the decision, we would attack.

I raised my spear. Every eye was on me. I pointed it at the men who were just thirty paces from us. Had any turned they would have seen us but their attention was on the walls. I spurred my horse and he leapt forward. Sir Alfred and Sir Richard did so at exactly the same time. We knew each other's minds. We three rode warhorses and they raced ahead of the others. The thundering hooves made men turn and from the wall, I heard a cheer. I concentrated on heading towards the sergeants who were busy trying to mount their steeds. One mailed sergeant had just managed to get his leg over the high cantle when I rammed my spear into his side. His mail was well made but the sharp head of my spear drove through the links, splitting them and easily slipping through his gambeson and into his side. I pulled back the spear and thrust it at the archer who was drawing back on his bow. He was so close that even a war arrow might penetrate my surcoat and mail. My spear struck him in the chest a heartbeat before he released. The bow and arrow fell from his lifeless hands.

The enemy began to run. The walls of the manor blocked an escape south and it was clear that was their intended route. The men we led were still fighting but Alfred and I had a clearer route thanks to my slaying of one sergeant and Alfred another. We rode after the fleeing men. I ignored those on foot as I tried to get close to the five sergeants who had managed to mount their horses. The men behind us could pick off those on foot at their leisure. The defenders of Elton hurled darts and loosed arrows at the fleeing men. One of the sergeants fell from his saddle, struck by an arrow and two darts at the same time. His cry made another of the sergeants turn. He saw me and tried to urge his horse to greater endeavours. My mount was a warhorse and, as we neared the corner of the walls of Elton, I was close enough to thrust my spear at him. He leaned forward and instead of striking him squarely in the back, I caught him obliquely. It was still a powerful blow and combined with his horse missing his footing made the sergeant fall from his saddle and crash to the ground.

It was as Sir Alfred and I turned the corner that we saw the bulk of the raiders. There had to be at least sixty or more who remained. I looked to the walls and saw my cousin Henry Samuel and Samuel. My cousin raised his sword in acknowledgement.

I reined in, "Alfred, we have to halt here."

Alfred looked at the men before us. He nodded for he saw that I was right. I turned in my saddle and saw that no enemies remained behind. Two of our men had fallen but the rest remained whole. Sir Richard joined us. His spear was gone and he held his sword. "They outnumber us two to one."

I nodded, "We have hurt them but not yet destroyed them."

Sir Alfred said, "Can we just wait here? Might that not make them flee?"

"It might but look, I think they plan to shift us."

As I pointed my spear I saw the knights who led them organise two lines. With their shields on their left arms, the defenders of Elton would not be able to help us much. Sixty men charging just twenty odd would result in our deaths.

"Form line."

We nudged our horses into a line. I would not precipitate a charge. Our horses had just climbed a slope and made one charge. They needed as much time to recover as we could give them. The two knights who led de Montfort's men did not give us long. Their horn sounded and they lumbered towards us.

"For King Henry and for the knights of the valley!" I pointed my spear and led my handful of men into the wall of steel. They were just fifty paces from us and neither side would be able to get up to full speed. It mattered not for they would sweep over us. My cousin's men sent arrows and darts at the enemy and a couple of horses fell but they would still outnumber us when we collided. I aimed my horse at the knight who led them. As I pulled back my spear, I heard a familiar horn. It was the horn that had sounded on the bluffs above the river. Henry Samuel was attacking from the rear. The charge slowed down those who were charging us and made even those at the front look over their shoulders. Henry Samuel and his sergeants had timed their attack to perfection and as they struck I saw many men fall.

I then had to give all my attention to the knight who had not turned and was clearly oblivious to the attack on their rear. The lance that hit my shield was longer than my spear and it was powerfully struck. I was unfortunate for my horse stepped on a body and slipped. I fell from the saddle. We had practised such falls and I held my shield before me but, even so, I was winded when I landed. The knight pulled back his lance to end my life as I lay on the ground, unable to move. Sir Alfred also had a spear and his blow was well-struck. He hit the knight in the arm. Blood spurted and his lance fell.

The knight heard the noise from behind and turned. He saw that they were surrounded. Lifting his helmet, the enemy knight shouted, "Back! To the river!"

Henry Samuel lifted his helmet and said, "Are you whole, cuz?" I nodded and waved him to pursue. He replaced his helmet and galloped off.

My squire, Alfred, brought my horse and dismounted, "I am sorry I was not closer, cuz." He held up his sword. It was bloody, "I was putting this to good use."

I had my breath back, "A squire should not risk himself. You have done well but this day is not over." I mounted and followed the last of my men as we hurtled towards Preston. This was now a chase. I saw that Alfred's father had forced the raiders to head away from the hall. Bodies littered the ground before the gates and riderless horses wandered. We were at the back of the pack of sergeants who followed Henry Samuel and Sir Richard of Hartburn.

It was the raiders at the back of those we pursued who saved the knights and their oathsworn. As Henry Samuel and Sir Richard slew the ones at the rear so those at the fore extended their lead. We gradually caught up with them. I found myself riding next to John of Parr. He grinned at me, "A timely arrival, Sir Richard. I would rather fight from the back of a horse than the walls of the hall."

Every horse was now weary and I wondered if the final battle would be on the banks of the Tees. As we neared the river, I saw that it was not meant to be. The knights had already mounted one of the two crude rafts that lay moored in the river. Even as the second one was loaded the first began to head downriver. The current was strong and as we reached the water's edge we saw that the first raft was fifty paces downstream. We were impotent to either harm or stop them for we had spears and swords only. The two knights waved their swords at us.

I reined in next to Henry Samuel. We both took off our helmets. Our squires, the brothers Alfred and Samuel, greeted each other. Henry Samuel held out his arm and I clasped it. He beamed, "Thank you for your timely arrival. Had you delayed then they might have used darkness to enable them to close with our walls."

"Thank you for your warning, when was it? This morning?"

He nodded, "I knew that you would understand."

I looked across the river. The smoke had long since disappeared, "Sir Geoffrey?"

He shook his head, "Dead along with his sons and his men. We cannot catch Guy de Ferars but we can bury our dead."

"Guy de Ferars?"

"The brother of the knight who ambushed us. If any of these men live, I would question them and find out more. I have his name etched in my memory now. Sir Geoffrey and my nephews will be avenged, that I swear."

I nodded and dismounted, "Then let us begin our walk now for my horse needs to rest after this day."

It was getting on for dark when we reached Stockton. My father greeted us, "We saw the rafts as they passed. The archers managed to hit some of them." He pointed across the river, "They left the rafts there and cut the rope for the ferry."

I sighed, "Sir Geoffrey and his sons lie unburied. Henry Samuel and I thought to bury them."

Ethelred knuckled his forehead, "My lord, we can use our punt to ferry you and my sons and I can repair the rope. We will have the ferry ready in a few hours."

I looked at Henry Samuel who said, "Aye, we will be on foot and we will take men at arms but let us cross and do what is right for the dead of Thornaby."

We waited until twenty of us had crossed before we walked up to the bluffs. We passed a couple of dead men. They had obviously succumbed to their wounds. We went warily but I doubted that our enemy would have hung around. They would be heading south as fast as they could. As we neared the dead we heard the scurrying of foxes and rats feasting on flesh. It spurred us on. We recovered twenty bodies. The rest were either too badly burned or in too poor a condition and we headed back to the river. We were weary beyond words but we owed it to the dead to do this. Ethelred had repaired the ferry. It was almost midnight when we reached the castle. We placed Sir Geoffrey and his sons in the chapel, they would be buried the next day but his men who had fallen were buried that night. Lady Rebeka insisted upon their commitment and we all stood in a sombre circle as the defenders of Thornaby were buried.

Chapter 14

Henry Samuel

The changing of the guard

Thornaby was abandoned. My brother, Alfred, might have had it for his manor but he did not want it. We cleared the ground and the bodies that remained were buried together. The place became somewhere to be feared. Men said that ghosts haunted it. The enemy dead were also buried. There was a more practical reason for that. We had enough foxes and rats without encouraging more. We had all lost men but thanks to the prompt action of my brother, my cousin and my best friend, far fewer than might have been expected.

We did not decide that the threat was gone immediately. We sent men south, as far as East Harlsey first. It was there we discovered that the raiders had continued their journey south. Two of the wounded we captured told us who the attackers were. Sir Aubrey had been wounded by me and the wound had become poisoned, he had died and when Simon de Montfort sought a lord to send north he and his nephew, Sir Aubrey's son Geoffrey, had eagerly volunteered. The two sergeants had been badly wounded. One had lost his hand and the other would never walk again. I gave them two sumpters we had captured and sent them on their way. I knew that they would end up back in Montfortian country and it would do no harm to let the earl know that Sir Geoffrey and his sons apart, he had done little harm to us.

It was April when the ladies returned to their manors and by that time we had cleansed Elton of every sign of the battle. We chose April as we knew that the king's supporters would be landing in Pembroke and, hopefully, our defiant stand would have kept him with one eye upon us.

One direct effect of the attack was that there were no longer any doubters. We had volunteers to fight alongside us and men came from Yorkshire to become warriors of the valley. Some came from Whorlton. We more than made up for the men we had lost. The second effect was that my uncle realised he had not covered himself in glory. When we went to pick up our wives and daughters, he told us all in his great hall that while he would retain his title of Earl of Cleveland, it would be me who made all the important decisions. Sir Geoffrey had been his friend and his death had hurt him. I had no special title but I had a greater responsibility. When we went to war, and now that the landing in Pembroke had taken place, then war was inevitable, I would lead every warrior from the valley.

Sir William de Valence had told us to stay in the north until May but not precisely when in May. As we had heard that he and the others had landed and by now the Earl of Leicester would know that we survived, I chose the first of May as the date we would head south. I sent my brother Alfred to inform the bishop but also said that I would not wait for the whole muster. This time we would not be sneaking through Montfortian land, we would be travelling with banners and trappers on our mounts. The world would know that the knights of the valley were going to war.

I would be carrying the banner of Cleveland. I had chosen my brother Alfred to be the standard bearer. The women of the valley sewed surcoats and trappers for our horses. I had the weaponsmith and tanner make a leather and iron shaffron to protect Duncan's head. The dead from the raid yielded mail and weapons as well as their horses. Rather than hurting us, the attack had made us better armed. The weaponsmiths repaired damaged mail and we would have more men with hauberks than before the attack. The extra horses we had bought from Abel had now been well schooled and some of my sergeants would have a spare horse. Ned and the archers had a good supply of arrows as well as spare staves for the bows.

We held our farewell feast at Easter at Stockton Castle. Eirwen was the only lady who did not live in the castle and when we arrived my mother and the other ladies made a real fuss of her and my daughters. The two girls were becoming young ladies and the squires who were not her cousins made a real fuss of both of them. To Eirwen's annoyance, they were delighted. Isabelle, Thomas' sister, was the only one with a shadowed face.

I spent some time with my brothers in my uncle's solar. Having handed over the reins of power to me he left us alone. His decision when the raid had taken place could have been disastrous and he knew it. The delay would have resulted in the fall of Elton and our deaths. William had found maps of the west country. "You had some of these made, Henry Samuel, while others were grandfather's. The Severn is the river that will decide who wins and who loses this civil war. See how it divides Wales from England. There are few places to cross it and they are well guarded with castles. If the king's men hold them then you can deny de Montfort the ability to manoeuvre. The danger will be the Welsh."

Alfred nodded, "And you have had the beating of Llewellyn, brother. When he sees your banner, he will know he has a hard fight on his hands."

I shook my head, "Our route south to join our friends will take us perilously close to North Wales and we know that is where he has his strongholds. We may find ourselves ambushed before we reach the rendezvous and we have now lost our Welshmen." The men who had fallen at Lewes had included our Welsh archers. We would no longer have local knowledge.

William nodded, "I have a route which should see you safe. See, if you head first for Chester, then you will enjoy the protection of that castle. Head south and east to Stoke which lies on the Trent and then directly for Ludlow. It will add a day to your journey but keep you free from the danger of ambush."

I had fought the Welsh for King Henry and his son many times but William had the stories of the times that our grandfather had fought them as well as the Warlord. We would be as well prepared as any when we went to war.

I was seated at my uncle's right hand and when prayers were said before we ate, they were both longer and more pointed than usual. The knights who would be carrying the banners of the valley were each named and when we all said amen the word echoed around the hall, for each of us knew that this war might be the one that ended the line of the Warlord. All the males of the family, my uncle and brother excepted, would be going to war. When they had done so for King Richard only my grandfather had survived the Battle of Arsuf. We were all aware of the danger.

I found my mother watching me as I ate. She was on the other side of Eirwen and both of them seemed intent on watching my every mouthful. I sighed as Samuel took away the platter of bones, "Why do you watch me eat, mother? Am I doing something wrong?"

She smiled and shook her head, "I see little of my eldest, my son, and while all my boys are special to me you are the one who looks most like your father. He was taken too soon and I was remiss to spend my life here. I should have been with you at Elton."

I felt awful for my outburst, "I am sorry, mother, forgive me for my hasty words. I am unused to this attention."

She nodded as Samuel brought the next course, "You are like your father. He too was a modest man. It seems to be a trait of the best of men in this family. I want you to know that I am proud of you, Henry Samuel, and always have been. My heart swells with pride when I hear of your deeds. I know I do not gush and weep like some," I smiled for I

133

knew she meant my Aunt Mary, "but know that in here," she touched her chest, "I am cheering and singing your praises. Your father, in heaven, would be proud and I know that your grandfather thought you to be the perfect knight. I just wanted you to know this before you leave and to tell you that you need not risk all in this war. You have done more than enough for this king and his son already. I pray that you win and that this is an end to your travails for the Plantagenets."

Eirwen nodded, "Amen to that."

This time I was not asked to sing but Louis was. His father had sent him to England so that he could become a knight. My cousin Thomas had told me that he was ready for his spurs. This was not the time for such a change but after the war, my uncle had promised him that he would be knighted. The old tradition of learning to play the rote and sing for the ladies was revived and Louis sang a beautiful French song about a maiden taken by a dragon and rescued by a brave knight. To me, it sounded like the story of St George but this was a French version. He had a good voice and even my daughters, whose French was not as good as it should be, were enchanted by the melody and the words. It ended the night well.

When I bade good night to my mother and we hugged it was longer than was the norm. I felt a tear from her eye drip down my cheek. She shook her head, "Louis has a good voice. He has made an old lady weep." I was not fooled, the tears were for me.

We left the valley in the last days of April. The muster was at Elton for we would be heading west and not south. We would cross the river at Piercebridge and cross the Pennines. We would head for Middleham Castle. It had been built by Ribald, son of Odo, Count of Penthièvre but there was no knight there. Lady Matilde and her mother lived in Richmond but there was a small garrison there. The castle was large enough to accommodate all my men. The hardest part of the journey was when we left Middleham to cross the highest part of the land to reach Clitheroe Castle. There Roger de Lacy would afford us a good welcome. He was a young knight but I knew him to be a loyal man. Those forty miles were the hardest we had to endure.

My knights and I dined with Sir Roger. "You are joining Sir William early then, my lord?"

"We were told to be there by May. I would not delay for this war will need to be won or we will have to endure a civil war such as we have not seen for a century."

"I have the men of the Honour of Clitheroe to lead but they owe the king just forty days. If we leave too soon then they may be disbanded before they are needed."

I shook my head, "The men I lead will fight for as long as it takes to rid this land of Simon de Montfort."

Sir Richard of Hartburn asked, "Were you at the January Parliament, my lord?"

The young knight looked uncomfortable, "I was. I felt I had no choice but to attend."

"And were you offered a reward from Simon de Montfort if you joined his alliance?"

Sir Roger sighed and nodded, "I was tempted, my lord, but I did not accept his offer. I was offered, Middleham Castle."

I said, quietly, "That castle has an heir who is a young maiden."

His eyes widened, "He would give me a castle that is owned by a young maiden. Where is the honour in that? It shows me that de Montfort is a Frenchman without honour."

I smiled, "And I have heard that a Neville is courting Lady Matilda. There will be a strong knight to watch over that land in the future."

He looked relieved, "Then I made the right decision."

As we headed for Chester, the next day Dick said, "I wonder what would have happened had Sir Roger been offered a different castle."

Sir Richard snorted, "He would have taken it in a heartbeat. Middleham is a strong castle but the manors are not rich ones. There are just sheep and a few horse farms. The jewels would have been given to Lusignans and Frenchmen. De Montfort seeks to make England into France."

We did not reach Chester in one day. We stopped at the crossing of the Mersey, at Wallintun. There was no bridge and it took time as well as coins, to cross the river by ferry. It meant we reached Chester Castle just after sext. This was a royal castle and I knew it well. We were afforded a fine welcome and having done the hardest part of the journey, I decided that we would have a day of rest before heading for Stoke and then Ludlow.

It was at the small manor of Stoke that we heard of the movements of Simon de Montfort. We stayed at the Benedictine Priory there. The fare was simple but the lodgings were cheap and I felt safe in the cloistered house of God. The prior was a knowledgeable man and he told us that the Earl of Leicester had sent his son to the south to hold Winchester and the rich lands there while he had crossed the Severn and was gathering an army at Hereford. He planned, so we thought, to stop the men of the west from crossing the river.

While we ate, my knights and I spoke.

"Where does this leave us, cuz? We do not have enough men to fight a battle and if the Earl of Leicester controls the crossings of the river then …"

I nodded, "I know, Dick, we have a dilemma but we were asked to come in May. It is now May and we have to trust that William de Valence, Baron Wigmore and Gilbert de Clare have a plan. Would you have us return home when we are less than forty miles from Ludlow?"

"No, but once more we are placed in a difficult position. We are isolated."

"It is true that thus far we have not seen vast numbers of men supporting the king but that is to be expected. Those who are loyal and ready to fight will already be heading for Ludlow."

"The men of the Palatinate did not arrive in time, brother."

"I know, Alfred." I sighed and spread my hands on the table, "It is true we have few knights but we have squires who have proved themselves in battle. We have more than forty sergeants. All are mailed and the equal of many knights. The fifty archers we bring are all well-mounted and as skilled as any, Ned is a good captain and he is ably supported by others. It is true that we cannot face an army but if an army came to face us then that would tell us many things, not least that de Montfort would be taking a sledgehammer to crack a walnut." They smiled. "I do not think he will do that. We are a burr under his saddle and that is all. He has more important worries. We will ride on the morrow ready for war if it comes, but I believe that if de Montfort is in Hereford and his son in Winchester then the dangers will lie south of the Severn."

My words seemed to set them at their ease.

Ludlow Castle was a mighty fortress guarding a crossing of the River Teme. I knew that Geoffrey de Geneville, 1st Baron Geneville, was a loyal knight and a supporter of King Henry. The king had given him vast estates in Ireland. The only worry I had was that he had not fought at Lewes and I wondered why.

He made us welcome and when I sat with him to enjoy some wine it was clear that he had expected me. He was part of the conspiracy that had engineered the return of the king's allies. It put my mind at rest. He was in a confident mood as he entertained us in his lavishly appointed Great Hall.

"We have the Welsh to thank, at least in part for this opportunity. When they began to raid the marches, after Lewes, the Earl of Leicester, the man who would be king, had to release men like Roger Mortimer of Wigmore. We prevented the Welsh from gaining land but we were also able to send messages to our exiled friends." He leaned forward, "And soon, there may be even better news."

I was intrigued but there were other ears in the hall and this secret was best kept from all. I suspected it involved the rescue of one of the three royal prisoners. De Montfort had wisely kept them all guarded separately and the rescue of all three would be impossible. One, however, would give us a figurehead, a leader around whom the country could rally. That night I slept better than I had for some time.

The castle was large but not big enough to accommodate either all my men or the ones arriving to follow the baron. It was almost summer and they camped in the two baileys. The horses were taken out each day to graze by the river and to be given gentle exercise. They soon recovered from the journey and whenever this war began, they would be ready.

It was the last week in May when the secret was finally revealed. Aided by Lady Maude Braose, the wife of Baron Mortimer, The Lord Edward had escaped captivity. It was a bold escape and the heir to the throne rose in my estimation. At the same time, we learned that King Henry was being held by Simon de Montfort. The Earl of Leicester was keeping the king close.

Baron Geneville also gave us the news that Ludlow was to be the place where all our plans would be finalised. The war had come and while it had not started in earnest, we knew that it soon would.

Chapter 15

Henry Samuel

The Ludlow Council of War and the road to the Severn

John de Warenne was the first to arrive, along with Roger Mortimer. He greeted me warmly. "You played your part well, Sir Henry. I am sure that The Lord Edward will be pleased." He frowned, "Did you lose any men?"

I nodded, "A manor, my brother-in-law and two nephews. We paid a price but if order is restored then all will be well."

"I know we shall win. De Montfort has divided his army and we are united. We have all our men here between Wigmore and Ludlow. I do not doubt that we will seal off the one escape route that is open to the earl and then we can take his two armies piecemeal."

For the first time since before I had left England to seek an audience with the Pope, there was a positive mood in the king's camp. When The Lord Edward arrived he was greeted like a conquering hero. He glowed with confidence and I suppose having escaped his fetters so easily then he had every right to do so. He strode into the room and spread his arms. We all duly applauded. He turned to the men he had brought with him and who had been part of his escape. "I will speak to my lords and I shall see you all later." As they went out, I saw that one had the build of an archer. There was an intriguing story here.

John de Warenne bowed, "And we have begun the muster, my lord, Baron Elton is here already and now that you have escaped we can send for the others."

He looked at me and nodded. It was clear that he had not forgotten the incident with the archers of the Weald. I consoled myself with the fact that we did not have to like each other, just be able to cooperate on the battlefield. Gilbert de Clare had sided with the barons and fought alongside them at Lewes, but I knew from my visit to his castle that he and the next King of England liked each other. Having said that it was he who pressed The Lord Edward, "My lord, we are pleased that you are free but we must know your mind. We have men ready to fight de Montfort and the earl has helped us by dividing his men but what do you intend and what is the future for England?"

138

This was a moment that would echo long into the future and there was silence. I was amongst the greatest lords in the land and I wondered at my inclusion. I was not the Warlord.

"My friends, we shall observe the old laws that served England so well in the past and remove the vicious customs imposed upon us by foreigners. Those same foreigners shall be denied both office and castles. England shall be governed through the loyal efforts of Englishmen." He stopped, "Does that suit, de Clare?"

"It does, my lord."

"And now, what plans are put in place? I know the muster has begun but what of de Montfort and his son?"

"Now that you are here we can ride to the Severn and destroy all the bridges across it. The Earl of Leicester and his prisoner, your father, are trapped on the other side. Worcester is ripe for the plucking and then Gloucester. His son causes mischief in Wessex. We can do little about that, my lord. We believe, and we hope that you concur with the opinion, that we must cut the head from the hydra. Simon de Montfort has to be defeated before we do anything about his son."

"I agree and I am ready to march. I exercised during my incarceration and as my horse proved, we are both eager for war. Let us take our host and march to Worcester." His hawk-like eyes scanned our faces and he said, "Return to your men. Worcester is less than a day away. We leave before dawn and surprise them."

We all cheered. Here was a prince freed from the shackles of his father. Perhaps his imprisonment had allowed him to reflect. Was he like the butterfly that needs to be cocooned before it can blossom and fly?

He turned to speak to de Warenne, Roger Mortimer and de Clare. I left and went to find my men. There was a buzz of excitement in the camp. Everyone had seen the arrival of the royal hope and speculation was rife. I was the first of the leaders to emerge and I was surrounded by knights and nobles.

I held up my hands, "Those to whom you owe honour and allegiance will soon come and speak with you. All I can say is that we ride on the morrow and the battle to free England from Lusignan chains begins then." There was a cheer and I was allowed to get to my men. Ned, Jack, Joseph and John of Parr stood with my knights and I saw intrigue on their faces. "We ride for Worcester in the morning. The Lord Edward has returned in good humour and a positive frame of mind."

Ned said, "I saw the archer Warbow with him. It is said that England's next king is close to an archer. Is that true, my lord?"

139

I shrugged, "I know an archer was involved in the escape but why should you be surprised, Ned? Every knight worth his salt knows that a battle is rarely won by horsemen alone. You and your archers will have an important part to play in this war."

We had rested long enough and my men were eager to march to war and fight as soon as we could. This was not our border and was unfamiliar to us. I was not alone in wanting to get home as soon as I could. The loss of Thornaby was a grievous blow and while we wanted revenge all of us wanted the lives that Sir Geoffrey and his sons would never have.

It was the archer known as Warbow who sought me out. It was said that he was the finest archer in England but this was the first time that I had seen him. That was not a surprise. Hitherto I had seen The Lord Edward close to men like Lord Henry Almain, his uncle and the most senior of knights. He had the slight twang of Welsh in his voice when he spoke, "Sir Henry Samuel?" I nodded. "The Lord Edward would like a word with you."

"Of course."

He led me to a small chamber just off the main hall, "I will watch without, my lord."

"Thank you, Warbow."

He began almost as soon as the door was closed as though he had to get something off his chest. "You and I have rubbed off one another before now, Baron, and I do not think that we shall ever be friends but I have spoken to the Earl of Surrey and know that you played a vital part in the plot to fool de Montfort. You should know that I am grateful and that gratitude will result in benefits for you and the knights that you lead."

"We have ever fought for your family, my lord. I was imprisoned in Rome for your father. We know duty."

He frowned, "And yet at Lewes, you fled."

"I was ordered to flee by your father." I saw the surprise on his face. "You could not have known, my lord, but when the Earl of Cornwall was defeated the king ordered every man to save himself. Had I not obeyed him then Simon de Montfort might have been waiting in Pembroke."

"Just so. I can see that I have harboured a grudge these past months that I should not have. You obeyed orders. Let us begin anew. I want you and your knights as close to me as my oathsworn. This war will need men with quick minds and the ties of blood. You have both." He held out the hand of friendship. There was none to see it and I doubted that any other than his loyal archer would know of it but we two did and in his eyes, I saw something I had not seen before, trust.

He was a man newborn. He pushed us hard and we reached Worcester before any of the men summoned by the Earl of Leicester could respond. We were just a week into June and already the royal army had the initiative. We took the town and the castle without any hurt. At Worcester, I was present with de Clare, de Warenne and Roger Mortimer. The words they spoke told me, quite clearly, that there were spies in the enemy camp. I did not discover who they were then but I would soon.

"The earl has summoned his men to meet him at Gloucester. We have the chance to stop them gathering on this side of the Severn. We ride for Gloucester. I will leave a garrison here."

John de Warenne said, "My lord, we have not yet the full muster. More men are coming from the Palatinate, Yorkshire and Cheshire."

"We have enough here to take Gloucester. It is not my father leading this army, Surrey, it is me and we shall strike hard and quick."

A week after we had taken Worcester, we reached Gloucester and surprised the knights who had already gathered there. The town fell but the supporters of the Earl of Leicester managed to reach the castle. A siege began but The Lord Edward made it quite clear that we would not bleed our lives away on its walls. We would attack but in such a way as to weaken the defenders and not risk our men. It was the archers of the army who gradually weakened the resolve of those within.

We knights were observers. Five days after we had begun the rain of arrows I stood with my familia. We did not even have to wear mail for the enemy had long since used up their limited store of arrows and bolts. We watched as Ned and my archers sent arrow after arrow at any knight or sergeant who dared to peer over the battlements.

"This was where our grandsire often visited." I was speaking to my sons and brother.

"How do you know, father?"

"Your Uncle William told me before we left. He has discovered many letters sent during that civil war and he knows that Empress Matilda and the Warlord spent many days here in this town. We are stepping in the shadow of the man who saved England."

Sir Richard said, "Do not be so modest, Henry Samuel, you will have more than a hand in saving the kingdom for this king and his son."

"Let us not get ahead of ourselves."

In the end, it was the archers who defeated the garrison. They surrendered a fortnight after the siege had begun, at the end of June. More than a hundred knights and nobles surrendered. There were negotiations and it was The Lord Edward who led them. I was standing close to him as he spoke to those behind the walls of Gloucester Castle.

"Surrender to me and, if you swear not to bear arms against us for forty days, you shall be allowed to return to your homes."

As they discussed it, Sir Roger Mortimer turned to me and chuckled, "Clever, eh Sir Henry? We might not get their ransom but these knights cannot now fight against us and we have forty days of grace to defeat de Montfort. His already weakened army is now even weaker."

The Lord Edward's spies, whom I had still to see, reported that Simon de Montfort had given away much land in Wales to Llewelyn ap Gruffyd and de Clare's lands were being devastated. The earl was across the Bristol Channel and was seeking to cross that waterway and join up with his son in Hampshire. We moved so quickly that even I was taken aback. We raced to Monmouth which we took without a fight and then headed to Chepstow. This was a battle of wits between the Earl of Leicester and the next King of England. De Montfort was losing.

Being as close as we were to our leader, only his oathsworn were closer, meant we were privy to many of the decisions the rest of the army only heard about in hindsight. I was there when Gilbert de Clare announced that he had procured some ships and he intended to fill them with men and prevent de Montfort's small fleet from rescuing their leader from before our very noses. Three of them were pirate ships from Ireland and it begged the question of how the Earl of Gloucester came to know them.

"Baron Elton, how about we put some of your men in the ships? I am sure that they would give a good account of themselves."

The Lord Edward snapped, "I do not intend to lose this conroi in a sea battle. Put men with no mail in them. All that they need to do is prevent the ships we see from reaching Newport."

We could see the rebel banners beyond the bridge over the Usk. Was this to be the battle we sought?

The Earl of Gloucester shrugged, "I doubt that we shall lose a vessel but we obey you, my lord."

As the men were without mail it did not take long to pack as many as we could on the little fleet that headed out to sea. We could see the enemy fleet as it approached. I had never seen a sea battle in English waters and I was intrigued.

It was clear that this would be a one-sided affair as the ships were coming across the channel empty. They had few fighting men on board. They would have to use guile and cunning not to mention great skill if they were to reach Newport. The three pirate ships gave us the edge and

their captains knew the waters well. They cut off three of the larger
vessels and boarded them. Their colours struck, they were used by the
pirates and effectively ended the battle. Less than half the Montfortian
fleet escaped and eleven ships were sunk or captured. The Earl of
Leicester was stuck in Wales.

"Now we strike for Newport while they watch their ships sink."

"My lord, what of the men we boarded on our ships?"

"They can follow de Clare. We use our mounted men. Let us take
Newport Bridge and with it, de Montfort."

The imprisonment seemed to have given The Lord Edward more
drive and purpose than enough. He was desperate for action. Once again
it was my knights and sergeants who followed closely. De Montfort had
seen hopes of rescue dashed and he was already falling back over the
river as we galloped up. I saw men with faggots and kindling under the
bridge.

"My lord, he intends to burn the bridge."

"Does he, by God? Come, Sir Henry Samuel, let us see if that
Scottish warhorse is the equal of mine."

It was madness, of course, but I could not let the heir to the crown
ride into a mass of knights. I followed as did Lord Henry Almain and
five of The Lord Edward's familia. My handful of knights was close
behind me and it would be we few who would crash and smash into the
Montfortian horsemen. I do not think that it was calculated but the
horsemen we fought were sergeants. The knights were fleeing across
the bridge to join the earl before the bridge was fired. I think it was the
pent-up frustration of having been a prisoner for so long and the chance
to wield his sword in anger that drove him on.

Duncan did not let me down and kept pace with the prince's horse.
The blow I struck the sergeant was so hard that despite his shield
coming between us he was knocked over the back of his saddle and his
weight, added to the force of Duncan, meant that his horse fell too and
crashed into the sergeant next to him. My brother Alfred had an easy
kill as the sergeant had to flail his arms to keep balance. The bridge was
saved by the sheer number of sergeants who blocked it. Had they turned
and ran then we would have crossed too but they did not want swords in
their backs and they turned. They were brave men and they
outnumbered us, but there is a difference between numbers and skill.
We were all better mounted, armoured and armed. When the wall of
flame leapt up behind them then the twelve sergeants who survived
surrendered.

I was close enough to see that the heir to the English crown was not
happy. We had been a bridge's length away from taking the prize that

was Simon de Montfort. He turned to me and gave a sardonic smile, "It seems my brother-in-law gave you a fine horse, Sir Henry Samuel, and I am pleased that you and your knights pressed home the attack hard."

"We have lost de Montfort, my lord. Do we pursue him in Wales?"

He shook his head, "We bar the river to him and retire to Worcester. Our enemies are divided and we are not. Each day sees more men arrive to swell our numbers." He pointed his sword at the sergeants, "Dismount and walk your horses. You shall enjoy the walls of Gloucester as your home until your master is dead, or, like you, a prisoner. Earl Gloucester, I want every bridge along the Severn destroyed. We shall meet you at Worcester. This first part of the campaign has gone well but the task is yet half completed."

Chapter 16

Henry Samuel

The spies in the camp

Worcester was back in England and we trudged along the Severn to cross the river at Gloucester. With the sergeants imprisoned and their horses now ours we continued on to Worcester. I do not think that I had entered the inner circle of the great and the good that commanded the army, I was a northern outsider but each of them knew the role that I had played and when they discussed strategy or heard the news then I was summoned to their side. We heard, in the third week of July, that young Simon de Montfort, the earl's son, had taken both Winchester and the mint there. He had not headed west to join his father. The Bristol Channel was now the Earl of Gloucester's and any ships that tried to cross it would be doomed to fail and the war would be over.

Roger Mortimer was always keen to fight a battle. He had nearly died at Lewes and he hated the de Montforts more than anyone I knew, "My lord, let us take our army and fight this cockerel. He must come along the Oxford Road and there the people are loyal."

The Lord Edward nodded and sipped his wine, "And if he does not, Sir Roger, and slips west while we head east, what then? The worst thing that can happen is that the son and his father join up. Then we would have a battle on our hands. I intend to battle the earl but on my terms. We had them at Lewes and lost. The next battle will decide who rules England, my father or the earl."

All of us knew that the one who would rule England would not be the king but his son. He had been reborn in captivity.

He looked at John de Warenne, "It is time for you, Sir John, to find out the enemy's plans."

Sir John nodded, "If I might suggest, my lord, we use Sir Henry Samuel and his brother."

The next king of England turned and looked at me, "He has proved his loyalty more than enough and shown that he is resourceful. Aye, but just Sir Henry and his brother, Sir Alfred."

"Of course." He stood, "Come, Sir Henry, we have a ride ahead of us."

I was intrigued, "Go where?"

He smiled, "You do not think that we are blind to the plans of the enemy? We have spies who are close to them. It is how I knew the threat that you posed to the earl. The three of us will ride this night to a secret location. I will not swear you to secrecy for both you and your brother have proved your loyalty and discretion enough but you tell no one what you are about to learn."

"Not even my familia?"

"Not even those. The future of England lies in the balance, Sir Henry. Do not ride your warhorse. And shun your surcoat. We ride with cloaks, cowls and coifs."

When I reached our camp my knights and our squires were watching the servants we had brought prepare the food. It was the middle of the afternoon and, as our army awaited news, we had finished all the work necessary by the end of the morning. I was greeted with smiles and waves. I would have to deceive them and I did not like to do so but I knew, somehow, that this was not a trivial little night ride. This was something that could win or lose the war for us.

I waved Alfred over. "Fetch your hackney and lose the surcoat. You will need a cloak and just your cowl. We ride this night," I shrugged, "And I know not where but it is a command of The Lord Edward and secrecy is all." I saw him open his mouth to speak, "You were asked for by name."

He nodded, "I suppose all will become clear in the fullness of time."

Sir Richard approached, "What is amiss, Henry Samuel?"

"Nothing but Alfred and I will take a ride with the Earl of Surrey. You will command in my absence. Do not worry if we are away overnight."

"Take care, my friend. You and your family have been overused before."

I went with Samuel and we saddled White Sock. "Where do you ride, father?"

I shook my head, "I know not but when I can tell you then I shall. I go to serve England that is enough."

We headed north out of the camp but as soon as we reached a crossroads and were beyond sight of our camp and observation we headed east. The road was quiet and the long days of July meant that we could ride a long way before darkness enveloped us. The earl rode between us.

"We have a spy, that is to say, we have two. I will not give you their real names for you need not know them but one is a lord who is close to Henry de Montfort. He has his own reasons for betraying the de Montforts. It goes without saying that their work is parlous. We use

146

them sparingly but we need to know what the younger de Montfort plans."

Alfred said, "I can see all that, my lord, but why bring along my brother and me?"

"The spies are mine. I recruited them. I found one and he brought the other. I am too well known now and each time I visit with them then I take a risk which is why we shall arrive in the middle of the night. Your brother Alfred here is as yet unknown. Apart from the foray in Gascony, he is not seen as a threat. Sir Matthew and Sir Richard were your squires and men might remember them. The Lord Edward and I have been planning to hand over the spies to another. Now seems the right time." He smiled, "All will become clear to you, I promise."

I did not mind being the one taking risks but I did not like Alfred becoming embroiled in the prince's plots. We reached the manor of Studley after dark. I only knew where we were because of the signs at the crossroads. There was a burnt-out shell of an old motte and bailey castle. It looked to have been derelict for some time. There was a manor house but we did not ride up to it. Instead, we stopped and the earl asked us to dismount.

"Sir Alfred, walk up to the door and ask for the master. When he comes say, *'I have travelled far and seek shelter.'* You will be asked, *'Do you need a bed'* and you will reply, *'Just a stable will do.'*"

Alfred looked confused, "And then what?"

"You will be taken to the stable and you will fetch us. Your brother and I will wait by yonder oak tree. Come and fetch us."

I looked at Alfred and smiled, "You can do this." He nodded.

The earl said, "You have the words?"

"Aye, my lord." He led his horse and headed for the door. We walked our horses and stood in the shade of the mighty oak's shadows. The hall had no wall around it but there were ornamental bushes and a bridge over a ditch. I heard Alfred's boots as he crossed it. He knocked on the door and I saw him illuminated by the light from within. He was too far away to make out the words but I saw the nod from the man who led Alfred around the side of the house. A gate was opened and they entered. It seemed an age before the gate reopened and Alfred, now without his horse, walked over to us. He gesticulated for us to follow him and we did. When we were through the gate Alfred closed and barred it. He led us to the stable. It was empty. There was not even an ostler there. We unsaddled our own horses, watered them and ensured that they had food. Alfred led us to a side door. It was small, in fact so small that I did not think it was a door. Alfred knocked on it. He used four knocks and then a single one. The door creaked open and a hand, lit by a candle from within, beckoned us. We had to duck beneath the lintel.

A voice said, "Close and bar it behind you." I was the last one through and I obeyed. The passage was low and narrow. I could not walk upright. At the end was another door and it was opened. I was the last one inside and found myself in a cosy room with a table and six chairs. It looked like a private dining room.

The man who greeted us was about my age and he did not look happy. He spoke to the earl, "My lord, this is dangerous."

"But necessary, Ralph."

He started, "I do not know these men, my lord. I risk betrayal."

The earl shook his head, "These two knights are as loyal a pair of men as you will ever meet. Now we have ridden far. Some refreshment before we speak."

He nodded, "Forgive me, my lords. Take off your cloaks and I pray you to sit."

As we did, he left by the other door in the room. I said, "He is right, my lord. You risk all by bringing us here."

"And that is why I needed your brother. You, Sir Henry, are not needed but young Alfred is. You need to trust me as, I hope, Ralph does."

When the door opened again a servant girl entered with a tray. She was beautiful but, for a girl, quite tall and she also had short hair. She wore a cloth cap over it but I could see that it was not coiled beneath the cap. I was used to ladies like my wife and others who wore their hair long and coiled. I suppose it meant less care had to be taken if the hair was shorter. I did wonder at her presence. She would see the earl and if he was to be a secret then it was out already. The earl smiled, as the door closed, "Good to see you again, Margoth."

"And you, too, my lord. I told Ralph that my services would be required once more but he thought our work was over." She sat and poured the wine.

I was confused and I could see that Alfred was too.

The earl spoke, "We know that young de Montfort has left Winchester and is heading north. I am guessing that he will be heading to Kenilworth. The Lord Edward needs to know when he arrives."

I sipped the wine and watched the two of them. Ralph was the more nervous of the two and the woman called Margoth, who looked to be just a little older than Alfred, seemed well at her ease. It was the man who spoke, "You want me to ride to the young de Montfort and rejoin the army? Will he not be suspicious?"

"He might be but you will ride to Kenilworth and wait for him there. You will tell him that you have discovered that The Lord Edward plans on crossing the Severn to fight the Earl of Leicester."

Ralph frowned, "But he does not, does he?"

"It is plausible intelligence and it may spur him to attack while we are away. The point is it will be your welcome to allow you into his inner circle. You send Margoth to our camp when de Montfort arrives. She will go directly to Sir Alfred here."

She smiled and nodded to Alfred who reciprocated.

"Will that not alert others? If a woman rides into our camp and speaks to me then everyone will know who she is."

The three of them smiled and the young woman, Margoth said, "When I see you next I shall be a youth riding a horse as a man does. My name will be Ralph, the same as my brother. I will ride in from the west. Trust me, Sir Alfred, the deception has worked many times but my brother is quite correct. We do not overuse it for fear of discovery. It is dangerous for us both."

The Earl of Surrey said, "So, you will be able to supply the information we need?"

"We will but you need to ensure that The Lord Edward plays his part in the deception."

"Do not worry, we shall spread the word in our camp over the next days that the army is preparing to move. We will drop hints that it is to be to the west. If Simon de Montfort has spies in our camp, then they will hear of it."

Margoth smiled, "Then we will leave on the morrow." She stood as did Ralph.

We were leaving. We headed back down the passage to the dwarf's door. At the door, Margoth said, "Look into my eyes when I next see you, Sir Alfred. I can disguise many things but these blue eyes with the violet tinge are distinctive. Greet me as an old friend."

"I will and I pray that you stay safe."

"I will and when this discord is at an end and I return to a normal life think of the memories I shall have. Few women will have enjoyed a life such as mine. Say nothing till you are well beyond the village. It may be that the villagers think that you are de Montfort's men. Speculation merely helps us."

She closed the door and we returned to our horses.

We heeded her words and spoke not a word until we were five miles down the road. The earl said, "Now do you see why you both needed to attend? We must keep the identity of our two spies secret."

"But my men will wonder when I am greeted by an old friend they have never seen before."

"Remember Hugh of Bala?"

My brother nodded, "He was the sergeant who warned us of the attack on Eirwen's family."

"You and he got on, did you not?".

"Aye, but the others knew him too."

"But not his family. If you and I say, when Margoth rides in, that it is Ralph, Hugh of Bala's brother then they will believe that."

"But we will be deceiving our family."

"Sir Alfred, when this is all over and peace returns to this land you can tell them everything and the part your family played. We serve God and King Henry. All else is of lesser importance."

I looked at my brother, "This is the bargain we make when we become knights, Alfred. Only our brother William does not have to compromise. We all choose our own path and yours is now chosen."

A few days later we heard that the Earl of Leicester and a starving army had finally reached Hereford. He had taken the precaution of gathering his army behind the walls of both the castle and the town. The Lord Edward would have to risk a siege if he wanted to bring the earl to battle. Our council of war determined that we would stay where we were. If either of the de Montforts made a move to join up we could stop whichever one we chose. The two enemy armies combined were larger than ours but we outnumbered each of theirs.

It was on the first day of August, in the early morning while we were still rising from our tents that Margoth rode in. As luck would have it only Alfred and I were up, along with Samuel. The others had shared a night watch and were allowed a lazy rising. We were just dressed in breeks and boots and were making water close to the sentries when she rode in. Had I not been anticipating a slight rider coming to our camp I would not have known her for a woman. She wore a woollen cap and her hair was tucked beneath it. She rode a hackney as well as any knight and had a sword hanging down her side. She looked like a young gentleman.

I said to the sentries, "I know this young gentleman, let him pass."

"Aye, my lord."

She glanced at Samuel as she reined in and then dismounted. "Samuel, fetch us some mulled ale."

"But…"

"Just do it."

Leading her horse we headed for our tent. Margoth leaned in and smiled, "I would know him for your son anywhere, Sir Henry Samuel.

Your family has striking features. I will be brief so that I may be gone before the camp rises. Simon de Montfort the younger arrived last night with his army." We held our breath and she smiled. "They camp outside the castle in open fields. They have not embedded stakes." She then described, in detail, their camp. It was such an accurate picture that I could see it in my mind.

She stepped into her stirrup, "Mayhap this might be the end of it but keep a watch for me, eh, sir knights?"

She swung her leg over the saddle and then headed out of the camp.

Samuel arrived with the three beakers of ale and looked disappointed. "Where has the young squire gone, father?"

"He had other errands to run. Now let us go back and you can help me dress." We did not need to tell a lie as only Samuel knew of the visitor.

My son was burning with curiosity but I had to impart my news to the others immediately. We had a chance to eliminate young Simon de Montfort as a threat.

It was terces when I reached the castle where The Lord Edward and the other leaders were accommodated. I was, of course, admitted immediately. They were all at breakfast. I rushed in and knelt next to The Lord Edward. My words were quietly spoken and I knew that only he, de Clare and the Earl of Surrey would hear them.

"The young de Montfort is at Kenilworth and his army is camped in the open. There are neither stakes nor ditches to hinder us."

The Lord Edward grabbed my shoulders and bodily raised me to my feet, "Then we have him. De Clare, de Warenne, I want every man who can ride mounted and ready to move. Do not let them know where we ride. It may well be that our enemies have spies and it will be difficult enough as it is to hide so many men. God willing we shall surprise our enemies."

De Warenne rubbed his hands, "Let us see if the seeds that were sown sprout. Hopefully, our movements will tell the Earl of Leicester that we are heading for Hereford."

The Lord Edward left scouts to watch the crossing of the river at Kempsey and he loaded infantry in wagons to speed up our journey. We headed north towards Bridgenorth before taking a side road east to head more directly towards Kenilworth. We carried our mail, weapons and helmets on our sumpters. Riding in mail would tire both men and beasts. We did not leave Worcester until the middle of the afternoon and so when we turned east we seemed to disappear. Margoth had told us that the two large areas outside of Kenilworth, one to the east of the castle and close to the priory and a second one south of the castle, was

151

where the enemy army camped. I spoke of this to the earl and The Lord Edward as we rode. I could almost see him making his plans.

"We will attack before dawn. Our horses will be able to have some rest and the enemy will not be expecting such an attack. I do not wish to waste time reducing such a fine fortress for it has a great body of water protecting it. When we have hurt them sufficiently, we will return to Worcester. I do not doubt that the Earl of Leicester will take the opportunity of our departure to make a determined attempt to join up with his son."

Samuel was astute and there was no fooling him. He rode behind me and when we stopped to water our horses at Redditch he waited until we were alone and said, "That young man who arrived this morning was a spy, was he not?"

I looked at him and said not a word.

"You can trust me, father."

"Is this something that will prevent you from sleeping?" He shook his head. "Does the young man's identity cause you a problem?" He shook his head again. "Then this is just an itch that you cannot scratch and I will not indulge you. Tonight we go to war and this will be hard for we fight knights and sergeants who believe in their cause every bit as much as we do. None of us will have the time to look over our shoulders to see how you squires are doing. My sons will have to fend for themselves. Concentrate on that for I do not want to be the bearer of sad tidings when we return home."

He nodded, "I understand. I am learning much on this campaign, father. Will tonight be the final battle? When it is over will the enemy be defeated?"

"No, my son, for the Earl of Leicester is still at large. He and his army are wounded but there is nothing more dangerous than a wounded, cornered wolf."

He dropped back to ride next to Roger and my other son, Alfred. I knew that the three of them would speculate about the young man but I could do nothing about that.

We were weary when not long after lauds, we halted in the small valley to the south of the mighty fortress. There we donned our armour while our squires tightened our girths. We drank from our ale skins and ate the food that my sergeants had managed to bring. We shared everything so that we all felt part of the same conroi. In death we would all lie together so why not in life too?

We moved into position as the sky began to become lighter in the east. We moved in a long line of horsemen with the men on foot behind. We would break through any defences they might have erected since

Margoth had left and the men on foot would simply destroy the ones left behind. This time I was not as close to the royal standard as I had been hitherto. I had my spear and my shield was held close to my body. I rode Duncan and Samuel rode White Sock close behind with a spare spear. Roger also had a spare spear although I did not think that I would need them both.

The Lord Edward was eager to get to grips with the enemy. This time they would not escape. The only place they had to run was the castle. Those who were camped near to the priory would have to cross the artificial lake made by damming the stream. Gilbert de Clare and Sir Roger Mortimer, with their border lords, would ride to the right while I would be with the Earl of Surrey and head to the priory. The Lord Edward would bear the brunt of the attack. We headed for the camp in a long line.

The enemy warriors in the two camps were alerted. They could not but help hear our horses as they thundered up the valley but they were asleep and perhaps thought they had a bad dream or that it was thunder. Whatever the reason they emerged from hovels and tents to be confronted by more than five thousand horsemen and many foot soldiers racing from the dawn towards them.

As my men and I peeled off to the left, and towards the priory, we found ourselves spearing men in their breeks. Some held spears or swords but it made little difference to the outcome. The hooves of our horses also did terrible damage. Some men died without even knowing that there was a battle. As we neared the priory I saw knights emerge. Some were dressed while others were dressing. I recognised the younger Simon de Montfort for I had captured him at Northampton. He ran to the patch of water and hurled himself in half-naked. He swam to the castle. The walls of the castle began to fill with men armed with crossbows and bows but there were few of them and we were too far away for them to hurt us. Some of the knights tried to follow de Montfort but Jack and my sergeants saw their attempt and prevented their escape. They surrendered. Knights have that luxury, the commoners did not. We did not slay all. In fact, those who just ran and evaded our spears we let go. I did not think that the commoners would pose a real threat to us. They would wake in the night for the weeks to come dreaming of the terror of the attack by royal horsemen.

The attack lasted less than an hour and the enemy camp of soldiers was completely destroyed. I took off my helmet so that I could better survey the scene, "Take weapons, mail and anything which might give the enemy comfort." I estimated that less than a quarter of their knights had made it into Kenilworth's walls. We had taken sergeants prisoner too and The Lord Edward ordered them to be marched back to Worcester. The carts carried our foot soldiers and the loot we had taken. We gathered before the gates of Kenilworth. No words were spoken but every knight was bare-headed so that young Simon de Montfort would know who had done this. There were still men in the castle who might aid the Earl of Leicester but now, when we met him on the field of battle, we would outnumber him. We took everything of value from the camp including the banners. We had the banner of the young Simon de Montfort and when he rode to war he would be without the symbol that would rally his troops.

We left after sext and headed back to Worcester. Not a man from the valley had been lost and we had taken ten horses as well as helmets, hauberks and weapons. When we returned to the north, we could equip our own army. It took all day to reach our camp and when we did, we were greeted with the news that the Earl of Leicester had used a ferry to cross the river at Kempsey and was heading for Evesham. He and his son could now join up but his son had been badly hurt by our raid. The captured knights were incarcerated in the castle. When we won the battle then they would pay a ransom but they were now prisoners of war and had to be guarded. Worcester needed to be guarded for Kenilworth still had a garrison. We would not be taking every soldier we had but we would have every knight, sergeant and archer. The Scots who had fought at Lewes had shown us all that common foot soldiers, no matter how brave, would not stand up to a charge of heavy cavalrymen.

Chapter 17

Henry Samuel

The Battle of Evesham August 1265

"This is a different man who leads us. He has changed and he does not have the constraint of his father. He has made all the decisions thus far and I cannot fault them, can you?"

He shook his head, "Yet he has enjoyed luck. We were fortunate to find the enemy camped outside of Kenilworth's walls."

"That was not luck, Dick. I was privy to the information and the next King of England acted promptly when he discovered that the enemy had made such a mistake. Nor did he tarry at Kenilworth. Our race back to Worcester prevented Simon de Montfort from taking advantage of our absence. I trust The Lord Edward but I am under no illusions, the rebels will be a hard foe to fight and they will fight hard. I cannot see them surrendering as easily as our knights did at Lewes."

Thomas was the quietest of my knights, he always had been. When he spoke the others would turn and listen to him, "Cuz, it matters not who leads the army for it is you that we follow. It is you that we trust. At Lewes, it was you who saved us. We will follow your banner and we will protect your back for if we do then we all have a better chance of survival."

The nods I saw from the others were both reassuring and a weight. I had more responsibility than I could handle. As we returned to our horses to continue the night march I said to Samuel, "Stay close to your brother and Louis when we fight, eh?"

He smiled, "Yes father, but I am more confident this time. When I rode through the carnage of Lewes I was terrified, but once I had wielded my sword and was not wounded I gained in confidence. I am not a fool and know that I am young and have much to learn but so did you, and my cousins."

I added, "You too, Roger. This is your first major battle and you will have seen nothing like it in your young life."

"Yes, my lord."

Our last halt was at the hamlet of Mosham where Gilbert de Clare's scouts reported that while there were scouts north of Evesham there was no sign of either Simon de Montfort or his son. They had not joined up on the road to Alcester. I ordered my knights and sergeants to don their mail. The sumpters would be led by my archers and when the battle lines were arrayed they would be tethered. Today there would be no horseholders. Our speed and the tiring ride had been worth it. We had de Montfort trapped below us. The question was would he fight or would he run?

At Chadbury, as the sun rose ahead of us, we paused to tighten girths and for those who had not done so at Mosham, to don armour. I was summoned to the side of our leader. De Warenne was already there and he looked eager. "Now is our time eh, Henry Samuel?"

"I pray to God it is so, my lord."

The Lord Edward was calm as he spoke. This was a far more mature man than the one who had tried to chase the Londoners back to London. "We shall be in the centre. There is dead ground to our left and right. The Earl of Gloucester and Lord Mortimer will flank us but be behind and hidden in the dead ground. We will fly the banners of the Earl of Leicester's son and those we captured at Kenilworth. I want him to see a small number of horsemen so that he will fight us. I would not have him run. We draw him to us for he will soon realise that it is not his son that comes this day but destiny. I want him to charge us and for that reason, we will hold our ground and endure whatever the enemy throws at us so that our two wings may ride unseen around their flanks and trap them. When I give the command then, and only then, will we charge. Now return to your men and, God-willing, this night we will say prayers in Evesham's churches and its abbey. We will then thank God for this victory which I am sure will come."

De Warenne nudged me in the side, "This is a leader to follow to the ends of the earth, eh?"

"He is, indeed, my lord."

When we reached our men I told them of the plan and we followed the banners towards the rising sun and the hill we later learned was Green Hill. De Clare headed due east while we rode south and east to rise up the slope. When we stopped, we saw Evesham nestled in a loop of the Avon. There was just one bridge across the river and I saw beyond it a village, Bengeworth. It was the only escape route for we straddled the Alcester Road. We heard the bells in the Abbey sound the alarm as our lances appeared above the skyline. There would be a delay as the confusion of seeing friendly banners was replaced with the horror that the royal army was here. The banners were for confusion. The Lord Edward could not be mistaken for young Simon de Montfort. We formed ranks. We were to the right of The Lord Edward and John de Warenne the left. I was aware of de Clare moving his men into position but the dead ground they occupied would hide them from our enemy.

It was terces when Simon de Montfort led his men from Evesham. They were coming to fight and flight was not an option. As they moved into position, I reflected that this was the opposite of Lewes. There the rebels had held the higher ground and we had charged. Now it was de Montfort who would lead his army up the slope to engage us. He had no Londoners and we had no Scots. The knights who faced each other were the same ones from the first battle.

I have learned, over the years, that a knight never sees the whole battle. That is only seen by men like my brother William who studies accounts from both sides and men who fought all along it. I would have no idea what de Clare and Mortimer did until after the bloodshed was over. Once we engaged then I would not even know how the Earl of Surrey or The Lord Edward fared for I would be fighting the men I saw before me. I studied their banners as they formed their lines. We would be facing knights and sergeants. Simon de Montfort was in the centre and we would not be coming into contact with him. He would try to get to our royal standard which had replaced the one that had tricked them. I would be facing an old enemy for I recognised the banner of de Ferars. The man whose brother I had slain after Lewes and whom I had defeated at Elton had moved his men to charge towards me. He had seen my banner and chosen vengeance rather than obeying his lord's orders. That would be my battle. I looked to my left and right. Sir Richard was on my right and Dick on my left. Alfred and Matthew were to my right too and Thomas was on the left side of our line. Jack had placed himself next to Thomas as had Joseph while John of Parr was close to Matthew. My sergeants were as close to my family as I was. The rest of our sergeants were behind our squires. Being the extreme left of our line and, until de Clare joined us, the sergeants extended beyond Jack and Joseph. None of us had yet donned our helmets. That would be the last thing we did. The helmet gave protection but was hot and did not allow you full vision. We would survey the land before we put on our helmets.

Matthew asked, as we waited, "We stand here and hold them. That is all?"

I shook my head, "Only a fool takes a charge at the standstill. The Lord Edward will order us forward to meet them lance to lance but we have the slope and need not tire our horses or ride recklessly and lose the cohesion of our formation."

Sir Richard said, "This battle will be one which is more even for the enemy have ridden almost as far as we have."

I saw that they had a narrow formation of horsemen. They were just forty men wide and eight ranks deep. The Earl of Leicester was not in the front rank. Next to him, I recognised the banner of Sir Hugh Despenser and then, behind the horsemen, the main body of the enemy, the men on foot led by Sir Humphrey de Bohun. Their lines extended well beyond the narrow wedge of horsemen. I saw that he had with him some Welsh allies. They would be the archers that might cause us trouble and spearmen who were hardy. It was then that I saw King Henry. He was still a prisoner and had been brought to the battle. He had neither sword nor shield and his horse was held by two sergeants. I wondered why de Montfort had brought him.

I turned to Sir Richard, "Simon de Montfort is bold. He intends to punch a hole in our line with his best men and make it a duel between him and The Lord Edward."

"Then he is in for a shock. He cannot see that we have two wings ready to enfold him."

The horn sounded and de Montfort's battle lines headed up the slope. We donned our helmets. The Earl of Surrey waited until he was sure they had committed and then ordered his squire to sound the attack. I could only imagine the horror of the spectacle of two bodies of horsemen, both as large as the one that faced the earl, rising like steel-dipped death from his flanks. Whatever else his faults were, de Montfort was no coward and he came on.

Couching my lance I moved forward at the walk. We kept a steady pace. We spurred on and began to trot, still keeping our line. The thunder of de Clare's horsemen from our left sounded like a death knell being tolled. It was then that de Ferars made his move. His men were to the right of Simon de Montfort. He spied my banner and spurred his horses on. I heard his scream above the sound of hooves, "Death or glory! Vengeance shall be mine!"

As soon as he did a gap appeared between him and the Earl of Leicester. Even as we headed towards the banner of de Ferars, the Earl of Leicester and his oathsworn veered left. The single column of horsemen had become two and while the Earl of Surrey and The Lord Edward would have half to deal with, my men would have the other half. I realised as we closed with the enemy lances that this would allow de Clare and his horsemen to plough into the Welsh and English footmen who were now unprotected from a flank attack.

Although we wanted a straight line, I needed to use all the power of Duncan to help me make a clean strike. He pulled a little ahead of Richard and Dick. It allowed Guy de Ferars to charge directly at me, his black stallion eager for battle. I had the slope and a horse in whom I had total confidence. I heard a mighty crash from my right and knew that de Montfort and The Lord Edward's men had crashed together. I pulled back my lance and with my shield held tightly to my body punched as hard as I could. I aimed between his horse's ears. I had learned that ears were a good guideline. He aimed at my head. I saw the lance's head as it came towards my helmet. Both our weapons struck at the same time. His was a well-struck blow and so powerful that the helmet flew from my head, exposing my coif. Mine was equally well struck and the head slid towards his middle. His shield did not stop it and the head drove into his middle. The mail links were no hindrance to the triangular head that Samuel had sharpened the previous night. Both of us reeled from the blows but it was the coming together of our horses that proved to be our undoing. As they crashed into one another, biting and snapping their mighty jaws we were both thrown from our saddles. I let go of my lance which was, in any case, embedded in Sir Guy's middle and kicked my chaussee from the stirrups. Samuel had polished and oiled them. Had I been wearing boots they might have stuck but they were metal, and shiny. I felt myself heading to the ground. I tried to relax as I had been taught but there was a maelstrom of hooves and horses all around me. I had to trust in God and in the skill of the sergeants who were following me.

The shield broke my fall and I rolled on my back. I looked up and saw that Alfred and Samuel, my sons, as well as Roger had stopped their horses behind me. I was protected. Glancing down the slope I saw that Sir Richard and Dick had also closed together. I was safe, for the moment, an island but one which threatened to be swamped by the battles around me.

Samuel took a foot from his stirrup, "Here, father, ride White Sock."

Drawing my sword I shook my head, "I will fight on foot, see, others are doing the same."

He glanced to our right and saw that de Montfort and his oathsworn were in a circle on foot and Roger Mortimer and his oathsworn were heading for them. The Lord Edward and the Earl of Surrey were hurtling down the slope to join Gilbert de Clare in smashing into the enemy line of foot soldiers.

I pointed my sword at Sir Richard, "Guard Sir Richard and my banner."

It was not blind courage or a quest for glory that made me do what I did, we had the battle won and Sir Richard needed to join The Lord Edward and destroy the men on foot. Simon de Montfort would be surrounded and he would be forced to surrender. We had victory in sight and I would have to fend for myself.

My sons nodded and spurred their horses. My sergeants followed. Ned and the archers were joining de Clare to swarm down the flanks and harry the foot soldiers with arrows. They could not target the two hundred horsemen who were gradually being surrounded by Sir Roger and his men.

It was one wearing the livery of de Ferars who rode at me with his lance. From the livery, I took it to be the son of the knight I had killed, Sir Aubrey. Clearly, the normal rules of chivalry had been abandoned for it was considered dishonourable to charge an unhorsed knight. I put my left foot forward and held the shield from my body. Without a helmet, my head would have been a better target but he clearly lacked confidence in his own skill for he aimed his lance at my shield. It meant he had to move his reins to the left to allow him to punch. That eliminated the threat of his snapping horse's jaws. I held my sword above and behind me. I knew when the lance would strike and I braced. It was a good strike but I angled my shield and the head scraped and scratched along it. I brought my sword down and hacked the wood of the lance in two. He was left with a stump. I heard the thump as two arrows slammed into his shield. There were still archers behind me. I whirled to face his next attack. The two arrows had clearly discomfited him. He drew a mace and rode at me. With a mace, he could batter me into submission and with no helmet to protect me I would not last long. I held my shield up and kept my sword ready for a counterstrike should the opportunity arise. He swung the mace and my arm was jarred when it struck. I knew that the blow from the lance and the one from the mace would weaken the shield. Without a shield, I would last for moments only. He then made a mistake. Standing in his stirrups he made his horse rear, intending to have the hooves crush me. As soon as he stood and pulled back, I knew what would happen and I moved. It was a risk but as soon as the hooves rose and while the knight was unsighted I ran to the other side, the knight's shield side and even as the hooves were coming down I hacked into the chaussee on his left leg. The sword sliced through the mail links and into flesh. He screamed and being off balance anyway tumbled from the saddle. His horse galloped off.

He was lying on his back and I could have slain him there and then but I had been trained to fight honourably and I said, "Either surrender or rise and fight me."

His voice was distorted from behind the facemask, "My uncle and I swore an oath that you would die as painfully as did my father. There will be no surrender."

I allowed him to rise and he advanced towards me. He had lost his mace and he drew his sword. It would be sharper than mine but his leg was bleeding and I did not think he was as skilled as I. It was weird because we were almost alone. There were bodies around us, including

160

his uncle and some of their sergeants but there were two battles. The one, close to me on the slope, was between Mortimer and de Montfort and the louder one, further down the hill, was fought closer to Evesham where the commoners were being slaughtered. I kept the upper slope. I had given him as much courtesy as I could. I had given him the choice of surrender and he had shunned it.

He was cunning and knew that he must have hurt my shield. His first blow was a mighty one and again my arm shivered but he was below me and put so much effort into the horizontal strike that he failed to raise his shield. I brought my sword down onto his helmet, I dented it and he reeled. He stepped back and I backhanded my sword across his middle. His arm barely blocked the blow and he took another step back. He was on a downward slope and when I advanced his spurs caught and he tumbled down the slope. I headed purposefully after him.

To my right, below me, I saw Henry de Montfort, the earl's son hacked in two by one of Roger Mortimer's household knights. I heard the king cry out, "I am Henry of Winchester, your king, do not kill me."

As much as I wanted to go to the aid of the king I needed to end this fight. When I reached him young de Ferars had risen to his feet and he launched himself at my middle with his sword held in two hands. Stepping aside I brought my sword down to hack into his neck. I must have broken some bone for he fell dead like a butchered bull. I hurried back up the slope and was just in time to see a sergeant raise his sword to end the life of King Henry.

"Stay your hand, sergeant, that is King Henry."

The sergeant looked down at me as though I was speaking a foreign language. Then he saw my red cross and my surcoat. He shook his head as though to clear the blood lust, "I am sorry, Sir Henry, I did not recognise him."

"Then guard our backs while I take him to safety."

Sheathing my sword I took the reins of the king's horse. "Thank you, Sir Henry Samuel, once more I am in your debt."

There was a scream and I looked around to see that Hugh de Despenser had been stabbed through his eyehole by a dagger. Simon de Montfort was fighting three men. I wondered why they did not demand his surrender. A sword blade appeared from his middle as one of the knights stabbed him from behind while another hacked into his leg. Then, as the earl shouted, "Dieu, merci!" Sir Roger Mortimer took his head. As his body was hacked and slashed, I turned away. There was no honour in this and I led the king back up the slope with the protective sergeant behind. The battle was over and I had seen enough. Before I

161

had turned, I had seen the horsemen and foot soldiers butchering the rebels as they tried to cross the bridge to safety. Few would make it.

When we reached a place of peace where there were no dead, I stopped and the three of us were able to view the bloody battlefield. Sir Roger Mortimer and his men had stripped the earl's body and the baron held the earl's head in one hand and his manhood in the other. Even the king looked shocked. I heard a neigh from behind me and turned to see Duncan approaching. Letting go of the king's reins I grabbed his muzzle, "I am glad you survived, my friend." Dropping the shield, which was almost a ruin, I mounted and surveyed the battlefield.

The king nodded, "It is over then?"

"Almost, King Henry. Your brother is a prisoner in Kenilworth of the earl's son. Simon de Montfort is there with almost as many knights as fought here but the figurehead is gone and the spectre of Lewes can be laid to rest."

The tolling of the abbey bell told me that the whole battle, from lining up to its now, clear end, had lasted less than two and a half hours. I could see the bodies of the main enemies of King Henry and his son lying down the slope, de Montfort and his son, Henry, Hugh le Despenser and Humphrey de Bohun. There was just the younger Simon de Montfort, sheltering behind impregnable Kenilworth who was the king's opposition. The war was over.

The king said, "I saw you fight de Ferars, Sir Henry Samuel. They seemed desperate to get at you. Was there some sort of blood feud?"

I nodded, "There was, King Henry." I told him of the clash on the road, the brief fight and then the attack on Thornaby.

He shook his head, "Sir Geoffrey was a loyal knight, along with your grandfather he kept my northern marches safe. And his sons?"

"Dead, my lord."

"When this is over and by that I mean when all the strife in this land is done, we shall take the lands of those who rebelled and give them to men who deserve a reward for their loyalty. You shall have de Ferars land. He was a rich knight with a good manor."

I shook my head, "I will not leave the north."

He laughed, "There are many Scottish lords who have manors in England that they rarely visit but they live north of the border on the proceeds. The de Brus family and the Balliol families are two such."

The income would be welcome and perhaps knights like my brother might enjoy running the manor for me.

The king nodded at the now naked and despoiled Earl of Leicester, "I was treated well by him although he learned his lesson and I rarely rode a horse that could carry me away, like my son. I was kept close to him in Wales and saw the mischief he caused there. He devasted de Clare's lands and made an unhealthy treaty with King Llewellyn that gave away huge tracts of land. Even when England is at peace, Sir Henry, we shall have to send men to Wales to recover that which was given away." I looked into his eyes and he nodded, "Aye, we shall need the knights of the north to go to war again. You are victim of your own success, Sir Henry, as was your grandfather. You are the most loyal of families and my son and I know that you will never knowingly let down the crown. My son and you will butt heads but you will never be discarded."

"Yet, King Henry, we will be used."

He sighed, "I was barely a child when your grandfather saved me and the kingdom. I am the anointed king and that means God smiles on me. You serve God when you serve the king. We are all set on a path that is ordained by higher powers than we." He smiled, "You would not be a king, would you?"

I laughed at the thought, "No, King Henry. When my uncle passes on and I become, with your permission of course, Earl of Cleveland, that is as high as I aspire."

"The permission you shall have but we could make you Sherriff now if you wished."

"No, King Henry, I am content."

It was my men who reached us first, leading their horses and with spare horses laden with mail and weapons they trudged up the hill. I saw that we had lost sergeants. Fewer than I expected but more than I hoped. One was from Hartburn and two from Stockton. The valley archers were whole and I silently thanked God.

Sir Richard of Hartburn's face broke into a grin that made him look like a youth again, "And even though we have had a great victory, Henry Samuel, this is the greatest sight I could wish for, you safely on the back of your horse."

He had clearly not noticed the sergeant and the king. King Henry said, mildly, "Not even the survival of your king, Sir Richard?"

All of them dropped to their knees, "I am sorry, King Henry, I did not recognise you and..."

He laughed, "Rise. The knights of the valley are bluff and honest men. I know that no insult was intended. If you would honour me with an escort, Sir Henry, I would see my son. He may not know that I am safe."

I nodded, "Sir Matthew, Sir Alfred and Sir Thomas, come with us. For the rest, we had best make camp. Evesham looks too small for a host such as this and I would rather camp than be in a crowded and raucous town. We lost few men but I would mourn them in silence."

We headed down the hill towards Evesham and the scale of the victory was clear. Almost all the rebel leaders had perished but their supporters had paid an even greater price. There were swathes of bodies through which we rode. Even if the earl's last son wished to continue the fight, he would struggle to find an army to do so.

Chapter 18

Henry Samuel

The pain of victory

It was a great victory. Guy de Montfort, the earl's son had been
wounded and was a prisoner. Few others had been taken prisoner such
had been the ferocity of the fight and that had all come from three men,
The Lord Edward, Gilbert de Clare and the vengeful Roger Mortimer.
They had expunged the dishonour they felt the Earl of Leicester had
done them.

There was also news to take home. Amongst the bodies found in the
slaughter near the abbey was my aunt's husband, Sir Robert. He had
clearly not been in the battle but it was Sir Richard who found him
amongst the men who fought on foot. He was not mailed and his sword
was still sheathed. He had taken service with the rebels but was not
committed to the fight. That had not saved him from warriors with
blood lust on their minds. We did not find the treasure he had stolen. Sir
Thomas had lost his father although, as we spoke, he pointed out that he
had lost his father long ago.

"It is my mother who will grieve. She loved him and I know that she
missed him. She hoped he would return home but that was not meant to
be. She can now start a new life and it will be with me in Norton. I will
seek a bride and give her grandchildren." Sir Thomas had been
damaged by his father but now he was fully recovered and I hoped his
future and his mother's would be brighter.

"And what of your sister, Isabelle?"

His face darkened, "I fear, Henry Samuel, that there is a flower that
will never bloom. When you took me from Redmarshal I was glad but
the one thing I regretted was leaving my little sister there."

I wondered then at how I had missed seeing the dark side of Sir
Robert. Even as the question rose in my mind I answered it. I thought
all knights were like my family and I had been away so often that when
I returned to the valley I saw what I wanted to see; smiling faces. I
would have to make a better effort when I was an earl. That my uncle
had not seen the faults in the knight was no excuse. It was only then that
I realised the power of my grandfather. Thomas and Isabelle had been
happy when he had ruled the valley. I determined to be more like the
hero of Arsuf. He had ridden to war for the valley even when an old

man. It had been he who had led the column of knights to save me when I had been besieged. I would not do as my uncle had and use a wound as an excuse.

We prepared to head back to the north. The king had been given his service and we owed him nothing. The flames of rebellion that still flickered could be snuffed out by others. My men were all richer as a result of the battle and all wished to return home. Some had plans to marry while those of my men who farmed saw the opportunity raised by the extra funds to buy animals and enlarge their homes. They were warriors but they were also men and some would now start to raise sons and daughters of their own. It was not meant to be. King Henry might have happily let us depart but his long incarceration by Simon de Montfort had shifted the balance of power to his son. It was Edward who ruled and made the decisions.

We were ordered to Kenilworth to secure the release of the last royal prisoner, Richard of Cornwall. It took until September for the rebels in the castle to agree to release the King of the Romans. We discovered the reason for the delay when the son of the Earl of Leicester was found not to be within the castle. He had fled to the Isle of Axholme in Lincolnshire. The Lord Edward was furious and he personally led men in pursuit.

He called a council of war and I, of course, was invited. "We will surround this watery refuge and end this rebellion once and for all." He outlined his plans and then dismissed us. He remained with the Earl of Surrey and I hovered nearby.

He looked up, "Yes, Sir Henry, was there something else you wished to say?"

I nodded, "My lord, we have been with this army now for much longer than the service that was asked of us. We began in May and now it is September. Surely you can use men from the land closer to Lincolnshire."

"Do you presume to tell me how to command now?"

"No, my lord, I would never do that but, as the earl will testify, the men of the valley began to fight for you long before the fight at Kenilworth and the battle of Evesham. We bled for you so that the earl and your allies could land in Pembroke."

Sir John de Warenne nodded, "It is true, my lord, and had the knights of the north not been a threat then our invasion might have been snuffed out in the west."

The Lord Edward nodded, "My father speaks well of you, Sir Henry and has bestowed upon you the manor owned by de Ferars, Alfreton in

Derbyshire. If I am reluctant to let you depart it is because you and your men have proved over and over how dependable you are."

"And there are others, my lord, who might rise to the challenge. I know that when you go to reclaim Wales you shall need my men and we will come willingly, but grant us some peace, at least for a while. If a sword is overused then weaknesses appear. You do not need the men of the valley to winkle out de Montfort from his swamp."

"Very well, go but remember that when I have need of you, I shall call and you must respond to that summons quickly."

I bowed, "Of course, my lord." I backed out, eager to tell my men and begin the ride home. We would be in the valley within a week and then we could truly celebrate.

As we headed north, now free from the fear of ambush, we spoke of the change that would come over our land. King Henry had been draconian and all the rebels whether they lived or died had lost their lands and their incomes. There was no more earldom of Leicester. It was now a royal castle. King Henry was making the rebels pay for his humiliation.

It was while we rode north that I learned of the battle I had witnessed from afar. Sir Richard had led my men well, as I knew he would. He was like my twin in many ways. We had an understanding of each other that was unique. I learned that Samuel, Alfred and Roger had heeded my orders. Riding behind the knights they had done as I had asked and used their spears to stop any of those on foot from harming them. Louis was another squire who had done all that was asked of him and more. He had slain a knight and that alone merited his spurs that had been promised before we left Stockton. My cousin Thomas had fought alongside Dick and Matthew as a mailed wedge and they had carved a passage through those on foot and were amongst the first to reach the bridge. It was they who told me of the deprivations and atrocities committed by Sir Roger's men. Some of the survivors took sanctuary in the abbey. The sanctified nature of the building did not stop Sir Roger's men from slaughtering them. It was a shameful act as was the butchering of the body of Simon de Montfort. I had not liked de Montfort but I had respected him. I did not mourn his death but the manner of it. I heard that Sir Roger had sent the head with the genitals stuffed into the skull's mouth as a present to his wife Lady Maude Braose. I thought that unnecessary. That our men had shown restraint and taken prisoners was a testament to the way that my grandfather and those before him had raised us.

We did not race north. We had time to stay in castles and abbeys rather than camping. We did not exhaust our horses. We now had another six captured warhorses. Their masters lay dead at Evesham and their bodies had been buried in the abbey grounds. My men had only taken the mail and weapons of those we had slain. All the de Ferars family had died at Evesham. Their widows were now childless and that line was extinct. It was a sobering thought.

Our slow speed meant that we heard news of the conflict that still raged in the south. Simon de Montfort and the men he had taken from Kenilworth were in the Fens and trying to cause trouble. Those who still resided in Kenilworth were acting like bandits and many of the disinherited had taken shelter in the woods around Chesterfield and the Sherriff of Nottingham had been forced to send in archers after them. The war was not yet over but our part in it was. The Lord Edward would punish the transgressors but first, he and his father were in London where they were punishing the Londoners. The Parliament held by the Earl of Leicester had made changes in the way the land was governed. The Lord Edward and his father left in place all the local laws. What they did revoke was the power of Parliament over the king. I knew, from my words with him, that he would be a better king now. The barons would not need to rebel. Indeed, when we were in Lincoln and I spoke to the castellan, I pointed out that if King Henry had forgiven the rebels and merely fined them then the land would be at peace. The ones who fought on were the disinherited ones.

We reached Stockton at the end of September. I had sent riders ahead of us to warn them of our arrival. It was not that I wanted fuss, far from it, but I knew the women of the valley would be worried and my men rode hard from York to give them a few days' warning. The people of the town lined the river to greet us. It would not be a quick crossing as there was only one ferry. I allowed Sir Thomas and Sir Matthew along with their men to be the first to cross as they had the furthest to travel. Sir Richard of Hartburn was next followed by Dick and Sir Alfred. I chose to be last as I hoped that the crowds would have dispersed by then. I did not like the fuss.

When I stepped ashore it was with a welcome party of all my knights as well as my mother and every lady. I glowered at Thomas and Matthew, "I thought you and your men would have been long gone by now."

They both grinned and my mother stepped forward, "Did you not think that we would save the greatest welcome for the man who saved the life of King Henry?"

"He was in no danger."

Sir Matthew shook his head, "The sergeant told us that he would have killed the king had your hand not stayed him. Even the king knows

168

that he owes his life to you. Come, cuz, take the accolades for you deserve them."

My mother put her arms around me and hugged me tightly, "Your father would be so proud." She turned and invited Eirwen to join the hug. I could feel the emotion in my wife's body. She said not a word. We would talk back in Elton.

I looked around, "Where are the earl and Lady Mary?"

The smiles turned to frowns and my mother said, "William is confined to his bed. It is probably just a summer cold. We had rain in early September and the air was pestilential. Your return will make him improve."

I hoped that she was right.

We stayed that night in the crowded castle. My uncle did not leave his bed and so I went to speak to him. It looked to me like more than a simple summer cold. Lady Mary was there with him and, of course, Dick and Matthew, now that they were returned, came with me. Perhaps my cousins did not see the sick man I saw before me for they sat on his bed and bubbled on about their successes in battle, the men they had slain and the treasure they had taken. To me, he looked shrunken and smaller. Lady Mary never let go of my uncle's hand and her eyes studied his face.

The earl smiled at his sons and then said, "Take your mother down to the Great Hall. She has spent over long here and she needs fresher air and smiling faces."

"I am content, husband."

"And I still command here, do as I say. My sons have done well but I would speak to the man who led my warriors and who was closer to those in command. I still have a duty to this land and our king."

I smiled, "I am sure that my sons and my other cousins would like to speak with you, Aunt Mary. I will entertain Sir William and wait here until you return. He shall not be alone."

She rose and after kissing her husband's fevered forehead came to me. She held my right hand in her two and put her mouth close to my ear, "We do not leave him alone."

I kissed her cheek and said, in her ear, "What ails him? This is something worse than a simple cold."

"The doctors and the healers do not know. He has been bled and that did nothing. He has taken purgatives and every remedy that there is but this ailment sucks the life from him."

"What are you two whispering about? Wife, go."

She shook her head and said, a little louder, "You will have to excuse Sir William for his lack of manners, Henry Samuel. The ailment appears to have made him lose them."

The door closed and I sat on the bed. He looked into my eyes and said, "You are not fooled by the words of the others are you, Henry Samuel? You see that death is at my shoulder."

"The doctors?"

"They said, at first, that the coughing was a sign of a cold but after a week when I became much weaker, they knew that it was not." He patted his chest, "There feels to be a weight here on my chest." He winced and closed his eyes as a sudden pain struck him. "And you do not get such pains with a simple summer cold." He opened his eyes. "I have made my peace with God and William has helped me to write my will." He smiled, "He has been as a rock. He has listened to the stories of my youth and he has written them down. It seemed to help me as though I was unburdening my soul. I have seen that we are all part of a larger tapestry. Some, like my brother and your father, flash and shine gloriously but briefly. Others seem to be part of the patchwork but all play their part. I know that I am dying and I will go to God with my head held high. I may not have achieved the glory of my father but I have not let down the memory of the Warlord."

I held his hands in mine, they were icily cold, "You never could."

"When I am gone and you are earl, I beg you to allow Lady Mary to live here with your mother. They are good for one another and Dick and his wife do not need her tut-tutting over the way they are raising their son."

"Of course. You still intend me to be the earl?"

"It was meant to be you. My son's words of the battle of Evesham and Kenilworth tell me that it is right and proper. Dick is a good boy and warrior but he does not have the vision that is needed. You and William do and besides, the earldom would have been yours by right had not your father been so foully taken. I was the steward after my father died but he recognised you as his real heir. You were the one who rode to war at his side."

The door opened and my brother William entered. He had a tray with food upon it, "There is a feast below, brother. I have persuaded my aunt that she should be the hostess with our mother and that I will sit with Sir William until the feast is over. I still have much to learn, eh, uncle?"

"You are a good boy, William, and I am honoured that you were named after me. Go, Henry Samuel, and enjoy the plaudits of this night. I am sure that you deserve them."

I rose, "I will see you later then, uncle."

As I passed William he said, "Make merry this night, brother, for both our aunt and our mother are low in spirits. They know that Sir William will not see the bone fire."

My heart sank to my boots. My uncle had less time than his appearance gave. As I left the doctor was approaching. He had with him his satchel containing his potions, salves and medicines. He stopped and I said, "What really ails him, doctor?"

"I do not know nor do the other healers who live close by. There is much about the body that we do not know. He is losing weight. No matter how much food he eats he grows thinner and smaller each day."

"He has a worm?"

"Not the one you think of. This is something far more sinister. We thought, like you, that it was a worm in the gut and so we gave him a purgative. It had no effect. We studied his stool and it is speckled with blood. It is as though he has a wound inside yet he has not fought a battle these many years."

"William says he will not see the bone fire."

"He will not see the end of the week, my lord. He has hung on to see his sons and nephews return. He is in great pain although he tries to hide it. All that I can do is dull the pain." He hesitated, "I know you wish to see your home, my lord, but your place is here. Sir William needs you."

I nodded, "Of course."

I too had a duty. I dared not enter the Great Hall looking like I felt inside. All the euphoria of an almost painless victory and the knowledge that our enemies were defeated had evaporated in that bed chamber of death. I would need to smile and speak cheerfully although my heart would be filled with tears. Eirwen waited for me outside the hall. Inside I could hear the laughter and the chatter of husbands and sons reunited with mothers and wives. They believed the story that we had been given. If my aunt could play a part then so could I.

Eirwen threw her arms around me and kissed me, "How are you?" She leaned in, "I know."

I could talk to Eirwen, "I never expected this. My grandfather was hale until the end. By comparison, my uncle is a young man. He has not yet seen sixty summers."

"Life is not fair for your father was much younger when he died. Your uncle has enjoyed three times the lifespan of his brother. The manor is in good hands and we shall stay here as long as it takes. I fear it will not be long."

"Then the others know?"

171

"Your mother gathered all in the Great Hall when you sent your message. She told everyone that your uncle had just a common cold and there were to be neither tears nor dark looks. She said that the warriors of the valley deserved smiles and not scowls."

"Then I shall play my part too."

"First, let us change you from these clothes, as much as I love you, Henry Samuel, you stink of horses." She led me to a chamber where fresh clothes, brought from Elton, were laid out. There was a bowl of water and when I had undressed, she helped me first to wash and then to dress. She placed a small bag of lavender and rosemary inside my tunic and squeezed it. The aroma of herbs sweetened the air.

"Now you are ready. Sir William told us all that you are now the heir. You are the lord. You need to play that part from now on."

As we entered, smiling and arm in arm, we were greeted with a cheer and I gave a half bow. I saw the nod of approval of my mother. She was seated at Lady Mary's right hand and Eirwen took me to sit next to her. After Grace, we sat and enjoyed a feast. We had not starved on the campaign but we had spent most of our time in fields and eaten hunter's stews. We had drunk ale and wine but from coistrels and not goblets. We had not been seated and in fine clothes but clothes that stank of horse sweat. I glanced over and saw Sir Thomas seated with his mother. She was dabbing at her eyes. He had told her of her husband's death. I knew my aunt and she would dry her eyes and put on a face for the feast. When she grieved it would be when she was alone. Isabelle looked lonely and alone on the other side of Thomas. I had much work to do now that I was home and this was work that would be new to me.

My mother had made the decision that the squires would not be the ones to serve us and servants from the castle and the town fetched the food. I smiled as my daughters, now grown almost to women, glowed as they enjoyed the attentions of their brothers and cousins, not to mention the handsome Roger. I was asked to tell the tale of the saving of the king. I was mindful of the presence of the ladies and also my duty. I avoided any indelicate mention of the blood and, instead told it simply. The ladies, the wives of my cousins, applauded thinking, I do not doubt, that we would benefit from such action. I knew we would not. It had been my duty and the royal family expected nothing less.

Dick said, "And there is another manor for your son, Lady Matilda. A rich one."

My mother looked at me, "It is no more than you deserve." She was an astute woman and said, "And who shall run it for you? I know that you have the blood of the Warlord in your veins and will not leave this valley."

I had spoken to Matthew, Dick, Thomas and Alfred on the way home. I knew that none of them wished to move from our heartland. All eyes were on me and even my chattering daughters were silent. I smiled, "We have that decision to make but as Sir Thomas' squire Louis distinguished himself, he must first be given his spurs and perhaps he might choose the manor." His sister, Alfred's wife, squealed when I made the announcement and the other ladies smiled.

Louis stood and bowed, "Thank you, Sir Henry. I prayed for spurs but I must decline your offer. When I came to England with Sir Thomas there were two purposes. I wished to watch over my sister and learn to be a knight. Mary is now a mother and part of this valley. I am a knight and a Gascon. The recent wars have shown me that my homeland is still not secure. My father," he smiled at Mary, "our father, will need help and I have learned much from Sir Thomas. When I am knighted, I will journey back to Gascony. With your permission, of course, my lord."

"Of course, a man has a duty to his family and while you will be missed, we all understand your need."

The announcement drove all thoughts of the dying earl as well as the battle of Evesham. Everyone spoke of the knighthood and the future.

My mother leaned into me and said, quietly, "And you have avoided the question but who will manage your new manor?"

I had already made up my mind but I said, "Who would you suggest?"

She gave me a smile, "I can see that you have a name in mind and wish me to confirm it for you. Let me see, it could be Alfred or Dick but you know that Alfred and Eleanor are settled here as are Dick and Margery. You would not wish to have the two bachelor knights, Matthew and Thomas leave their manors. Isabelle will need her son and it is good that she shall live with him. That leaves just one of your sergeants and my guess would be Jack or John of Parr."

"You read me well, mother. It shall be Jack but I will give him his spurs first. He has deserved them and King Henry will need every loyal knight he can get."

"I thought the war was over or is there something you have not told me, yet?"

"The king has disinherited all of the rebels. I think that is foolish for they will harbour grudges. So long as Simon de Montfort's two sons live then there is a heart that beats rebellion. We will be safe here in the north for, if nothing else, we have shown the rebels the futility of trying to cross swords with the men of the valley."

"And soon you shall be the earl."

I shook my head, "I do not wish the death of my uncle."

"Yet that is as certain as the coming of winter. We cannot stop it or even slow it. All we can do is what you did before, give him comfort."

And that was what we did. For the next fortnight, I stayed in Stockton. Sir Thomas, Sir Matthew, and Sir Richard of Hartburn returned to their manors but I spent time each day with an uncle who gradually slept more than he was awake. It was heart-breaking to watch him waste away. He was dying piece by piece. In battle, even the butchery of a death such as the Earl of Leicester's was swifter than this one. Sir Geoffrey and his sons had been butchered but it had been over quickly. Even Sir Robert had enjoyed a quick if savage death. My poor uncle suffered and lingered on, dying by inches.

We knew when death was upon him for Lady Mary and William, who had both shared the watching of the earl, summoned us. His sons were there as well as my mother and me. The priest had given him the last rites and he looked to me, dead already. Lady Mary was weeping silent tears while the rest of us just stood. I had spoken to him every day and said all that needed to be said. This was the time for his wife and him to share. Matthew and Dick were fighting back the tears. Suddenly Sir William opened his eyes and smiled, "I come, brother." His eyes closed and my uncle died.

William put his hand on my uncle's neck and then his ear to his mouth. He stood, "The earl is in a better place, now, Aunt Mary."

She stood and Dick embraced her, "I would not have him dead, my son, but it pained me to see him suffer so. He is at peace and I can now grieve for the man I have loved for most of my life."

We buried him in the chapel alongside the Warlord and the rest of our family. King John and the Bishop of Durham had done their best to despoil it but thanks to my grandfather the chapel was now a fitting memorial to the family that was begun by Ridley.

After the funeral and by way of celebration, we knighted Louis. I had already spoken to Jack and he was knighted the same day. As Earl of Cleveland, I did not have to ask anyone's permission to do so. I had the task of taking my uncle's will to Durham so that the Bishop of Durham could give his approval. I already had King Henry's and the visit to Durham was a courtesy.

I had much business to conduct for my uncle had been ill since before we had left for Evesham. I spent three days with William and Edgar going through all the documents that I had to. Dick did not want Elton and so Alfred became Alfred of Elton and he and Mary, along with their son Henry and daughter Matilda, moved into Elton and I took over the chamber of the Lord of Stockton. I did not feel that I deserved it but everyone else did. When Jack left, with John of Parr, who had chosen to follow his old friend, and young Walter as his squire for the new manor, we had barely a fortnight before Christmas. Louis also left for Gascony. The valley seemed emptier. The year had been a momentous one and I hoped for a quieter year to follow.

Chapter 19

Henry Samuel

Dousing the embers of the rebellion

If we thought that the year 1266 was going to be a quiet year, we were wrong. Simon de Montfort and his brother Guy had fled to France where they used their father's money to ferment discord. The rebels in Kenilworth were under siege and both Ely and Chesterfield saw rebels using the wilderness and the woods as bases from which to terrorise the land. I thought that we would not be involved but in April of the new year, Sir John of Alfreton, my former sergeant Jack, rode in with his squire Walter. It was an unexpected visit but a welcome one. Jack had been at my side longer than Eirwen.

"A welcome sight, Jack."

"And I am pleased to be here, my lord, but I come with a request."

"The Lord Edward?"

"No, my lord. Lord Henry Almain has been charged with the scouring of the forests of Chesterfield. The rebels there are causing much mischief and his lordship asks if you could send your archers and some knights to aid him."

"He did not specifically ask for me?"

Jack smiled and shook his head for he was an honest man, "He asked for archers, my lord, but as he came to me first, he was able to speak privately and he asked me to deliver the message and ask if you could aid him." He sighed, "I think that this is the first time he has been in this position. The Lord Edward is in Hampshire dealing with the rebels there and I think that Sir Henry would like your advice."

Samuel had been listening and he smiled, "You know, father, that you would not send the knights of the valley off along with the archers without you there. My brother Alfred and Dick both have young families. You know that it will be Matthew and Thomas who go."

He was right, of course, and I nodded, "It will not be long will it, Jack?"

"There are many rebels but they are not natural woodsmen. We can easily winkle them out but it needs Ned and our archers to do so. It is the sort of country where we found Robbie and his sons. This task was made for them. For you, my lord, it will just be a time to watch your men."

176

"And when did that ever happen, Jack?" I sighed. I had to go. I owed it to Jack and Lord Henry had known that. We will leave tomorrow for Chesterfield is some days away." I hesitated, "Is this part of our annual muster?"

Jack was now a knight and understood such matters, "No, my lord, the Sherriff of Nottingham will pay each archer six pennies a day and each knight a shilling. The sergeants you take will also be paid as archers. Sir Henry said that he would only need ten mounted men."

I smiled, Lord Henry Almain was saving the Sherriff money, "Good for we have worked without pay too many times ere now."

This time felt different as we prepared to head south. I would be leading as the Earl of Cleveland, the bishop had confirmed the title. I would have the banner carried by my grandfather. I doubted that I would need Duncan and so I used White Sock. Thomas now had a new squire, Robert. His father had been a sergeant who had fallen at Lewes. Robert wished to walk in his father's footsteps. Matthew had made Redmarshal a better manor. We had not recovered any of the fortune taken by Sir Robert and so the income for his archers and sergeants was welcomed. I would let Sir Matthew supply the men at arms. Joseph of Aylesbury had become my captain and he was still learning to exert his authority. The other sergeants had followed Jack and John of Parr for many years. Joseph just had a different style. We would take all forty archers from the valley. Ned would lead them. We had plenty of horses and the sergeants who remained in Stockton and the other manors would not need them. The one-hundred-mile journey would take no more than three days by riding.

We left before dawn to make as much time as we could. Samuel and Roger rode with young Robert as they knew what it was like to be a new squire. I was easy with Matthew for he had been my squire. The one I knew the least was Thomas and, as we rode south, I tried to get to know him. We had the spectre of his father to get over first.

"Is your mother settled, in Norton?"

"She likes the manor, my lord. It is larger than Redmarshal. The mill and the pond are places she likes to visit and, of course, the church is bigger than that at Redmarshal. She and my sister visit the church each day and pray for my father's soul. It grieves my mother that he may not have been shriven before he was untimely taken."

"Yet he died in the abbey, surely he will be given God's grace."

"He stole, my lord, and he abandoned his wife and family."

"Yet, Thomas, I do not think he did murder."

The young knight sighed, "I did not like my father. There I have said it and if that makes me a bad son I care not. I do not think he liked me either. If it had been left to him, I would never have become a knight."

"Would that have been a bad thing?"

He became quite animated, "That is the point, my lord. I did not think so until you took me to Gascony. My life is better now and it is thanks to you and not my father. I mourn his death for I am of his blood but I do not grieve for his passing."

I nodded, "I just wanted to know how you felt."

"I pray that when I find a wife that I am a better father than he was."

Matthew nodded, "Aye, you and I are in the same boat, Thomas. We both seek a bride but all the eligible ladies are our relatives."

I laughed, "I found my bride in the most unexpected of places as did my brother Alfred. Remember Sir Thomas' tales of the Baltic and the three sisters who weave."

"Is that not blasphemous?"

I shrugged, "Thomas, I have seen nothing in the Bible that speaks of such women. What I do know is that accidents have a way of changing men's lives."

England was largely a land at peace. Certainly, the north had not been touched. The islands of rebellion have drawn the disinherited and the defeated. King Henry tried to break down the walls of Kenilworth but he had been too slow to begin the siege and they had food and war machines. They had already destroyed some of King Henry's stone throwers and there would be no swift end to that siege. I was more hopeful about the other three. The Lord Edward had shown his true colours at Evesham and he would defeat the Hampshire rebels. I knew that Lord Henry Almain would take advice and with my help, we could take Chesterfield's rebels. Ely would fall in the fullness of time, if only because of the damp and the pestilence that would eat into their bodies and weaken their resolve.

We stopped in Sheffield at the castle. I was pleased that Lord Henry Almain had not taken advantage of the quarters there. The castellan told me that the son of the Earl of Cornwall was camped with his men. When we left the next day, I waved Ned and Robbie to ride with me.

"You two are the archers, how would you organise this campaign if you were Lord Henry Almain?"

Ned nodded to Robbie, "We have spoken of this on the way south, my lord. Robbie here has lived in the woods and he has his ideas. I defer to his opinion, my lord."

I looked at the man who had lived as an outlaw close to Leicester, "The men who live in the forests have certain advantages, my lord.

They can move from one part to another. When you found us, we had just moved camps. There will be men preparing camps even while they are living in the existing ones. This will be more than just archers. There will be knights and sergeants. They have horses and they will need both grazing and water. You do not seek the enemy but you control the places that they can use. If you restrict their movement then they will suffer and may be forced to come to you."

"What about ambush? I know from my time with you that archers can blend into the trees while a knight or sergeant wearing a surcoat can be seen from some distance."

"That is true, my lord, but what an archer gains in disguise he loses in range. An archer cannot send an arrow as far as the trees are in the way. If they ambush us then they will be close and a man on a horse can catch a man on foot."

Ned added, "And one more thing, my lord, we do not think that they will have many bodkins. If they have a workshop and a weaponsmith then that will be easy to find. Those of you with mail should be safe from harm."

I had their ideas and knew that when we met Lord Henry Almain I would be able to give him a plan. He had sent for me and as Jack had said, on the way down, it was my mind as much as my archers that he needed.

Sir Henry was waiting for me as Jack's squire had ridden ahead to warn him of our arrival. I had not seen the king's nephew to speak to for a long time and like his cousin, Edward, his incarceration had changed him. He was now a more confident leader.

He beamed when he saw me, "Congratulations, Sir Henry, now you are an earl."

"I would that my uncle was still alive and healthy, my lord, but he is at peace now."

Sir Henry Almain made the sign of the cross, "I am pleased that Sir John here found you and persuaded you to join us."

"We have fought them before, my lord, and the difference is that now we shall be paid."

He laughed, "As I recall, Sir Henry, you and your men always profited from war."

"And we shall do so again. Now, my lord, what is your plan?"

He waved towards the house he was obviously using as his headquarters, "Come within and we will speak."

I turned to Sir Richard and Jack, "Have the men housed and see to their needs. Samuel, come with me and you can act as a messenger. Roger can tend to the horses."

"Yes, my lord."

Once inside his servant brought us wine and then the three of us were left. Lord Henry Almain glanced at Samuel and I shook my head, "You can trust my squire for he is my son also."

"Of course, I thought I recognised him. The truth is, Sir Henry, that the rebels are like will o'the wisp. By the time we find them they are gone and we raid empty camps. Worse, we are ambushed when we move through these forests. We are losing more men than our foes."

"Then stop looking for them." His jaw dropped. I smiled, "I have spoken with men who lived as outlaws. We use our men to find the places that they might choose to use. Places with water, game and grazing for their horses. Put men to watch the roads in and out of the forest and have any who might offer succour, imprisoned. Bolsover Castle has space enough to hold them."

"That will not be a swift course of action nor will it be a popular one."

"The men are rebels, my lord, and nothing that we do will be popular. As for the speed, we will end this in the time it has taken Sir John to ride north, find me and return south. I do not intend to spend more than a fortnight away from my home. We begin tomorrow," I hesitated, "with your permission, of course."

He nodded, "If you use a gamekeeper then it is as well to heed his advice. Of course, I have local men who know the forests, they will take and hold the places you suggested would make good camps. And you, my lord?"

"I will take my men and we will be the swift sword that seeks the enemy. I intend to start them so that you and your men can catch them. I do not think this will be one battle, my lord, but a series of skirmishes. We whittle down their numbers and destroy their ability to fight. We may not catch them all but so long as the bulk of Chesterfield's rebels is taken then we will have succeeded."

We both had much to do and before Samuel and I ate we visited first my archers and then my sergeants and knights. Jack and his handful of men would, once again, fight alongside us.

By the time we ate my stomach thought my throat had been cut and I devoured the hunter's stew and then wiped my bowl with bread. I turned to Jack, "You know this land better than any of my men, Jack. Tomorrow, we ride to find them. If you were me and wished a quick victory, where would you go?"

"As you know, my lord, I am not a literate man and maps are just so many squiggles and lines that I do not understand but I have hunted these woods before the rebels took them over. There is one place that they have not used, as yet, it is called Arkwright for there was a house there once and a charcoal burner of that name lived there. It is a ruin but there is water close by and horses could be grazed. I think that they will try to use that as a camp."

"If it is so attractive a place why have they not used it before?"

"It is said to be haunted, my lord. The last charcoal burner killed his wife and then hanged himself. People are fearful."

"But you think that they may be forced to use it." He nodded. "Then we let Lord Henry take his men and occupy the other attractive sites and close the roads. We will disappear."

Sir Matthew said, "Disappear?"

"The rebels will have their spies. We stayed in Sheffield and passed through Bolsover. They will know that the Earl of Cleveland has brought his archers south and they will be watching for us." I waved a hand and said, "They will be watching us even now. Tomorrow morning, when Lord Henry orders his men forth, we use the confusion to ride, not as one body but as small groups. We simply blend in with the other men leaving Lord Henry's camp but instead of following them we enter the forest and all meet up. Jack, you have eight men with you, we will divide into nine groups and each of your men can lead one of our groups. We will take food and ale skins so that we can live for a few days in the forest if we need to. We will leave our mail and helmets here. Coifs and arming caps shall be our only protection. You choose the rendezvous point."

"Me, my lord?"

"Yes, Sir John, you."

The division of my men was easy. I would be with Jack along with Robbie and eight archers. We did not rise earlier than the rest but joined the milling men as Lord Henry of Almain issued his orders. If he wondered why some of my men joined his he did not comment but I saw the intrigue upon his face. As luck would have it or perhaps Jack intended it, we followed the son of the King of the Romans and headed along a well-used track. We rode at the rear and Jack suddenly waved his arm and led my small band through the trees and off the track. He stopped just twenty feet into the forest and we waited and watched. No one followed us but Jack was a wily fox and he waited long enough for the sounds of the other men to fade into the distance. When we heard bird song once more, he took us through the trees. All of my men had skills that I could only envy. I would have been lost within a few paces but Robbie and the archers were as confident as Jack and it was Samuel, Roger and me who brought up the rear.

Eventually, we found ourselves upon a hunter's trail and Robbie dismounted to examine the ground. He rose with a piece of dried horse dung in his hand, "Horses have used this path, my lord, within the last week and they were shod. Rebels have been here."

We continued until, by noon, we reached an open space. Sir Thomas was there with the men he had led and one of Jack's men. Jack said, by way of explanation, "Lord Henry and I found this camp a few days before I was sent for you, Sir Henry. I reasoned that they would not return here soon. We can use this for our camp as there is water and while the grazing may be poor, it will only be for a day or two."

"The oats we brought will feed the animals." I dismounted, "Tether the horses but no fires and no hovels. We rough it."

My men nodded and Robbie said, "Aye, my lord."

The rest of our men arrived within an hour of us and all were confident that our departure had been unobserved. I held a council of war with my knights, sergeants and four senior archers. "Jack, how far away is Arkwright?"

"No more than two miles, my lord, but there are few trails and we will not reach there quickly."

"Speed matters not but stealth does. We will not wear surcoats but just plain cloaks that will disguise us. Any men we find will be enemies and we know each other. There will be no confusion."

Thomas nodded, "Aye, some of those killed at Evesham were slain by our own men for they did not wear the red cross."

Matthew said, "Then our handful of men is a good thing."

"The squires will have the hardest task for they will have to act as horse holders for the archers." I saw the disappointment on their faces but they would do as I had ordered.

We kept sentries watching at night but the fact that we heard the sounds of animals in the night told us that we were alone. This time we did rise well before dawn. We were aided by the fact that we had an uncomfortable night on hard ground. We dressed, made water and then ate a cold breakfast. We walked our horses through the forest and followed Hob, the local man Jack had chosen as his scout. Jack was right, our journey was not a quick one. Not only were we walking but we were not using a good trail. It sometimes petered out and we had to take detours. It was noon when we smelled smoke and heard a noise in the distance. If we could hear others then we could be heard. I used hand signals and the squires took the reins, not only of the archers' horses but ours too. I saw Samuel take charge and he signalled for the horses to be tethered. Roger and he worked well together. While the archers strung their bows, I took my shield from my saddle and drew my sword. I knew not what we might find but we would be prepared.

I waved my sword and we spread out in a long line. There were more archers than knights and sergeants so I walked between four archers, Alan, Walter, Rafe and Ted. We stepped as carefully as we could to avoid crunching dead twigs but the noise from ahead grew. It was clear to me what was happening. Lord Henry Almain's sweep into the forest had started the game and Jack had been right. The rebels were forced to use their last resort, Arkwright's. From what Robbie had told me the men ahead would be making the new camp both defensible and habitable. There would be no women with them. I would, of course, give them the opportunity to surrender but I doubted many would take the offer. This was their home and they would be confident that they could evade us.

Hob held his hand up and we all stopped. He disappeared into the trees ahead. I saw my archers each choose an arrow. They would be war arrows. I doubted that the men ahead would be mailed. I heard the neigh of horses and that was confirmation that we were, quite literally, on the right track. When Hob returned, he mimed for Jack and for me. There were forty men ahead of us. More than thirty were men of the woods while the rest were soldiers. I nodded and, looking down my line of men, waved them forward. The two ends spread out so that a gap of ten feet appeared between us. It might give the illusion that there were more of us than there actually were. We outnumbered them and I hoped that they would surrender.

They had no sentries set and that made sense. Their purpose was to make camp. I heard the sound of wood axes as trees were hewn. I saw men, stripped to the waist burying stakes to deter horsemen. It all made sense to me. When we were less than forty feet from the nearest men, I held up my sword and our line stopped. The archers lifted their bows but did not draw. My voice sounded inordinately loud as I shouted, "Surrender in the name of King Henry."

The reaction was as I expected it. The woodsmen picked up their bows to string them. The men who were horsemen ran to their mounts.

"Loose!" Even as I shouted the command I was moving forward. Robbie had been right and trees affected the range but my men were loosing into a clearing. An arrow slammed into the tree next to my head. I heard cries as my archers' arrows found flesh.

Whoever led these men was no coward and he shouted, "Follow me!"

He rode his horse directly towards us. My voice was the focus. His men followed him. One was knocked from his saddle by an arrow but

183

the rest came on. These men all wore simple helmets and had swords, spears and shields. I did not think the leader was a knight for I saw no spurs but then again a forest was no place for spurs, Robbie had also been correct about the problems the terrain presented horses. There was no direct line for them to use and the riders could not generate enough speed. We had trees behind which we could take shelter. The leader came for me. I used a tree to my left to aid my shield. He had a spear and he rode at me. My head was an attractive target as I wore no helmet. He did, a round-topped one with a nasal. I could have moved behind the tree but that might have allowed him to escape. I concentrated on my blow as I heard the sounds of dying men all around me. Even as I brought up my shield to deflect the spear I was slashing with my sword over the horse's head. It was a blind strike but I knew that if my sword cleared the mane it would also clear the cantle and allow my sword to strike at his middle. He struck his spear well but my shield deflected it to strike the tree and the head was buried in its trunk. My right arm jarred as my sword hit his middle and rasped into flesh. I lowered my shield as his horse galloped off and looked down at his body. My sword had not killed him although it had given him a mortal wound, his head had struck the bole of a nearby tree and he was dead.

I looked up and saw that the fight was over. I shouted, "Are any hurt?"

There was a pause and then Matthew shouted, "I think not, my lord, but half a dozen escaped."

While we gathered the bodies, I sent six archers back for the squires and our horses. None of the horsemen had survived. It was clear that they were all sergeants and that none had experience of fighting in a forest. They had paid the price.

We camped that night at the eerie charcoal burner's house. I am not a superstitious man but I was glad, the next morning, when we quit the place and headed through the forest. So far the plan was working but it was far from over.

Despite our victory, we still moved stealthily and when, late in the afternoon, we heard the clash of arms from ahead we stopped. I gave the order for the archers to dismount and this time they tethered their own mounts. I turned to Jack, "Does that sound as though the battle is getting closer?"

He nodded, "Aye, my lord, and Lord Henry was driving from the west. As we are in the east we may have the enemy between us."

"Nock arrows. Horsemen, we will hold the line. Be prepared to charge."

It became clear to us all that the battle was moving in our direction and there sounded to be more men involved than in our little skirmish. I saw women and children fleeing.

"Let the women and children pass."

They saw us when they were just fifty paces from us and took off north, not risking our blades. They did not know that they were safe. There had to be forty or fifty of them. The men who came towards us were not so lucky. My archers could not allow them to close with us and they sent their arrows into them. They had not seen us mounted on our horses and it took eight dead men to warn them of the danger before they stopped and those with shields, there were precious few of them, raised them. My archers changed their aim and arrows struck unprotected limbs. One of the enemy warriors must have decided that we posed a lesser threat than the ones following. I suspect that had they seen my banner they might have thought otherwise. They charged us.

My archers were to my right and so I shouted, "Charge!" and led my handful of horsemen to our left. It made the men facing my archers turn a little and that exposed their right sides. As with the horsemen we had fought earlier, we discovered that the only advantage a horse gave you was height. That was enough and we carved our way through them hacking at heads and shoulders. The shields that they had were not up to the task and merely slowed our blades.

When I heard the horn from ahead and recognised it as Lord Henry Almain's I shouted, "Save the slaughter and surrender. You are finished. I am Sir Henry Samuel of Stockton and I give my word you will be treated fairly."

I still do not know what made them surrender, the thought of imminent defeat or my offer. Weapons were thrown down and fifty men were saved from certain death.

Lord Henry Almain lifted his helmet as he rode over to me, "The nest of vipers is no more. Your plan worked, Sir Henry. Once we have secured these prisoners then your work is done."

I sheathed my sword and pointed north, "Their women and children fled north."

"I know, we took more than fifty of them prisoner at their camp. We will let them go. We have destroyed their ability to ravage the countryside around here and I can join my cuz. Perhaps we can end this war before the year is out."

We had enjoyed success but it was down to the skills of my archers and my former sergeant. Lord Henry Almain would have spent all winter hunting the rebels but for our arrival.

Riding north we spoke of the strange and brief campaign we had just fought. Ely and Hampshire were two other such conflicts and they resulted from King Henry's desire for vengeance. Lord Henry Almain had told me, in confidence, that The Lord Edward had not wished to disinherit the rebels. He had felt that a fine was more than enough but his father was adamant. The brief sojourn away from our home had cost us nothing and whilst the pennies the archers had accrued were not as much as they might have been, horses and weapons somewhat compensated. The men were in good humour as we rode into Stockton. It was there that we parted from those men who had served me in Elton and who had not uprooted their families to move with me to Stockton. For one thing, the land they farmed was better than that which was available in Stockton. The best plots had all been taken. Sir Matthew and Sir Thomas took their men back to their manors and I settled into Stockton.

My duties as Lord of Elton were as nothing compared to being the earl. I had assizes to organise and disputes to settle. Edgar was a godsend and he eased me into the task but my greatest ally was my brother William. He knew the manor better than even Edgar. He had studied the past and was at pains to tell me how to avoid some of the mistakes made by my grandsires. He also advised me to make a weekly walk around Stockton.

"I believe that the Warlord did so when he was not fighting for Empress Matilda and Prince Henry. I went on one such walk with Sir William and you cannot believe the effect it has. It shows the people that you are not remote, you are one of them and, of course, you can get to know them." He looked serious for a moment, "I have read how spies came to stay in a Stockton inn and almost caused the downfall of the castle. It was discovered because the men of Stockton were vigilant."

I realised that it would do no harm and to be truthful I did not know enough people who lived in Stockton. It was the largest manor and had a commercial side that none of the other manors did. There were tanners and potters. Stockton clay made good pots. The other manors came to our market to buy such things. The trade made Stockton richer. There were merchants who imported and exported using both the river and Herterpol. As the Earl of Cleveland, I needed to know these people. The taxes that they paid made the manor richer. The richer the manor the more men I could employ to defend it and keep it safe. William and I took Samuel with us for while he might never be earl it was part of the process of becoming a knight. Roger stayed with my sergeants for he was keen to become a better warrior.

That first walk opened my eyes. I had seen Stockton, of course, but it had been just as I passed through, normally on a horse. Walking through the houses and businesses I saw the people. They knew William and he was warmly greeted but the welcome for my son and I bordered on adulation. I had not known that my name was renowned. Men were desperate to speak to me and show me old scars earned while fighting for my uncle or grandfather. Women came to speak of the kindness of my mother and her good works with widows and orphans. By the time I returned to the castle I was exhausted, but I also felt overcome by the affection the town had for my family.

William said, as we sat in my solar, "It is the connection to the past, brother, that makes this place strong. You have spent the last few years with your eyes on the south. To those who live in this valley, the threat is always from the north. We are lucky that we live in a time when the Scottish border is quiet and, thanks to you, we have a Scottish king who looks on us as his friends." He paused dramatically, "King Alexander is a good man but he has no sons. What happens when he dies? Will the maid, Margaret become queen and rule? She is a child. I pray that the Scottish king has a son and that he lives a long and happy life but life can be cruel. It is good that you are home."

"And The Lord Edward has subdued the rebels in Hampshire. He has even taken the leader into his band of knights. I hear that he is now at the Cinque Ports to gather a fleet and take on the rebels of Ely."

"That just leaves Kenilworth." He looked at Samuel, "You have young eyes and have seen the castle, describe it for me."

As usual, William had his wax tablet and as Samuel spoke, he began to draw the lines of the walls and the buildings.

"Stockton has a river to protect it but Kenilworth has a lake and a moat. They have an outer bailey with a good wall and a single bridge over the moat. You could camp an army within that bailey. Then there is a barbican that leads to a causeway bridge to the wall which encircles the inner bailey. There are towers along the wall. There is another wall within the inner bailey surrounding the donjon and that is a mighty one with towers protecting it. There is another bridge over the moat."

I nodded, "It is very much like the one at Alnwick, brother, but far bigger."

William nodded, "It looks like that?" He showed the drawing he had made to Samuel who nodded. "Then King Henry will be there for more years to come."

"When his son has rid the land of the Ely rebels, he might be able to use his tongue as a weapon. He has the problem of Sir Roger Mortimer."

"Baron Wigmore?"

"Aye, he hates all the rebels as does Lady Maude. He would have executed every rebel if he had his way. The king is swayed by him."

I found my talks with William most illuminating. As the year passed our talks became a regular event. Each day I found time to sit and speak with my clever little brother. It was in August that we had the news that while the siege of Kenilworth was not yet resolved, The Lord Edward, aided by a papal envoy, Ottobuono Fieschi, had organised a sort of Parliament to resolve the problems. I was invited to join it, which is how we heard of it but I was not happy about being away for who knew how long and I sent my apologies. In the end, it was a balanced group that debated the issue, bishops of Exeter, Bath and Wells, Worcester and St. David's, the earls of Gloucester and Hereford, and six barons, Philip Basset, John Balliol, Robert Walerand, Alan la Zouche, Roger de Somery and Warin Basingbourn. Balliol was, I think, my replacement. They decided that the disinherited had been unjustly punished and instead of losing all their lands rebels were subsequently fined five times the annual yield of their lands. The exceptions were the Earl of Derby who was fined seven times the annual yield, and the castellan of Kenilworth Castle, Henry de Hastings. The fines were to be paid to the royal supporters who had been given the lands and now had to give them back. It took until October for all to be resolved and then the king called a Parliament at Marlborough to establish rules about the governance of England. It seemed, as Christmas approached, that our land was at peace.

Eirwen and I sat with my mother and William, "We ought to celebrate, my son. When you won at Evesham, that was the light behind the black clouds. Now we can see that the clouds have gone. We should celebrate and in doing so we can honour the memory of Sir William."

It was a good idea and I endorsed it knowing that all the hard work would be done by my mother and wife. My only part was to take my archers to hunt in Hartburn woods and provide the meat for the feast. I took the knights and squires with me. We all enjoyed a hunt. We had great success and it was as we were roasting the hearts and kidneys of the kill while our servants prepared to take the carcasses back to the castle that Sir Thomas came over to see me, "Cousin, now that you are the earl I suppose it is you whom I must ask the question."

I was somewhat distracted by the smell of the cooking kidneys and said, "Question, cuz?"

"Aye, marriage."

The others had been chattering away but Thomas' words silenced them all. I looked at my cousin, "Marriage?"

He nodded, "Our talk when we rode to Chesterfield planted seeds in my mind. You were right about accidents for while I did not actively seek a bride my mind was more receptive to the idea. You know the de Brus family who have lands around Herterpol?"

"Of course and they also have lands in Scotland but I did not know there was a daughter of marriageable age."

"There is not." He sighed as he explained, "My mother misses my father but she knows that what he did was wrong. She asked me to take her and my sister to the convent just outside Herterpol to enable her to provide the nuns with funds to help their work with the poor of Herterpol. When we were there we met a cousin of the de Brus'. Anne de Botercourt is an orphan whose father died in Gascony. The French king claimed the lands and his widow and daughter came to Herterpol to stay with their cousins. Lady Botercourt died not long after landing and as the hall was without a lord living there, Anne stayed in the convent. I think that she might have become a nun…"

His voice tailed off and Matthew said, "Had not a handsome young knight appeared."

Thomas shrugged, clearly embarrassed, "While mother spoke with the nuns we walked the grounds of the convent and…you were right cousin, accidents do happen. I fell in love and she responded. Before I seek permission from the de Brus family I would have your permission."

"Your mother?"

"Is happy beyond words."

"Then I happily give you my blessing but rather than seek the permission of the de Brus family I would suggest a speedier method would be to ride to Durham. Herterpol is in the Palatinate and the bishop can give permission. I am sure that both your mother and your bride-to-be, not to mention every lady in the valley, will be desperate for a speedy marriage."

Chapter 20

Henry Samuel

The Battle of Alnwick

Both the bishop and Baron de Brus gave their permission for the marriage and there was even a dowry. Anne's mother had brought a chest of gold with her and Baron de Brus was happy to have an unmarried relative now part of the powerful clan that was my family. Anne was a delight and I could see why both Thomas and his mother thought so highly of her. I saw poor Matthew looking wistfully at her. He was now the only bachelor knight and that such a prize had been on his doorstep must have galled him. The wedding was held on the shortest day of the year. We would still celebrate Christmas but anything that brought life and colour into the small number of hours of daylight was to be welcomed. Despite the fact that we had lost Sir William the end of the year was the best of times. Even Lady Mary laughed and smiled once more. Lady Isabelle now had a daughter-in-law and the prospect of grandchildren to fill the void left by the death of Sir Robert. When the castle emptied at the end of December, I felt sad. My mother confided in me that this might be the best thing to happen for Thomas' sister, Isabelle. The poor girl had been affected badly by the departure of her father. That, in itself, was strange for she had not appeared close to him while he had lived in Redmarshal but even I had noticed that she was sad. Thomas' conversations and the conversations I had with young Isabelle all came together. My mother thought the presence of another young woman in Norton might cheer her up. My Aunt Isabelle and her daughter spent long hours in the church praying for Sir Robert's soul. My mother, wise woman that she was, did not think that this was healthy in a young woman.

"She is young, perhaps Anne's love of life will make her come out of her shell."

The new year was both cold and wet. I preferred hard frosts where we could walk on solid ground and not slip and slide on mud. The joy of the wedding faded. Thomas, his mother, wife and sister were at Norton and we missed them. We could not even visit as the rains made the roads almost impassable. We were somewhat isolated. The rest of the world seemed to be so far away as to make us an island in the north. When a ship arrived at the end of February, I was surprised for few

ships came up the river in winter. The captain had been sent by The
Lord Edward himself to deliver a missive. I entertained the captain
while he waited for the next tide to take him downriver.

"Yes, my lord, I was one of the captains hired by The Lord Edward
to rid the Fens of the last of the rebels. The ones that were not taken fled
to France where de Montfort's boys are trying to raise an army to
invade. Now that I have delivered the letter I was given I can sail home
to Folcanstan. What is the point of earning good money if you cannot
spend it on your family? Now that we have peace in the south, I can
earn my living by carrying cargo and not warriors."

I waited until he had departed before opening the letter. William and
Samuel had been with me while speaking to the captain and they were
interested in the contents. The Lord Edward had not communicated with
me since the Battle of Evesham and that was more than eighteen
months since. I had thought we had been forgotten. I broke the seal with
some trepidation for it was not a note, it was a long missive and I
recognised the hand of the heir to the throne.

My heart sank when I read it. William saw my expression and said,
"What is amiss, brother?"

In answer, I gave him the letter and then said to Samuel, "We go to
war. Sir John de Vescy, it seems, is not happy about the Dictum of
Kenilworth. Perhaps this was not a surprise. King Henry took his
northern lands from him long ago and he has ever been a supporter of
the de Montfort cause. He has raised the standard at Alnwick and defies
the king. The Lord Edward is heading here with loyal knights and he
wants the men of the valley to be with him."

William had read the letter and he waved it, "And I can see why he
wishes to dampen the flames of rebellion. He fears that the de Montforts
will take advantage and land in the north."

I nodded, "They cannot risk that until May at the earliest. It is one
thing to sail up the east coast of England from London but quite another
to bring an army across the sea from France. Once more we shall be at
the sharp end of a war. Tomorrow, we send riders to the manors. The
muster begins and even though the ground is a quagmire we must be
ready to ride north to Durham as soon as we can."

"When does The Lord Edward come, father?"

"He has his men boarding ships and they will be at Herterpol within
a fortnight." I looked at William, "So much for your peace in the north,
brother."

"At least we will not have far to march." He was ever the optimist.

It was the worst time of year to prepare for war. While it was still
too early to plant crops this was normally the time of year when fences

would be repaired and the fields enrichened with night soil. It would still have to be done but it would have to go side by side with ensuring mail and harness were whole. We had brought back weapons and helmets from Chesterfield and they would be put to good use. We would be taking everyone this time. The Lord Edward had made it quite clear that he wanted the men from the north to put down this northern rebellion. He would bring his household knights and that would be all. We would march to war.

We left as soon as the men were mustered. Poor Thomas had the hardest task as he had only been with his new bride for the briefest of time. The rest of us had endured the pain of parting already. We had eighteen miles to get to Durham where The Lord Edward would join us and then it would be almost fifty miles to the rebellious parts of the land. William guessed that Alnwick and Warkworth castles would be the places that de Vescy would defend. Newcastle could be blockaded by sea and besides was not as strong as the other two fortresses.

It was a wet and miserable march north. There was none of the banter and humour that normally accompanied us. We had thought the rebellion ended by the Dictum of Kenilworth and it had flared into life again. I said nothing to the others but it struck me that the only way it would end was when the de Montfort line was eliminated. So long as they festered in France fermenting discord there would be no peace.

It was when we reached Durham that I heard, for the first time, of the pope's call for a crusade. When Cardinal Ottobuono Fieschi had completed his negotiations for peace he had broached the matter with King Henry and his son. Louis of France was also committed. This war meant that preparations for a crusade could not go ahead. We had arrived before most of the other men who had been mustered and my knights and I dined with the Prince Bishop.

"So Sir Henry, you will join this crusade?"

"I believe my family has done enough crusading. The son of the Warlord went there first and then my grandsire Sir Samuel died there. Sir Thomas fought in the Baltic Crusades and I myself was with him when he went on the Baron's Crusade. Is that not enough blood shed for any family?"

He nodded, "You have done much but you still surprise me. I would have thought that fighting for Christ was the ultimate task for a knight."

I shook my head, "From the stories passed down in my family, Christian values are the last things to come from a crusade. The pope and, perhaps the kings, might have the right motives but others seek power and position. The Holy Land is now a tiny coastal strip. Jerusalem fell. Would you have men die to retake it?"

He was silent.

I sighed, "I have been on a crusade. I was there on the Baron's Crusade with my grandfather and uncle. If I am asked, I shall give my answer but I will not bar any knight from taking the cross."

He seemed relieved, "That is all that can be expected, Sir Henry. It is down to each man's own conscience."

I looked the bishop in the eyes, "And mine is clear, my lord." It struck me that no Prince of the Palatinate had yet taken the cross but they had encouraged many young men to do so.

When The Lord Edward arrived it was like a whirlwind had struck the north. He had with him forty knights and sergeants. Lord Henry Almain was one of them. For once I was greeted warmly by the future King of England. "My cousin has told me of your deeds at Chesterfield. We could have done with such endeavours at Ely but with your help and God's blessing, we shall end this rebellion quickly. I would quash the rebels before they attract others from overseas." He turned to the bishop. "Are the others here for the muster?"

"Most, my lord, but not all."

His face darkened, "The Earl of Cleveland has already done more of his fair share in this war against anarchy yet he arrives first and men who have squatted in their homes while others bleed for them are yet to arrive."

The bishop appeared to be unflustered by the anger of The Lord Edward and he smiled, "They will be here when they will, my lord."

"And do we know where the rebels are waiting for us?"

"It appears that they are in the Coquet and Aln valleys. The two castles, Alnwick and Warkworth are their strongholds."

"And that gives them fifty miles to ambush us."

I had been thinking of this and had a sort of solution, "My lord, the ships that brought you from London, where are they now?"

I thought that The Lord Edward was going to snap at me too but he just looked puzzled as he answered, "Herterpol where they await our return, why?"

"If those ships sailed up the coast to Warkworth Harbour and anchored there then it would do two things, it might make the defenders of Warkworth think that you were aboard the ships and that we planned to join up at Warkworth. And it would also mean that when this is over you were saved a fifty-mile ride south to Herterpol."

"And that would make them uncertain. They might send men from Alnwick to fight us when we landed or they might empty Warkworth and concentrate their forces at Alnwick. We have nothing to lose by the deception. Bishop, a clerk and parchment if you please."

de Montfort's Crown

While he sat and dictated his orders Lord Henry of Almain joined us, "We go on crusade you know. The Lord Edward, cousin Edmund, my father, all of us."

"The king?"

Shaking his head he said, "No, the king will not take the cross. His capture and the battles aged him. He was never a warrior king, as you well know. We have enough knights of renown but your presence would ensure victory."

I shook my head, "My grandfather took the cross, three times. Others in the family, including me, went on crusade, I will guard this part of England."

"The Lord Edward will be disappointed."

"The taking of the cross is not something you command, my lord. My conscience is clear."

In the end, I was not asked. Perhaps Lord Henry had been asked to sound me out, I know not but the matter did not arise again. We waited a mere two days for the last of the muster and to allow the ships to sail north and threaten Warkworth Harbour. I knew that at the very least the defenders of the castle would see the standards on the ships at the mouth of the Coquet and wonder. We headed north through what was, to me and Sir Richard, familiar territory. We had both been knights around Otterburn and guarded the lands there from the Scots. As we rode, I told The Lord Edward what I knew of the castle.

"Alnwick is like Kenilworth, my lord, in that there is water and a moat but there is no lake and they have just an outer wall and an inner wall around the donjon. Unlike Kenilworth, I do not think that de Vescy will have had time to build large engines."

"Nor shall I, Sir Henry. We will use escalade to take this castle. I intend to have men construct ladders and under a shower of arrows from your redoubtable archers, we will storm the walls. In my experience, a determined attack on the perimeter of a castle usually divides the defenders. I do not intend to spend long quashing this rebellion. I want England at peace so that I can plan my crusade. I shall take my wife you know?"

I looked at him and shook my head, "It is a hard land, my lord. I took the cross and know."

"The Lionheart took his bride, Berengaria, with him and Eleanor is determined that we will not be parted. We both know that a crusade might last years."

I hoped he was right and that we might take Alnwick quickly. I was less sure about the taking of the future Queen of England to Outremer. The Lord Edward took us to Swarland just six miles from Alnwick. The de Haslerigg family were loyal and whilst they had no castle, their hall was a spacious one. By now the defenders at Warkworth would know that we had headed directly for Alnwick. The ruse must have worked as we had not been attacked or ambushed on the way north. If Warkworth did wish to send men to aid Alnwick then they would be the ones who would be ambushed.

We rode, the next day, to Alnwick while the men we had brought on foot made ladders. The Lord Edward had brought as many knights as we had raised in Durham and we must have looked like an impressive sight as, with banners flying, we arrived at the wall around the town. Baron de Vescy had shown his colours and the walls were manned by his men and his townsfolk. As was usual when the men of the Palatinate went to war, we had with us St Cuthbert's banner and it was displayed behind The Lord Edward. He also pointedly had me at his side when we rode, bare-headed, through the barbican into the town. He wanted the townsfolk to see that the men of the Tees Valley were with him.

"Men of Alnwick, I have come from London to ask why the men of the north have raised the standard of rebellion. My father, the king, has obeyed the wishes of the pope and those who were disinherited are now returned to their lands."

I recognised Sir John de Vescy who defiantly answered us, "We are asked to buy back our own lands at half their value and that is deemed fair. I, for one, do not think so."

The Lord Edward shook his head, "Sir John, you sided with rebels and lost. Did you think there would be no price to pay for making war on your rightful king?" Silence greeted his words. "Surrender now before blood is shed and all will be well."

"Do your worst, my lord, for we have nothing to lose."

He turned to Lord Henry of Almain, "Except, perhaps, their lives. Surround the town."

Although there was a wall around the town it was not as high as the one around the castle. As I ordered my knights and those of the Palatinate into position, I was already estimating how long the town walls would take to fall. There were houses outside the walls and they had been abandoned. We destroyed those close to the walls but occupied the ones that lay beyond arrow range. A roof was a small but necessary comfort. Our foot soldiers arrived the next day with the ladders that they had made. It must have intimidated some of those within the walls to see the fires of our men encircling them. It took all day for our men to arrive and that night twenty men deserted Alnwick and abased themselves before The Lord Edward. Their leader was a merchant from the town, "My lord, Sir John de Vescy has pressed men into service. We do not wish to fight against the heir to the throne."

He smiled, "Good, then you shall fight for him instead. Lord Henry, these men will fight under my banner. Welcome." The looks on the faces of the men told me that they had not expected to have to fight but they now had no choice.

My men had their ladders but unlike many of the other conroi who would attack the walls, my knights and sergeants would be the first ones up the ladders. The men who fought on foot were brave and they had helmets and leather jacks but climbing a ladder without mail was inviting death. Samuel and Roger, as well as Alfred, also wanted to join me as we waited with the ladders but I shook my head, "This assault is for you to watch. See how we do this. Joseph of Aylesbury and the others who will follow me up the ladder know their business as do I. See how we fare first, eh?"

"Yes, father."

"Yes, my lord."

My knights had all told their squires that they would not be attacking. Lord Henry of Almain and the knights brought by The Lord Edward would assault the barbican and, like us, Lord Henry would be the first up the ladder.

The horn sounded the moment we all marched forward. The arrows from our archers rained down on the walls. They kept up a fast rate and the sound was like that of a murmuration of starlings. Carrying the ladder in our right hands we held our shields over our heads. Missiles did strike them but such was the effect of Ned and my men's arrows that they did no harm. There was no ditch and we planted the ladders on solid ground. Holding my shield above my head I began to climb. The arrow storm did not cease but it became more focused. Ned and my archers aimed at those threatening to harm us. I was blind to this for my shield protected me. The wall was just ten feet high and when I reached the top I stopped and drew my sword. I had to move my shield so that I could see the fighting platform and the spearman lunged at me as I did so. The arrow that slammed into the side of his head missed my right arm by a handspan. It allowed me to jump down to the wood of the fighting platform. The sergeant who came at me was from my left and he had to raise his sword to avoid the stone of the wall. I brought my sword over the edge of his shield and punched with my shield at the same time. His swing unbalanced him and weighed down with mail he tumbled from the wall to crash on the stones below. Joseph had been just moments behind me and with the two of us guarding both sides of the ladder, we had a toehold. Joseph more than made up for the loss of

Jack. He was as solid a sergeant as I had known. With Sir Richard
ahead of me I moved down the fighting platform. Already the men of
the town were fleeing. It was one thing to stand on a wall and try to
keep mailed men at bay but quite another to face them on a narrow
wooden walkway. We had the walls within fifteen minutes of the attack
beginning and the gates of Alnwick Castle were slammed before all the
defenders of the walls made it inside. It was a victory.

We opened the gates for the gatehouse had not fallen to the attack of
Lord Henry and his men. The Lord Edward ordered all the women and
the children from the town while the men were bound. We now had the
town and that meant we had food and that the castle would not. They
had not had time to take food inside the castle. We still had the sturdy
and daunting walls of the castle to climb and they would be harder than
the town walls but we had time to starve them.

The Lord Edward would not wait and more ladders were ordered to
be constructed. The walls were taller and the ladders would also need to
be longer. We would have to assault the walls and this time he was keen
for his men to take the mighty barbican while the rest of us would have
to take the walls, again. He was annoyed that it had been we who had
broken the tiny town's defences. His knights would have to show their
lord that they were worthy to be his knights. We lit fires within sight of
the walls and cooked some of the animals we had captured. Those
within the walls would be on shorter rations and the smell of cooking
meat would be an additional torture.

My sword needed to be sharpened as did the rest of our weapons.
The archers found undamaged arrows as well as damaged ones. The
heads were stored for future use and they prepared for another attack.
This time they would need bodkins. There would be more mailed men
within the walls. I was summoned to meet with The Lord Edward and
Lord Henry, "We will attack at dawn again but this time the horn will
signal the attack on the walls. Let them think that their barbican is too
difficult for us. When they have taken men from the barbican to
reinforce the walls then we will send the rest of our men to take the
gatehouse."

"We could wait a day, my lord. They will stand to for nothing. Let
us tire them out."

He shook his head, "This is the last nest of rebels in the land. I want
this ended so that I can return to the king and tell him that he has his
kingdom back. I have a crusade to organise."

I returned to my men. "We have to draw the enemy to the walls and
that means we use all the ladders, even the ones that will not reach the
top of the towers."

"What about the moat?" My brother had a sharp mind and saw the problems we faced.

"We demolish some of the buildings to make bridges, Alfred."

Sir Richard shook his head, "The earthen bank will sap our energy before we can even put the ladders into place. It would be better if we threatened the castle with a mine."

"The Lord Edward has made up his mind and we will just have to do the best that we can. Ned and the archers will be our salvation. We lost not a man when we attacked the town walls and that was due to their skill. Trust to them, Richard."

That night we retired as early as we could for the escalade had sapped energy and the morrow promised an even harder task. We rose in the middle of the night. The priests sent by the bishop heard our confessions and we broke our fast. We would, at least, be well fed. The days and nights were equally long and we were waiting at the moat before dawn broke. The braziers that the sentries had used to stay warm gave a glow to the crenulations. We saw their shadows as they moved along the walls. A horn inside roused the garrison. They would be ready for us. My archers had made pavise during the afternoon of the previous day and they stood behind them. From their elevated position archers inside Alnwick's walls could send arrows at us. They might not be as good as my archers but I wanted to bury none of my men.

We slid the rough bridges in place and then retired to wait for the signal. Both sides waited for dawn. Arrows and bolts were too valuable to waste in the dark and we had to await the orders from our lord and master. Samuel was behind me with his shield, helmet and short hauberk. It would afford him some protection and help to prepare his body for the days when he was mailed from head to toe. He would learn to wear the mail as though it was a second skin.

The archers had strung their bows but held their arrows in their hands. Each one of them was studying the walls and identifying the man they would try to kill. It was not cruelty that would make them accurate but necessity. If they did not kill them then when we climbed the ladders, we might die. The horn sounded and Ned shouted his command. The archers drew back and released in one motion. The archers each studied their strike but their hands held the bows still. Once they knew that they had the range they released in constant motion. Arrows slammed into the pavise but my archers knew how to protect themselves. The duel began. I waited until the arrows, stones and bolts heading in our direction slowed and then I shouted, "Ladders!"

These were longer ladders and we had more men carrying each one. Joseph had assigned one of the biggest sergeants, Alan, to plant himself at the bottom of our ladder to keep it secure. We crossed our rough bridge and then began the energy-sapping climb up the motte. It was hard work, made especially so by the need to hold our shields before us. The closer we came to the wall the stones that were hurled at us increased in number. Some were quite large ones. This time they were hurled by sergeants and soldiers who knew what the effect would be. If I had not kept my arm angled to deflect them down to the ground then my arm might have been broken. As it was, I had no idea the effect of the stones on those at the bottom of the ladder and so I forced myself to climb faster. This time there was more noise at the top and I made out words.

"Send for men from the barbican. These are knights that we face and it is the main attack."

"But Sir Harold, we weaken the barbican."

"They think it is too strong and are not attacking it. Have those pikes made ready."

The plan was actually working and I knew that as soon as the men were moved then The Lord Edward would lead his knights. It increased the danger for me and my men as we would have more men to fight and this time they would be both better armed and armoured. When I reached the stonework at the top of the wall I did not reach for my sword. I knew that if they were using pikes then they intended to push me from the ladder. A sword would avail me little. Instead, I waited. One pike struck my shield and I leaned into it. The second man with the pike saw his chance and lunged at my right shoulder. Leaving go of the ladder I grasped the pike below the head and pulled. The sergeant was already committed to the strike and his body came through the gap in the stone. His weight pulled him over and he tumbled, screaming, to the ground. I took the last step and hurled myself over the top of the wall. I drove myself at the man whose pike had rammed my shield and he was taken by surprise. He fell from the fighting platform.

I sensed rather than saw the pike coming down at me and I rolled towards the safety of the wall with my shield held over me. The pike came down and made my shield shiver. As the sergeant raised his pike for the killing blow, I swept his legs from him and as he crashed to the fighting platform was on my feet and drawing my sword. He saw the blow coming and rolled but, unlike me, he rolled the wrong way and fell into the bailey. There had been four men ready to fight me and three were gone. I lunged at the fourth man. He tried to deflect the tip of my sword with his pike. He partly succeeded but the end of my sword went through his chaussee and into his thigh. I punched at him with my shield. A pike needs two hands and my shield smashed into his face. I sank my sword into his middle and then waited until Joseph of Aylesbury stepped over the top.

I could see down the fighting platform and we were the only ladder to have breached their defences, "Joseph, stand back to back with me and we hold here until the rest of our men join us. Then we go to the aid of the others."

"Aye, my lord. That was sweetly done."

Ralph of Banbury and James Poleaxe joined us as Joseph and I fended off the pikes and spears. They were the perfect weapons to knock men from ladders but less useful on a narrow fighting platform. Joseph and I easily kept the jabbing heads at bay.

I felt a shield in my back and James Poleaxe said, "Ready, my lord."

"Then with me. Slow and steady." My aim was to enlarge the breach foot by foot. The more men I had behind me then the better chance we had of victory. I saw the pikes and spears ahead poking and prodding at my cousin Dick as he tried to gain a foothold on the wall. He was just six feet and two men away.

The man who faced me had dropped his spear and grabbed both his shield and his sword. He wore a round pot helmet with a nasal and I could see his eyes. He had the advantage that he could make a wide slashing swing at me and I had to use a downward strike for fear of hitting the stone of the walls. Knowing that I did two things. I lowered my sword and braced my shield for the sword that would come hard at my side. He was a big sergeant and a strong one. James Poleaxe aided me by swinging his war axe over my head towards the man's shield. The sword swing was well practised but his eye went to the axe. I lunged as his sword hit my shield and almost knocked me to the stonework. His eyes widened when he felt the sword slide into his body. James pushed his shield into my back and I turned my sword so that the dying man fell from my blade as he tumbled to the bailey.

The next man, and the last one before the two men trying to spear Dick, now had less room to manoeuvre and he still held a poleaxe. He had no room to swing it and he used it as a staff. He swung the bottom at my legs and then tried to bring the axe's head down on my helmet. James Poleaxe used his own axe to pin the poleaxe above my head. Like the first man this one wore a pot helmet and I brought my head back to butt him. I drove the nasal into his nose and blood spurted. At the same time I brought up my knee and, as he doubled over, dragged the edge of my sword across his neck. My shield pushed his dead body back and he crashed into the two men with pikes and spears. We had more room and James brought his axe down to smash into the helmet and skull of the first man while I had an easy kill into the side of the second.

We pushed forward and the two of us occupied the fighting platform. My brother Alfred was ahead but we needed Dick and his men to join us before we pushed on. He scrambled over the top and stood behind us.

"Thank you cuz."

"Take half of your men and support Joseph as he makes his way to Sir Richard. I will go to the aid of Alfred."

The task was made easier by the fact that the men had seen James and I rid the wall of the men who had been to their right. They now feared us. The fighting platform was just wide enough for two of us and we advanced with shields held before us and our weapons ready to strike at them. One threw his spear at us. We easily raised our shields but it afforded him the time to grab his own shield and sword. The man next to him held a spear and the two made a barrier. It was my younger brother who needed help and I would not allow him to be knocked to the ground.

I did not know James as well as I had Jack and John of Parr but we had sparred enough together to be familiar with each other's moves. That knowledge had already helped us and now we moved as one. The spear was intended to keep us at bay while the swordsman sought weaknesses. We did not allow them the initiative and we both stepped onto our left legs with our shields held out. James' axe smashed at the swordsman's shield while, having deflected the spear, I drove my sword up into the body of the spearman. As he fell James pushed his opponent to the bailey and I hacked at the pikeman who was trying to kill my brother. He died and the two of us stood to allow Alfred over the top.

As he stepped over he said, "Anyone would think we were not welcome, brother!"

I laughed, "Aye, we have a foothold now. James, take men and descend the steps we just passed. Sir Alfred and I will drive on to the small tower."

"Aye, my lord. Hugh and Alan with me."

We now had more than thirty feet of the wall in our hands and the defenders before us had retreated into a small tower. The door slammed shut. The archer on the top leaned over and drew back on his bow. Alfred and I acted instinctively and pulled up our shields. It was unnecessary as an arrow from below, loosed by Ned slammed into the archer's head. As I sheathed my sword I said, "Ned has saved us again, brother."

As he sheathed his sword he asked, "How do you know it was Ned?"

"The red and white fletch." We both picked up discarded pikes. Swords would be useless against a wooden door but a pike's head could gouge a hole in it. We both swung our weapons alternatively and wood splintered from the door. Behind us we heard the screams and shouts as more of my men poured over the walls. We had a breach and soon The Lord Edward would join us. When the gate was sufficiently weakened, we both used our pikes as rams to smash into the door simultaneously. When they broke it, we entered an empty guard room. The defenders had fled. We hurtled down the steps to the bottom.

The bailey was filled with milling men as the defenders fought the men who had followed James. "Alfred, take your men and open the gates."

"Aye, Henry Samuel."

I turned, "Men of Stockton, follow me."

The breach had caused confusion. The donjon would take siege engines to reduce it but as most of the men were on the outer walls the gates were still open. If we could keep them open then the battle might be over. We ran and our training came to our aid. My men formed up around me. Dick was to my left with his men and Joseph and James flanked me. We pushed men from before us or slashed at them to make them move away. This was a foot race. I heard voices, panicky ones, screaming for the gates to be closed. The press of men before us was too great and as we pushed into the back of them we found ourselves in the guard room of the donjon. We needed to do nothing more than to keep open the doors. We slashed, stabbed and slaughtered those in the guard room. The men who were following me cleared those trying to gain the safety of the stronghold. When Thomas, Matthew, and Alfred joined me, we had the donjon's entrance secure.

I nodded, "The men of the valley have done their part. Let others take the rest of the donjon."

It was The Lord Edward and Lord Henry Almain who were the ones to follow us. His bloody surcoat and sword showed that the next King of England was a warrior. He nodded at me, "You have made our task easier, Sir Henry. Hold here while we work our way through the donjon. It will take time but when we are done then the rebellion will finally be over."

It was late afternoon when Sir John de Vescy finally surrendered having been defeated in single combat by The Lord Edward. Lord Henry Almain told me how the two had fought but The Lord Edward had prevailed. Alnwick and Warkworth were ours and the rebellion was truly over. We could go home.

Epilogue

We had lost two men in the attack. Their loss was sad but it could have been worse. We were rewarded not only by treasure from weapons, mail and purses but The Lord Edward paid each of us from the treasury of Alnwick and Warkworth. The castle at Warkworth had surrendered when our ships had approached the port. We made our way home and the riders I sent to warn the valley of our arrival ensured a triumph worthy of a Caesar. It was the late afternoon as we entered the town. That we had not been away for too long did not matter. I saw people counting the men as we rode through the north gate. They would know that we had not lost many men and that would cheer them. Richard and Matthew carried on through the gates to head for their manors. They would reach them before dark. Edgar stood with the ladies who were all smiling. My mother, Lady Mary, Eirwen, Lady Isabelle and Alfred's wife Eleanor were all there. I dismounted and Edgar took both my reins and Samuel's.

"Welcome my lord." He waved over Cedric the ostler, "Cedric will tend to the horses, your mother has arranged a feast."

As I knew she would. I turned to the sergeants, "You have all done well. Tomorrow enjoy that rarity, a day of rest."

They cheered. Joseph said, "Thank you, my lord."

I hugged my mother first and then Eirwen. She kissed me and whispered in my ear, "Before you do anything else come to your solar. I need to speak with you."

Her tone made me worried. What had happened while we had been gone? I nodded, "Of course." I turned to the others. "I will go and rid myself of the stink of animals. I will see you all when we eat." I caught my mother's eye and she nodded. As I passed her, she squeezed my hand.

Eirwen said nothing as she led me to my solar. When we reached it I saw that my daughters, Myfanwy and Eleanor were with Isabelle, Sir Thomas's sister. What had happened?

My wife said, "Thank you, girls, you may go and greet your brothers. Your father is here now."

They rose and both came to kiss me, at the same time, on my cheeks. Myfanwy was the elder and she said, "I am pleased that you are home, father."

"As am I."

The door closed and my wife sat with her arm around Isabelle. She had always been a fey young thing but now she looked even more so. She was older than my girls but looked much younger. She had the look of one who was afraid of her own shadow. I could talk to lords and princes, nobles and warriors alike but here I was well out of my depth and I looked at Eirwen. She squeezed Isabelle, "The earl is here now, Isabelle. Know that he is a kind man and your cousin. You can tell him all that you told us. Be not afraid."

Her eyes were wide when she looked up at me, "You were my hero when I was growing up, my lord."

I smiled, "It is still Henry Samuel."

That made her smile, "I thought that one day a knight such as you would ride into the valley and I would be swept off my feet." She shook her head and looked at the ground. "That was not meant to be." Silence hung in the air and I found my heart beating as quickly as it did when I was riding to war. "I wish to join the convent in Herterpol. I would be a nun." She looked up at me, "My mother said that as head of the family I should ask your permission."

I was stunned. The commitment to a convent was not one to be considered lightly. "What about a husband? A family? Your choice means that you can have neither."

She nodded, "I will regret not having children but…" she shook her head. "This is for the best. I have been unhappy for some time and the only peace I have found was when I went to church with my mother. When we visited the convent at Herterpol I found solace."

"Is this because your father left?"

Suddenly her eyes flared and she spat her words out, "Do not mention his name to me. He has destroyed my life." She suddenly realised how she had spoken to me and put her hand to her mouth, "Forgive me, that was inexcusable."

I was stunned into silence and just looked at Eirwen, "Best that you do not know, my husband, but whatever death Sir Robert endured was too swift a death."

I nodded, "There is nothing to forgive. If you are set on becoming a nun then you have my permission but I would beg you to think long and hard before embarking on such a dramatic journey."

She smiled and was briefly the old Isabelle I remembered, "I have thought of nothing else since the Battle of Evesham when I knew that I was free."

Suddenly much more made sense to me. Thomas' unhappiness. My cousin Isabelle's turning to the church. Sir Robert had been a monster, exactly what kind I did not want to know. I liked to believe the best in people. Sir Robert had shown me that I had never really known him.

That evening, as we dined, I was even more convinced that participation in another crusade was not a choice that I would make. I told those around the table of the crusade. None chose to take the cross. I was content. While the next King of England learned for himself the futility of a war he could never win I would make my valley even more secure. I would ensure that in the future such a monster as Sir Robert would never ruin the life of any who lived along the River Tees.

The End

Glossary

Archae – legal documents relating to usury
Carter's Bread – dark brown or black bread eaten by the poorest people
Caparison or trapper – a cloth covering for a horse
Chevauchée - a mounted raid
Folcanstan - Folkestone
Manchet – the best bread made with wheat flour and a little added bran
Raveled or yeoman's bread – coarse bread made with wholemeal flour with bran
Raygate – Reigate, Surrey
Sergeant – man at arms
Shaffron – protection for a horse's head, leather cuir-bouilli with a metal strip
Socce – socks
Wallintun - Warrington

Historical Note

Jews were savagely persecuted by the de Montfort faction. Two high-ranking Jews were murdered by the bare hands of one Montfortian supporter. Northampton did fall because of a weakened priory wall but there was talk of collusion with the prior who was a Poitevin.

The royalists should have won at Lewes but The Lord Edward's pursuit of the Londoners cost them dearly. There were few knights killed at Lewes which, in comparison to Evesham, seems almost a civilised affair. When The Lord Edward was kept prisoner, it was Lady Maude Braose, Sir Roger's wife, who arranged his escape. He was sent a good horse and when he was out riding, he switched to the better horse and outran his guards. King Henry was kept close by Simon de Montfort after Lewes as was The Lord Edward's wife, Eleanor.

There were two spies who passed on valuable information. One was Margoth who was a cross-dressing woman. I made up the relationship with the other spy for convenience. It made for a tighter story. King Henry was mistaken for a rebel and was almost slain. Again, in the interest of storytelling, I have Henry Samuel rescue him.

The butchering of de Montfort and his leaders took place as I described it and Sir Roger Mortimer did all that I ascribe to him. It is not sure if the future King Edward condoned the act for all the men who went with Sir Roger were his men. The two sons of de Montfort who escaped both went to France where they spent the rest of their lives trying to undermine King Henry and his son.

The scouring of the forests of Chesterfield did take place and it is from this time that the legend of Robin Hood began. The Dictum of Kenilworth did end the war but Sir John de Vescy objected and the last battle of the civil war took place at Alnwick Castle. Sir John not only changed sides after that battle, he joined The Lord Edward on the crusade.

The end of this book references the crusade undertaken by The Lord Edward. I will not be writing about that for I have already done so in the book, 'The Archer's Crusade' (Lord Edward's Archer series). When I wrote that series, I thought that the title, The Lord Edward, was optional and omitted the The. I have read original thirteenth century documents since then and realised that the future king of England was always referred to with the definite article before his name.

Roland's song

Under a pine tree, by a rosebush,
there is a throne made entirely of gold.
There sits the king who rules sweet France;
his beard is white, with a full head of hair.
He is noble in carriage, and proud of bearing.
If anyone is looking for the King, he doesn't need to be pointed out.

This is only part of the song. Readers of my other books will know who Taillefer was. He was a troubadour and knight who famously asked Duke William of Normandy if he could begin the Battle of Hastings. The book is the first in the series, Conquest, and is called, **Hastings**.

Canonical hours

There were, of course, few clocks at this time but the services used by the church were a means of measuring the progress of the day. Indeed until the coming of the railways, there was no need for clocks. Folk rose and slept with the rising and setting of the sun.

- Matins (nighttime)
- Lauds (early morning)
- Prime (first hour of daylight)
- Terce (third hour)
- Sext (noon)
- Nones (ninth hour)
- Vespers (sunset evening)
- Compline (end of the day)

All the maps used were made by me. Apologies, as usual, for any mistakes. They are honest ones!

Books used in the research:

- A Great and Terrible King-Edward 1- Marc Morris
- The Crusades-David Nicholle
- Norman Stone Castles- Gravett
- English Castles 1200-1300 -Gravett
- The Normans- David Nicolle
- Norman Knight AD 950-1204- Christopher Gravett
- The Norman Conquest of the North- William A Kappelle
- The Knight in History- Francis Gies
- The Norman Achievement- Richard F Cassady
- Knights- Constance Brittain Bouchard

- Knight Templar 1120-1312 -Helen Nicholson
- Feudal England: Historical Studies on the Eleventh and Twelfth Centuries- J. H. Round
- English Medieval Knight 1200-1300
- The Scottish and Welsh Wars 1250-1400- Rothero
- Chronicles of the age of Chivalry ed. Hallam
- Lewes and Evesham- 1264-65- Richard Brooks
- Ordnance Survey Kelso and Coldstream Landranger map #74
- The Tower of London-Lapper and Parnell
- Knight Hospitaller 1100-1306 Nicolle and Hook
- Old Series Ordnance Survey Maps 93 Middlesbrough
- Pickering Castle- English Heritage
- British Kings and Queens- Mike Ashley
- Alnwick Castle

Griff Hosker April 2023

Other books by Griff Hosker

If you enjoyed reading this book, then why not read another one by the author?

Ancient History

The Sword of Cartimandua Series
(Germania and Britannia 50 A.D. – 128 A.D.)
Ulpius Felix- Roman Warrior (prequel)
The Sword of Cartimandua
The Horse Warriors
Invasion Caledonia
Roman Retreat
Revolt of the Red Witch
Druid's Gold
Trajan's Hunters
The Last Frontier
Hero of Rome
Roman Hawk
Roman Treachery
Roman Wall
Roman Courage

The Wolf Warrior series
(Britain in the late 6th Century)
Saxon Dawn
Saxon Revenge
Saxon England
Saxon Blood
Saxon Slayer
Saxon Slaughter
Saxon Bane
Saxon Fall: Rise of the Warlord
Saxon Throne
Saxon Sword

Medieval History

The Dragon Heart Series
Viking Slave *
Viking Warrior *
Viking Jarl *
Viking Kingdom *
Viking Wolf *
Viking War*
Viking Sword
Viking Wrath
Viking Raid
Viking Legend
Viking Vengeance
Viking Dragon
Viking Treasure
Viking Enemy
Viking Witch
Viking Blood
Viking Weregeld
Viking Storm
Viking Warband
Viking Shadow
Viking Legacy
Viking Clan
Viking Bravery

The Norman Genesis Series
Hrolf the Viking *
Horseman *
The Battle for a Home *
Revenge of the Franks *
The Land of the Northmen
Ragnvald Hrolfsson
Brothers in Blood
Lord of Rouen
Drekar in the Seine
Duke of Normandy

de Montfort's Crown

The Duke and the King

Danelaw
(England and Denmark in the 11th Century)
Dragon Sword *
Oathsword *
Bloodsword *
Danish Sword*
The Sword of Cnut

New World Series
Blood on the Blade *
Across the Seas *
The Savage Wilderness *
The Bear and the Wolf *
Erik The Navigator *
Erik's Clan *
The Last Viking*

The Vengeance Trail *

The Conquest Series
(Normandy and England 1050-1100)
Hastings
Conquest

The Aelfraed Series
(Britain and Byzantium 1050 A.D. - 1085 A.D.)
Housecarl *
Outlaw *
Varangian *

The Reconquista Chronicles
Castilian Knight *
El Campeador *
The Lord of Valencia *

The Anarchy Series

de Montfort's Crown

(England 1120-1180)
English Knight *
Knight of the Empress *
Northern Knight *
Baron of the North *
Earl *
King Henry's Champion *
The King is Dead *
Warlord of the North*
Enemy at the Gate
The Fallen Crown
Warlord's War
Kingmaker
Henry II
Crusader
The Welsh Marches
Irish War
Poisonous Plots
The Princes' Revolt
Earl Marshal
The Perfect Knight

**Border Knight
1182-1300**
Sword for Hire *
Return of the Knight *
Baron's War *
Magna Carta *
Welsh Wars *
Henry III *
The Bloody Border *
Baron's Crusade*
Sentinel of the North*
War in the West
Debt of Honour
The Blood of the Warlord
The Fettered King
de Montfort's Crown

de Montfort's Crown

Ripples of Rebellion

Sir John Hawkwood Series
France and Italy 1339- 1387
Crécy: The Age of the Archer *
Man At Arms *
The White Company *
Leader of Men *
Tuscan Warlord *
Condottiere*

Lord Edward's Archer
Lord Edward's Archer *
King in Waiting *
An Archer's Crusade *
Targets of Treachery *
The Great Cause *
Wallace's War *
The Hunt

Struggle for a Crown
1360- 1485
Blood on the Crown *
To Murder a King *
The Throne *
King Henry IV *
The Road to Agincourt *
St Crispin's Day *
The Battle for France *
The Last Knight *
Queen's Knight *
The Knight's Tale

Tales from the Sword I
(Short stories from the Medieval period)

Tudor Warrior series
England and Scotland in the late 15th and early 16th century

de Montfort's Crown

Tudor Warrior *
Tudor Spy *
Flodden*

Conquistador
England and America in the 16th Century
Conquistador *
The English Adventurer *

English Mercenary
The 30 Years War and the English Civil War
Horse and Pistol

Modern History

The Napoleonic Horseman Series
Chasseur à Cheval
Napoleon's Guard
British Light Dragoon
Soldier Spy
1808: The Road to Coruña
Talavera
The Lines of Torres Vedras
Bloody Badajoz
The Road to France
Waterloo

The Lucky Jack American Civil War series
Rebel Raiders
Confederate Rangers
The Road to Gettysburg

Soldier of the Queen series
Soldier of the Queen*
Redcoat's Rifle*
Omdurman

The British Ace Series

de Montfort's Crown
1914
1915 Fokker Scourge
1916 Angels over the Somme
1917 Eagles Fall
1918 We will remember them
From Arctic Snow to Desert Sand
Wings over Persia

Combined Operations series
1940-1945
Commando *
Raider *
Behind Enemy Lines
Dieppe
Toehold in Europe
Sword Beach
Breakout
The Battle for Antwerp
King Tiger
Beyond the Rhine
Korea
Korean Winter

Tales from the Sword II
(Short stories from the Modern period)

Books marked thus *, are also available in the audio format.
For more information on all of the books then please visit the
author's website at www.griffhosker.com where there is a link to
contact him or visit his Facebook page: GriffHosker at Sword
Books or follow him on Twitter: @HoskerGriff or Sword
(@swordbooksltd)
If you wish to be on the mailing list then contact the author
through his website.
at Sword Books

Printed in Great Britain
by Amazon

40364246R00126